ASLEEP

AT

THE

WHEEL

ALSO BY ERNEST HAMILTON

SHARK POINT
THE IMPOSTOR
FREE AT LAST
GO FOR THE GOLD
THE FORGIVEN
AN INVISIBLE HAND
THE ART OF LIVING

ASLEEP AT THE WHEEL

A novel

BY

ERNEST HAMILTON

ISBN-13: 978-1483954264
ISBN-10: 1483954269

Cover Design by Nancy Bell

Printed in the United States of America

April 2013

First Edition

Special Thanks

As always, my special thanks go to my wife, Nancy Bell, who continues to support me under all circumstances.

CHAPTER 1

Taxpayers were already at the front desk, asking questions or responding to a summons, when Jesse Hawkins arrived at the Internal Revenue Service office early Monday morning. He nodded at the office auditor behind the counter as he entered and walked down the hall toward the large area where the field agents worked. Most of the forty or so desks, positioned side by side, were occupied – not unusual for a Monday morning. The office manager didn't look up as Jesse made his way into the room and on to the far side. Memories of the weekend fishing and water skiing on the ocean and Intracoastal Waterway and the flight to Everglades City in his small plane, caused him to reflect on just how humdrum this work could be. In another few months he'd have his pension locked up – maybe 2006 would turn out to be his year. He'd quit the rat race and start his own tax business. He could work part-time to pay the bills if he had to. *Who knows – may even try out for the FBI again. If only I could get an exciting case.* The agent at the next desk looked first at Jesse, then at Jesse's desk, with a knowing grin.

Jesse noted the single file with the word "urgent" in large letters lying on top of his desk. He nodded at the agent and pulled the chair away from the desk, still looking at the unusual file. *Umm, maybe this is the one I've been waiting for – real excitement for a change.* Fraud? International money laundering? Offshore business financing? The World Trade Center came to mind. *Terrorists?* His heart quickened, but he masked the growing excitement. He removed his coat, draped it across the back of the chair and loosened his tie. He glanced at the coat and the slightly frayed elbow. Of his three suits this was the worst, but the others were well on their way to needing replacing soon.

The other agent continued to look at him. "Something wrong, Mike?" Jesse asked. "You know something I don't?"

Michael Gibson was like the evil scientist who salivated when he was about to come upon something particularly juicy. Mike seemed to love sticking it to the taxpayer every chance he had, as if it was a game with him to see who was assigned the better cases with the best chance of finding meaningful adjustments with the least amount of time spent. He figured promotions came to those who produced the most tax revenue.

Mike eyed the file on Jesse's desk. "No, nothing wrong. Just interested to see what the new case is about. Never seen one marked 'urgent' before."

Jesse looked around the room at the other agents who were into their own routine, most probably getting ready to visit a taxpayer somewhere in the county. "Did anyone else get one? You?"

"I didn't get one. Don't know about the others. Maybe you're something special, huh?"

Jesse thought about that question. Lately he had been assigned some fairly good cases, one recently turned over to the Criminal Investigation Division for suspected criminal fraud. He'd been working with special agents there for the last three months and, so far, it had been the most satisfying job he'd ever had. He had a yen to join that department and tackle the criminal element. Maybe those good cases came his way because he made extra effort to be thorough in his examinations while still being efficient. It was important to know when to dig further and when to quit. His decisions in that regard were right most of the time. Regardless that the brass held "quality-of-the-audit" as paramount, and the reason for the name change from Bureau of Internal Revenue to Internal Revenue Service, the agency was in business to raise tax revenue. That was still the main issue – get in and get out with the most tax and least effort.

Jesse flipped the file open and a small frown formed on his face. "No, I doubt I'm considered special by anyone." Without looking at Mike, he picked up the file and headed to the managing agent's office. He indicated to the secretary that he wanted to see the boss. She picked up the phone, spoke into it and motioned for him to go in.

The small office was sparse with a simple desk, two chairs in front, a low bookrack against the side wall and a picture of Daniel Feldman's family – wife and two small children hanging on the back wall.

Daniel looked up as Jesse entered. "Been expecting you."

Jesse walked to the desk and held the file in front of him. He stood tall, as he always did when facing his boss, trying without success to get his five-foot, eleven inch, 180-pound frame to measure up to Feldman's six-foot athletic frame. *Oh well, play with the cards you're dealt.* "Danny, why am I getting another Taxpayer Compliance case so soon? I just finished three, and I thought we were through with that project." He laid the file on the desk and pointed to the cover, "And why is it urgent?" He flipped it open to reveal the cover sheet indicating the type of examination.

"That case was originally assigned to Whitaker and, as you know, he's still in the hospital from the car crash. Likely be weeks before he's back on duty. Critical condition I hear. May never come back." Feldman moved the file in front of him and glanced at the cover sheet. "This report is due in the main office by the end of next week and I know you—"

"But I don't understand. The car crash was over two weeks ago. Why me?"

Feldman looked agitated that he'd been caught in a lapse. He closed the file. "Look, Jesse, it doesn't matter. I was looking for someone who could get on this case and get it resolved to everyone's satisfaction in the shortest time. I think you fit that bill. Do you?"

Jesse had already begun to rue his outburst and wished somehow he could eat his words and back out of the office as if the meeting had never occurred. "Yes." He reached for the file, his mind already rescheduling his other cases. "I'll get it done in plenty of time."

CHAPTER 2

It was already Friday when Jesse turned onto Hibiscus Street. It had taken him all week to arrange the appointment. With any luck it would proceed without a hitch and he'd soon be back on the ocean and in the sky.

Beyond the stately trees and sidewalks on both sides, concrete driveways, bordered by colorful plantings, led to upscale stucco and brick houses. He'd never been in this area of town and his mind began to compare the area to the tax return he had under examination – something didn't quite fit. This was a Taxpayer Compliance examination – boring at best. Every field agent had at least one a quarter without any opportunity to shift it to the back of the list. A simple task of verifying income and expenses – no proof, no deduction. Not much opportunity for finding fraud or other exciting adjustments – the fun part of this job. *What's odd about this one?*

He reached for his briefcase with the idea of perusing the return again when his attention was directed to police cars at the far end of the block. Groups of people stood on the sidewalk or in their yards, chatting and staring at the house with yellow tape staked in front. His appointment at house number 379 would be nearby. He hoped that whatever was going on wouldn't interfere with his planned meeting.

As he slowed to pinpoint the house he was looking for, a police officer waved him on. *My God, that's the house I'm going to.* With his mind absorbed by this information, he almost stopped, and the policeman ran toward him shouting and waving angrily for him to move on. Jesse finally realized what he was doing, then drove down the street and parked on the side.

With briefcase in hand, he approached the policeman who had been so abrasive. "Is this the residence of Julio Mendez?"

"You must move on, Mister."

"But I have an appointment with Mr. Mendez at two-thirty." He started to reach inside his coat for identification.

The policeman's hand went to the gun at his side. "I said you have to move on, Mister. Now do it."

"But, sir, I'm a Revenue Agent, and I just spoke with Mr. Mendez this morning. It's important that I speak with him."

"A Revenue Agent, huh?" The officer's demeanor changed. "You have I.D.?"

"Yes, sir." Jesse reached to his coat, hesitated, then moved his hand inside when the officer gave the okay. He extracted his card and presented it to the officer. "Jesse Hawkins, Internal Revenue Agent with the local office."

"I've got a problem with them." The officer's face showed deep concern. "Maybe you can help me. I have to."

"You were called?"

"Yeah. Said something about an office audit, whatever that is." He waved another car through. "I'm scared to death. What should I do?"

Jesse glanced at the car – a light blue BMW. His eyes stayed with it as it moved slowly down the street – the driver gawking at the scene. *Now that's my kind of car . . . one of these days.* He returned his attention to the policeman. "It's usually not a great problem. Just organize the material you used to prepare your return. Most of the agents are good people and will work with you to get through the examination. I wouldn't worry about it – just be prepared."

"Thanks a lot. That eases my mind some. You examining Mr. Mendez's return?"

"Yes, we were to meet this afternoon. What's going on? Robbery or something? Can I go in?"

"I'm sorry Mr. Hawkins but you'll not be able to see Mr. Mendez . . . he's dead."

Jesse's eyes widened and his mouth opened. "Huh? Dead?" He quickly recovered his composure. "What happened?"

"Appears to be murder."

CHAPTER 3

Jesse, his mind in turmoil over this turn of events, sat in his car and stared through the windshield as if in a trance. He'd never experienced anything quite like this in all his thirty-seven years – in any of his fourteen-plus years with the Service. What to do now? *Guess that ends the case.* He turned the ignition and shifted into drive, noticed his briefcase on the passenger seat, had a second thought and shifted to park.

The first page of the tax return indicated Mendez had filed as a single individual, which would now rule out continuing the examination. He started to close the file and head back to the office when his eyes dwelt on the types of income shown on the first page, a small amount of interest income and the rest, still not a standout amount, entered from Schedule C, the business schedule. That's what had been bothering him. Total income shown on page one didn't match the apparent lifestyle of the neighborhood and the implied standard of living.

He flipped to page two, was a bit shocked to see the large itemized deduction total and scanned the page to see zero tax due and none paid in during the year. As he contemplated this information his hand moved automatically to the ignition switch and turned the engine off. *Wait a minute.* He flipped to Schedule C, then to the remaining pages. No self-employment tax paid on the business income.

Information at the top of Schedule C indicated that Mendez was a real estate agent. The deductions were high and varied – some opportunity for adjustments there. As he scanned the itemized deduction schedule, he mentally compared them to total income reported. Net income as reported didn't leave Mendez much for living expenses. The small amount of interest income indicated few financial assets. He examined the depreciation schedule for types of assets used in the business. His eyebrow arched at the auto – a 2004 Cadilac Escalade. Back at the front page he noted the return had not been prepared by a professional.

Jesse laid the return in the file and closed it. As he reached for the ignition, his mind contemplated the total return and the events of the afternoon. There were definitely a few adjustments to be made and . . . Mendez was dead. Will the government want to pursue the examination and end up having to deal with the estate, which could take years and cost plenty? Were the few errors and the paltry tax to be garnered justification for a full audit? He started the engine, shifted into drive, pulled away from the curb, and glanced at the empty BMW parked on the right side at the end of the block.

Jesse's mind moved away from the idea of getting himself a BMW convertible and back to the case at hand as he pulled into the office parking lot. This Mendez was a real estate agent and, logically, when considering all the facts, appeared to have made more money than he reported on his tax return. *Maybe I should run over to the courthouse and check the public records. Who knows?* He looked at his watch – almost three-thirty. *What the hell? What've I got to lose?*

Jesse noted no other patrons in the Property Appraiser's office as he printed the two pages he'd been studying. He returned to the computer and screened another entry under the name of Julio Mendez. Totally absorbed in the research, he jumped when the lady approached and said, "I'm sorry, sir, but we're closing now. You'll have to return at another time. Did you get the information you came for?"

"Huh?" He turned to look at her, back at the computer, then back at her. The screen seemed to hold information with possible ramifications unlike the other information he'd garnered during the past two hours. "Could I have just a few more minutes? I'm almost finished."

The lady looked over at another woman standing across the room with the door open. "I'm sorry, sir. It's five-thirty now and my boss is giving me the eye. She's ready to lock up for the day. We're supposed to close at five. We're open at nine Monday morning."

"Okay. I understand." He made a quick note regarding the screen he'd been viewing, gathered the papers and placed them inside his briefcase. He stood and followed her to where the other woman was holding the door for him.

Jesse entered his car and tossed the briefcase onto the passenger seat. He was disturbed by the last bit of information he had been unable to copy, but glad to be finished for the day. As he started to pull away from the curb, he noticed the BMW parked on the other side of the one-way street – the man appeared to be reading something. The man, young, square-faced, and dark-skinned, reminded him of some Asian types he'd seen around. *Wonder if it's the same car? Sure looks like it.* He shifted into drive and glanced at the BMW as he passed.

Like the clerk in the courthouse, Jesse looked forward to a nice, quiet weekend and sighed audibly as he nestled his back against the seat for the drive to his modest quarters across town, where he'd lived since his divorce two years ago. A peaceful picture of his ex-wife and two children flashed across his eyes and was quickly blurred by the image of crying children waving goodbye as the car backed out of the driveway and drove away. His hands tightened on the steering wheel. That image always seemed to be not far out of his consciousness. The weekend was near, though, and he and the children would spend most of it on the boat – fishing, camping and skiing on the river. His hands loosened and the smile that tried to form was quickly replaced with a grimace.

The events of the day flooded back into his mind. Somehow this Mendez case had turned into something of an enigma – like nothing he'd ever been up against. The thought of something sinister kept making its way into the mix. Where did that thought come from? A product of his wild imagination? He tried to back away from the myriad pieces and analyze the individual facts.

First, the neighborhood didn't match the return data – too upscale for such modest income reported. Second, the taxpayer had been murdered the very day of the appointment – almost like somebody didn't want the meeting to take place. Third, although the recent purchase of two small parcels of real estate may prove to be explainable, that last bit of information, the purchase of a very large, expensive piece of property as trustee for some unknown entity or person, was very intriguing. Where had the money come from? Who was the owner? *Something definitely not right here.*

Jesse was still deep in thought when the truck horn behind him blared. He looked up to see the green light, then in the rearview mirror to see the angry face of the driver behind. *Good grief man – ease up.* He pulled through the light and turned right. The horn blew again as the truck passed and cut in front dangerously close, causing Jesse to brake suddenly. Through the back window of the truck the man showed a derisive finger.

Jesse tried to calm his nerves by again nestling his back into the seat, but his anger at the impulsive, impatient man would not abate. He hated his inability to control himself in such situations. Someone had said "he who angers you conquers you", and that was certainly true today. His hands were gripping the wheel again.

The sun had passed below the buildings and dusk was coming on fast as Jesse passed through an intersection next to a shopping mall. A small car came out of nowhere. He veered sharply to the right and found himself in the midst of two other cars with nowhere to go, then the truck from before plowed into the side of his car, propelling him over one car and broadside into another. His car had not quite settled on its roof when another car landed on top. His head, dangling dangerously close to the roof, jerked sideways as the truck pushed both cars into the parking lot and next to a building. Jesse, still not fully aware of what was going on, loosened his seat belt as the car on top exploded and burst into flames. Fire licked at him as he struggled to make his way through the broken window. Shards of glass tore into his skin. As the truck backed away from the wreckage, he could barely see people milling about and caught a faint glimpse of the blue BMW far across the parking lot. Everything went black.

Hamza Nazim, sitting in the BMW, stared intently at the burning heap across the parking lot, lit a cigarette, flipped his cell phone open and pressed a key. He grimaced as the phone on the other end rang and rang and rang. He grumbled to himself and started to close the phone when a man answered. "Yes, Hamza. What do you have?"

"I have the new one. It is over."

"How can you be sure?"

"He is under a pile of burning vehicles. No one could survive that. The accident was a bad one. He probably died before it started to burn. I am confident." Hamza inhaled deeply from the cigarette and blew the smoke out into the night.

"That is what you said about the first one who is still alive in the hospital."

"I will go to the hospital before I quit for the night. Do not worry. It is over. They will not assign another agent to the case."

"Inform Syed Rabia without delay."

Hamza closed the phone.

CHAPTER 4

Syed Rabia, in deep thought, continued to stare at the telephone receiver even though Hamza had disconnected. The soft, tonal beep in the phone finally brought him back to reality and he placed it on the holder. He started to page the secretary, realized that she had likely left by now, stood from the desk and walked over to the bookcase against the far wall, adjusting his tie as he scanned book titles. There weren't many in this case he hadn't read, but he would never replace them because he loved them so much. These books were his favorites. He had many more in his den at home and wondered what he should do with so many. He hated to dispose of them even though he continued to purchase more.

The report from Hamza returned to his mind and he walked back to the desk and the business at hand – his dinner engagement with his superior. Why did Abdullah insist that he receive information from the likes of Hamza? Syed despised working with such inhuman beings – people who could take the lives of others without blinking an eye. The taking of innocent lives was abhorrent, yet he had accepted it as a necessary alternative, at the present time, if they were to complete their mission.

The details of today's tragedy, the taking of another innocent life – an ordinary American trying to do his job, forced its way into his mind. He shuddered at the thought of the man in the hospital and his fate at the hands of Hamza. Would this really be the end of the killing? What was it about Mendez's tax return that had spawned such disasters? He was such a simple man – a recent convert and so very eager to learn his adopted religion. Why would such a tax return even spark an interest in the government, and what was the likelihood that ordinary revenue agents would ever detect his connection to the operation?

Syed reached for the telephone to call his wife, hesitated in thought, then turned and walked back to his beloved books. He chose one in particular, flicked the light on and sat in the easy chair near the window. The page appeared devoid of words as his mind mulled over his predicament.

The absolute hardest part of this mission was using his citizenship in this country to plot against it, but again, there seemed no other way to keep them from meddling in the affairs of his mother country – and the effect that had on their way of life.

He flipped through the pages and absentmindedly let his mind take him back in time – to his arrival in America – to the beginning of his adopted life.

It was 1992 and the excitement of the flight across the Atlantic had already begun to boil over when the plane turned on final approach to JFK International. As Syed stepped through the glass doors to the outside, he breathed deeply and watched in awe as the vehicles and people scurried about making their way in or out of the airport. He was in America. He pinched himself and fought to maintain a calm appearance.

His student visa was good for three years and could be extended for another two if everything went right. He would assure that it did. Within that period of time he could obtain the Masters in Business Administration he dreamed of. His father wanted him to return home and assume the family business, or seize the opportunity provided by family connections to enter government service to further enhance the business, but he already knew he would become a citizen of this great country before his time was up.

He breathed deeply again and watched as an airplane took to the sky. He ducked his head into the taxi and departed for the chance of a lifetime.

That was a moment in time Syed would hold dear forever. Within the three-year period, he had received the MBA and at the end of the fifth year in the United States, achieved the coveted citizenship, all before his twenty-fifth year.

Two years later, through the successful start-up of his own business, he'd been well on his way to the realization of his dreams when his father came to visit, along with a friend who wanted to acquire a business of his own. Syed was asked to introduce the friend to the business community. Imraaz Amed was especially interested in ports of entry, land transportation and chemical production. Syed's father had also introduced him to the unrest in his home country, and in the whole region. Mainly because of oil, the United States was deeply involved. The powers at home blamed the U.S. for coercing leaders to change the form of government, for the age-old grudge of installing Jews in the region, and for the continued unsettlement of the Palestinians. Then, two years later came the World Trade Center disaster and its aftermath of bias and blame – causing his whole world to crumble in confusion.

CHAPTER 5

Syed unconsciously adjusted his tie as he looked over the crowd of diners and, spotting Imraaz Amed, proceeded to the table in an isolated corner of the restaurant. During the five years since the New York disaster, Imraaz had also adapted to the American way of life while still clinging to his religious and mid-east heritage. He now sported a colorful jacket with a splashy tie. His complexion and the dark chin whiskers that proceeded in a thin line up his cheek to join his hair clearly identified him as a man of Arabian ancestry.

Syed studied the sixty-year-old man, pulled out the proffered chair and smiled. "So good to see you, Imraaz. I trust you have fully recovered from your recent illness." He glanced around the room to see that others paid them little attention. Meeting in a public place such as this caused in him an uncomfortable feeling.

Imraaz smiled, obviously pleased to see Syed, and reemphasized the chair with a wave of his hand. "Come. Sit. Sit. Yes, I am completely recovered. Ah, how do you say? Stomach problem, the doctor said. Nothing to worry about. And you are well? Your wife?"

"Yes, I, too, am well and Mary is likewise." Syed nestled into the chair across from Imraaz, leaving the chair in between for his superior who was due at any minute. The faint, pleasant aroma of cooked food reached him. "I have not seen you in some time. Business going well?"

"Very well." Imraaz smiled again and now looked at the others in the room. "You keep the money coming and I will see that it is invested properly." He adjusted the napkin on his lap. "How are you able to do it?"

Over the years Syed had washed millions of dollars and he was impressed that Imraaz had made good use of it all.

17

Imraaz, an important man in his own territory back in the old country, reminded Syed of his own father – important and influential with the right governmental connections. He certainly seemed the right man for the important job of acquiring local, sensitive businesses as part of the overall plan to win the war. Syed ignored the question about his methods. Imraaz didn't know about the recent deaths and would never understand how that affected Syed. "The money will keep flowing," he grinned, "and grow. We must . . . ."

The waiter came and handed menus to both. "Can I get you gentlemen something to drink?" The tall man looked at Imraaz and then at Syed, rubbed the white cloth draped over his arm and held a pen over a pad, ready to write.

Imraaz said, "There will be another coming." He looked at his watch, then at Syed as if waiting for confirmation to hold up on the drink.

The waiter placed another menu on the table. "Shall I bring you something while you wait?"

Syed looked to the entryway far across the room and spoke, "Yes, I will have a vodka martini with two olives." He looked to Imraaz.

Imraaz beamed, "A glass of white wine for me." When the waiter had departed he said, "Now that is what I like about you. Abdullah is always late and you understand that. There may be time for yet another." He chuckled.

When the drinks came, Imraaz held his glass up and toward Syed, glanced across the room and proposed a toast. "To our continued success and," he looked solemnly at Syed, "to this country that allows us so much freedom." He placed the glass to his lips but waited for Syed to do the same.

That remark about the country sent a pang through Syed's body. Was he not the only one to recognize the benefits derived from so many opportunities? He probed Imraaz's eyes searching for meaning. Seeing none, he touched the glass to his lips and sipped a drink. "Yes, to our continued success." The debate he'd had so often with himself over the question as to which country he owed allegiance raged again inside his head. Even Mary didn't know and would never believe that of the two he had chosen his mother country – the country of his birth, the country of his predecessors and his heritage – the country that promised to change this one. The choice would not have been so had it not been for the continued government harassment after the 9/11 incident. They sought information from banks, credit cards, telephone and Internet companies. Even this year his bank had received a National Security Letter inquiring about his account. All Mid-Easterners no matter how upstanding, were targeted, and not only by the government. His normal American friends began to treat him differently – some even shunning him altogether. One need only resemble an Arab to receive rebuke.

Imraaz sipped his wine. "I believe you said your wife was born in this country."

"Yes, we met while at the university. She is a citizen. Her parents and grandparents emigrated from Saudi Arabia before she or her two brothers were born."

"You never did tell me how you are able to acquire so much offshore money and how it flows Syed. Are you not allowed to tell me?"

"I . . . ." Syed looked past Imraaz to see Abdullah Zacaari speaking with the head waiter and then start to make his way across the room. "Uh. Here is our leader." He looked apologetically at Imraaz and stood as Abdullah limped toward the table. Abdullah, a university professor, had started out in the trenches and was severely injured when a bomb he had strapped to his waist in an Israeli restaurant misfired. He'd spent seventeen years in prison in Israel, and faced numerous interrogations and detention in the United States after 9/11, all to no avail to the enemy.

The waiter was there immediately and took Abdullah's drink order.

With the help of Syed, Abdullah adjusted himself in the chair and spoke as Syed retook his chair. "Please forgive me for meeting this way, here in this place, but I thought it wise even though government prowling has diminished considerably from the old days." Abdullah glanced around the room as if studying the faces of all the patrons, trying to ferret out any possible federal agent hiding within. He stared long at a poorly dressed man in a wall booth to his left. He spoke in a muted tone, "Let us keep our voices down." He glanced at the man again. "It has been a trying two months, but I am happy to say that most all is proceeding very well." He placed the napkin on his lap as the waiter returned with the drinks. "I especially wanted to speak with Syed about the recent events which have caused a furor in the top echelons," Abdullah looked to Imraaz and reached to pat his arm, "but I thought this was a great opportunity to have the three of us come together in a non-business setting to iron out any possible problems." He looked to Syed, then back to Imraaz and laughed. "There aren't any, right?"

Imraaz was the first to speak, "If Syed continues to provide money, as he has in the past, I will have companies across the whole country well before the planned date. I was just asking him about all that money. He—"

"We will discuss that aspect today, but first I wanted an update on the recent happenings with the Internal Revenue Service. I hope that issue is now resolved." Abdullah turned to Syed. "Can we move on?"

"I have not heard more. The last indication, as you know, was that both agents' lives had ended. We will not know if others will be assigned to the case until next week."

Imraaz broke in, "There have been killings? I have not heard of this." His look bore into Syed; then he turned with a questioning look to Abdullah. He looked again with an apparent new appreciation of Syed.

Abdullah spoke, "It is nothing that you should be concerned with. It cannot be connected to your operation. The Revenue Service was investigating one of our operatives and there was concern it could possibly lead further. It was deemed appropriate to end it now. And, it seems to be."

Syed's face was passive when Abdullah looked there for assurance. Syed said, "I am promised. I will know for certain next week." Syed looked apologetically at Imraaz trying to convey without words that he remained the same person who hated all violence and would go to all means to avoid it – especially the killing of innocents. The portion of their crusade directed to ridding governments of corrupt officials had almost caused him to reverse course on several occasions. He thought of the Prophet Mohammed and his quest to spread the word of Allah – war and killing was sometime necessary.

Abdullah said, "All right, Imraaz, bring me up to date on your operation. A moment ago you seemed to say you had more money than you could spend – that Syed was providing too much. Anything to add?"

Imraaz waved the waiter away then spoke directly to Abdullah. "We continue to move forward. Since the meeting last week, we have bought substantial interests in five corporations operating in our area of interest. We now have interests in well over one hundred companies across the country. There seems to be no lack of U.S. citizens willing to take board positions as they become available. We are on target to alter corporate policy at the appropriate time." Imraaz looked at Syed and smiled. "As money flows in, we will continue to invest."

"Allah be praised. It is well that you are so positive. We will talk more about the companies at our next meeting. The time for action is drawing near and may be sooner than we think." Abdullah grimaced with pain as he turned to face Syed. "First I want to express my deepest sympathy to you, Syed. I know how you abhor the killings, and I know how you must wrestle with your feelings, but I also know that you recognize and accept the necessity." His look conveyed his deep understanding.

Syed showed no emotion. He'd learned to master that ability over the years. Only these two men knew of his inner feelings. He peered into Abdullah's eyes. "Yes, I fully accept the duties that are required to accomplish the mission." His eyes never varied for a moment.

"You seem to also have the ability to acquire companies, and that was another reason for this meeting." Abdullah shifted his gaze from Syed to Imraaz who looked a little confused. "Syed has secured a substantial position with a company in England that does business, in a round-about way, with the United States. This company will provide funds to aid our cause and," his eyes moved again to Syed, "it has a sizable political connection in this country, which we may eventually utilize. This appears to be a coup that will resonate to the highest echelons of our group. You are to be congratulated, Syed." Abdullah reached to take Syed's hand in a gesture of admiration.

As the waiter approached, Abdullah said, "Enough business. Now let us dine."

The agent in the Homeland Security Office in Washington D. C. picked up the phone, engaged the recorder and listened to the voice on the other end.

"PB One, here. Zacaari meeting with Rabia and Amed in restaurant."

"Anything significant?"

"Nothing. Same old."

The agent paused and considered this routine. The agency had been tailing Abdullah Zacaari ever since he'd been cleared of collaborating with terrorists in 2002, all to no avail. The agent could not comprehend the order prohibiting telephone surveillance if the government still considered Zacaari a terrorist. For similar reasons the agency was prohibited from listening in on Syed Rabia's telephones. Imraaz Amed was tagged but apparently was only involved in legitimate business deals.

The decision was his, and he made it. "All right, stand down. Go back to regular duties. I'll call if the situation changes."

CHAPTER 6

Martin Walker half-listened to his fellow senator as they made their way out of the Senate conference room. The Senate Finance Committee meeting had been long and contentious, taking all his mastery to keep it on an even keel. They had accomplished in spite of the opposition. The meeting next week would be tougher – the outcome almost known beforehand.

He fretted continuously over the problem of Social Security and its impending deficit. Under the present plan, the program would be unable to pay full benefits for Social Security in the year 2040, and Medicare would be devoid of funds in 2018. The President had made a valiant effort with his idea for personal accounts, but in Martin's mind, that was not wholly the answer – there were better alternatives. Getting the panel to agree on a specific plan was the difficult job.

As they passed through the doorway and into the hall, Martin spoke through the banter of all the other senators and assistants flowing out of the Senate chamber. "We tweaked this one through, Gordon, but the next one's the real test. We have to pull out all the stops. Time to call in favors." He looked to Gordon for concurrence.

"I'm already set up to get it moving. Be a busy week." A man touched Gordon's sleeve and they all stopped. Gordon continued, "Martin, this is really a challenge, but one we must succeed at. Count on me."

Martin nodded at the man, a well-known lobbyist, and began walking again. "I'll call you the middle of the week, Gordon. Maybe lunch."

Through the glass double-doors Martin could see the press with their microphones and cameras. He would have to face them – his duty as Committee Chairman. He was about to go through the door when the familiar voice of his aide overrode the hum of voices. He turned to face the running aide. "Where were you, Tom? I thought you were supposed to be back in time for the meeting today."

Thomas Benson, panting from the jog down the hall, paused to catch his breath, then spoke. "Sorry, sir. I ran into unforeseen circumstances." He looked straight into Martin's eyes. "Not good."

Martin glanced through the glass doors at the melange of people, then back to Thomas. "What the hell are you talking about, Tom? I needed you here today. Damn near lost, too." His peeved look likely wasn't lost on Thomas. Martin had too many things on his mind that seemed to keep him in a snit most of the time.

"I apologize again, sir. I'm talking about your re-election campaign. As we've discussed, our funds are dangerously low," Thomas paused. "Too low, sir. I talked with—"

"I don't understand this talk, Tom. We've always raised sufficient funds. It seems you have undue concern. It isn't like you. You have personal problems you haven't told me about? Allied Paint will come through as always, as will others."

"That's my point, sir. That's the problem."

Martin's face showed momentary concern. Several press people pushed and shoved each other for position at the door. There had been some behind-the-scenes rumbling in political circles about his long association with that company. "Look, I've got to meet with these people before they tear the door down. I'll see you in the office at five. We'll settle this once and for all." He pushed through the door.

Martin, still in a peeved mood from the meeting with his wife and their lawyers, entered his office on the fourth floor of the Senate building, glanced at the young woman sitting on a chair in the corner and frowned at his secretary. *What the hell now?* His face mellowed, he nodded slightly at the woman, and walked briskly to the secretary's desk.

Still agitated, he gazed down at the pleasant looking, middle-aged, brunette woman who had been his secretary and most trusted confidant for over twenty years. Before he could offer a question, Sylvia Bauer, who conveyed her usual business demeanor, said, "The young lady there . . ." she flicked her eyes to the corner of the room, ". . . says she must have a word with you today. I said you were busy but that I would try. Could you take one moment and hear her story – it's heart-wrenching."

Martin managed to remove the frown and softened his facial expression as he looked toward the woman whose face seemed to be pleading for an audience with him. He looked questioningly at Sylvia then strode over to the woman who stood as he approached. "Miss, I'm sorry I don't have more time now, but Sylvia tells me you're in dire straits. Please have a seat." He continued to stand. "Let me have the basics."

The woman remained standing. "Oh. Thank you so much, Senator Walker. I just don't know what I would have done had you not given me a moment. I—"

"Please go on."

"I am a Canadian citizen and this country, where I have legally resided for close to thirty years, has ordered me deported." She wrung her hands and stared at the floor.

The immigration bill before Congress immediately flooded Martin's mind. This fair, blonde woman didn't seem like someone who needed deporting. He pictured the hordes of people lining the streets waiting to be picked up for some menial job. "Have you done something wrong? On what grounds are you being deported?"

"My husband of twenty years managed to get into trouble with the law, was sentenced to two years in the penitentiary and, because of his age and the thought that he was meant to die young like his parents, escaped. I traveled and stood by him during this time. He was eventually caught and returned to prison. I was charged with abetting a criminal. I paid a five thousand dollar fine and served four years probation." Tears welled in her eyes and she wiped them with a handkerchief. "Please forgive me. I can't seem to get over this. I have never knowingly broken the law. I have always respected this country's laws and traditions."

Martin's face betrayed his growing displeasure. "What did your husband's age have to do with not staying his term?"

Tears welled in her eyes again. "He was afraid he would die in there." She wiped the tears away, her lips quivered. "All his family died early."

Martin looked at his watch. "If my memory serves me right, you've paid for your crime and that's not cause to deport you. Is there something else?"

"Early last year, I went to visit a sick uncle in Bavaria, the home of my ancestors, and was detained upon my return. They said that felons could not come into the country. They allowed me in but I had to go to court where they made their decision."

Martin's face now showed his sympathy for this woman. "Aah. That is a law that has long needed changing. Maybe with your story we can get it changed." The door opened and Thomas Benson entered, looked at the woman and walked to the desk.

Martin said to the woman, "I must meet with this young man now, but I will arrange to meet with you later. Are you staying in town for a few days?"

"Oh. Thank you so much, Senator. I will stay as long as it takes."

He took her hand and led her to the desk. "Sylvia, I will try to help this young lady. Get her information and I will contact her tomorrow." He turned to the woman. "Sylvia will help you, and I will be in touch. Keep up the hope." Helping someone like her always made him feel good – the real value of this job – and the reason to keep it. With a determined resolve to keep his position, he entered his office followed by Benson.

Martin stepped to the window behind his large oak desk and stood for a minute gazing toward the White House. The sun far to the west sent shafts of light into the wading pond at the east end of the National Mall. He could be sitting in that building had he wanted, but here in the Capitol Building was where he felt he could do the most good for the country and its people. Here is where he had served for the past thirty years and where he planned to serve for another six at the very least.

He closed the vertical blinds and moved to his desk. Thomas Benson stood behind one of the chairs, the blank expression on his face masking the known anticipation and fears of the upcoming election. Martin nodded for Thomas to take the chair and settled into his own. "Okay, Tom. This old bull raising its head again, huh? I've been nominating Allied Paint for the Navy contract for the past ten years and the opposition has been trying to make something of it for that long. The company does an admirable job, and its people are some of my staunchest supporters. What's the beef now?"

"Well, I never have completely understood just how all that money ends up in our coffers, and until now I've chosen to ignore it. Now it's—"

"Until now? Are you trying to tell me something, Tom? You're not having second thoughts about getting me through this campaign, are you?"

"Absolutely not. We've been together too many years for that, but this time we may want to reconsider our sources. It's not just the old bulls raising their heads, it's . . . ." Thomas paused, apparently searching for the right way to present his information. Martin stared into Thomas's eyes but maintained his composure even though severe agitation rushed through his body. Thomas continued, "This time it's the press."

"The press? What do they have to do with it? What kind of story could they have? Which paper?"

"*Washington Post*. My contact, apparently at the urging of the opposition, has done some digging into the finances of Allied Paint and has found some disturbing facts. Even though they're funding you substantially, they're showing losses each year on their income tax returns. They've not shown a tangible profit in over ten years."

Martin frowned, stood and moved to the window where he peeked through the blinds and stared absentmindedly toward the White House, the view now fading in the diminishing sunlight. He had never thought it necessary to tell Thomas where the bulk of the money came from and how it came into the campaign coffers, but he suspected that Thomas knew. It never occurred to Martin the company might be using the direct payment to him for tax purposes. Surely Thomas could not know the origin of funds going into support groups in his home district and other crucial areas. He turned around and faced Thomas. "I really don't see how their financial situation affects us. The contributions come from employees, not the company. I don't see how the reporter can make a case out of that." He retook his chair and began shifting papers into his briefcase.

Benson said, "My contact has determined that Allied Paint has about a hundred employees which would, under normal circumstances, account for approximately ten to twenty thousand dollars. At least $150,000 came into our coffers in each of the three years before election." Thomas looked into eyes that were impassive. "I have not taken the time to examine our contributors but you can bet the reporter will."

"So, what are you suggesting? We give up the race?" Martin laid the briefcase on the desk and stood.

"I'm saying we should let the opposition know that we are no longer supporting Allied Paint for the Navy contract. Although we face stiff opposition at home and our contributors have dwindled, we still have a chance to win, and," Thomas stood also, "we don't have to face the possible tarnishing of an otherwise solid career."

"Let me think on the consequences." Martin headed for the door. "Thomas, I think you understand how important winning is for me." He placed his hand on the doorknob and looked into Thomas's eyes. Before Thomas could answer, Martin opened the door and walked out.

CHAPTER 7

Lying on the gurney in the emergency room, Jesse had time to reflect on the events of the afternoon. The doctors had found nothing wrong with him except for a bruise to the head and several lacerations on his arms and legs. He had been very lucky, they said. Lucky the two men were able to pull him from underneath the burning vehicles and lucky he had not sustained more injury – the cars were a total ruin. The woman and her two children in the top car had been consumed in the flames.

Did this all happen because of an irate truck driver? How was that driver connected to the car that caused the whole thing? What would've happened to him had those men not pulled him away before the cars exploded? The BMW flashed into his mind.

His inquisitive mind and desire for action got the best of him. Could there be a connection with the tax case? That BMW had been everywhere: at the taxpayer's house, at the courthouse, at the shopping mall. All coincidences? How about the taxpayer – murdered? How about Whitaker? He was the initial auditor and had ended up in this hospital – still here. *Good grief – am I next? What's going on?*

"How're you feeling?" Jesse jumped as the nurse took his wrist and mentally counted the pulses found there. "The doctor said you were very lucky. He said you're free to leave if you feel up to it." She placed the stethoscope on his chest, listened for a minute, let it hang from her neck and brushed a wisp of blond hair from her eye.

Jesse sat up. "Yeah. I'm ready to go." She aided him as he swung his legs to the side and stood for the first time in two hours. He felt momentarily dizzy and kept his hand on the side of the gurney.

"You okay?" The nurse took his arm. "Here sit in this wheelchair. We'll take you."

"Yeah. I'll be all right." Jesse followed her direction and sat in the chair. "Only problem is how do I get home? I guess my car was totaled. Can I use a phone?"

"Yes, I guess it was. Can I call you a taxi?"

"Let me use a phone if you will. I'll try to rent a car. Will need one anyway until I can buy another."

The eyebrow of the elderly lady at the hospital reception desk raised as she tried to decipher Jesse's unkempt attire. "Can I help you?"

Jesse looked at the torn coat sleeve and blood smears. "Forgive me. I just came out of the emergency room – accident. I'm—"

"Oh. I'm sorry. Are you okay?"

"Yes. I would like to visit Gary Whitaker if I could."

The lady looked away from Jesse and turned to the computer screen. "Whitaker." She seemed a bit perplexed after searching the database. "Hold on a minute." She picked up a phone and punched in numbers. "Can you tell me about Gary Whitaker? He was in room 406 but now I can't find him. Has he been moved?" A frown formed on her face as she listened. She replaced the phone and turned to Jesse, a wistful look gracing her face. "I'm very sorry, sir, but they tell me Gary Whitaker died today."

Feldman faced the back wall trying to align the painting of his family when Jesse entered the office Monday after his return to the courthouse. He laid the file on the desk. "Danny, you're probably not going to believe this, but our TPC taxpayer is," he flipped open the file, "dead."

Feldman's hand jerked and the picture frame tilted on the wall. Still holding onto the frame, he turned to face Jesse.

"What the hell are you talking about?" He straightened the frame and moved to the desk. "What's the matter with your head? Did you have an accident fishing?" A smile spread across his face.

Jesse remained serious and unconsciously rubbed the side of his head. "A little more than a fishing accident, but first let me explain about the taxpayer. When I got there Friday afternoon, the police had his home cordoned off. Couldn't get in. Cop said it looked like murder."

"Murder? Are you kidding?" Feldman picked up the file and breezed through the papers, closed the file and looked up at Jesse. "Good. Case closed. You can go back to your important things."

"Before you make such a hasty judgment, you may want to hear what I found out at the courthouse this morning." Jesse rubbed his head again. "And maybe you'd like to hear the rest of the story."

"What're you talking about, Jesse? The rest of what story?" Feldman fingered the file and took his chair.

Jesse sat in one of the chairs in front of the desk, removed his jacket and rolled up the sleeves of his shirt.

Feldman's eyes widened when he saw the lacerations on Jesse's arms. "What the hell?"

"Hear me out and see what connections you can make." Jesse proceeded to tell Feldman how it all began Friday afternoon including the first and later sightings of the BMW, the details of the crash and his brief stay in the hospital. "You told me Whitaker was getting better even though he might not come back to the Service – right?"

"That's right. What does he have to do with this whole story? What makes you think this story relates to some vast scheme to deprive the government of revenue? Come on, Jesse. That venturous mind of yours is playing tricks with you – always looking for that far-out case. We're tax collectors, Jesse, plain and simple."

Jesse looked intensely into Feldman's eyes. In his gut he knew this case was different – knew he could make a difference if given the chance. "When I was released from the hospital, I stopped by to see Whitaker. Wanted to find out what he remembered of his accident." Jesse hesitated.

"Well?"

Jesse shuffled uncomfortably in the chair. "Danny, Whitaker is dead. He—"

"What?" Feldman abruptly stood. "I just talked with his wife Friday. He was improving steadily. Talking about coming back to work." He retook his chair. "Are you sure? How did you find out?"

"The hospital told me when I asked to visit with him."

"Are you suggesting that his accident and yours are related? Are you suggesting that someone is trying to do you in? That someone did Whitaker in? The same someone that murdered the taxpayer? How are you able to jump so far?"

"I don't know all the answers to that, but get this. Mendez, in addition to purchasing several small pieces of real estate in his name, recently bought a rather large piece – almost a section – in his name as trustee – a little while before Whitaker was assigned the case. The trust is not named in the available court records." Jesse reached for the file and flipped it open. "Look at his return and tell me if you think he could afford such a piece, and why buy it as trustee?" Jesse stood and walked around behind the chair. "No, Danny. That kind of money is coming from somewhere else," he hesitated and focused on Feldman's eyes, "offshore. This is a case worth pursuing further. I want you to let me work on it exclusively – starting right now. This could be the case I've been looking for."

"Wait a minute, Jesse. I'm still trying to see how Whitaker is tied to all that happened to you. When you took over the case were there any indications that he suspected something?" Feldman took the file and flipped through the pages.

"Two things: the fact that he had an upcoming appointment with Mendez, and a note reminding him to visit the courthouse. Someone knew that an examination of the court records would lead to this property. I guess they thought that by taking him off the case the investigation would end. When it didn't, they took the additional steps, probably figuring they wouldn't be connected. I . . . . "

Feldman looked at his watch and stood. "I'm still not convinced that further examination is warranted. I'm under great pressure to get this case closed. I'm already getting flack from up top. This whole program should've been closed a month ago." He turned to glance at the picture of his family, walked to the coat rack, unhooked his coat and turned to face Jesse. "I've got an appointment now." He moved toward the door. "You've got two days. Report back Wednesday afternoon."

CHAPTER **8**

It was Tuesday afternoon when Jesse arrived at the Mendez house to conduct the examination. It had taken almost two days to get through the red tape and get the police and the Personal Representative to agree to let him into the house with access to financial information necessary for auditing. This was the first time he'd ever had to issue a subpoena. He involuntarily squared his shoulders in a sign of power. He was vexed, though; Feldman had only given him until Wednesday afternoon to come up with some reason to continue the examination – about twenty-four hours. Somehow he knew this was the case of his dreams; he must persist. He glanced up and down the street half expecting to see the BMW and, seeing nothing resembling the face he'd seen before – was it Asian or Arabian – released an audible sigh of relief. He had to force himself to stay calm. In his mind there was a killer behind every bush. He looked around again to be sure.

Yellow tape still circled the house, but the police officer, sitting in his car parked under a shade tree in the yard, merely waved Jesse on towards the house after giving a cursory glimpse to his identification card. A middle-aged man in casual clothes opened the door as Jesse stepped onto the porch.

The man, still holding onto the doorknob, partially blocked the entrance. "Mr. Hawkins?"

"Yes, that's right." Jesse again held out his I.D. card.

The man examined it, glanced toward the police car and stepped back to allow Jesse to enter. "I'm Ramon Mendez, Julio's brother and Personal Representative. How long do you think this will take?"

Jesse glanced around the sparsely decorated living room and noted a cardboard box on a coffee table in the middle of the room. Maybe Mendez *was* just an ordinary guy, buying a home a bit out of his reach and then conserving on furniture. "Couple of hours, maybe – if all the paperwork is there. Fairly simple case, I think."

The man brushed by him and stood by the coffee table. "I hope it's complete. It's all I could find. Will you need me? If not I'll take care of my chores around here."

Jesse laid his briefcase on the sofa. "Well, let's hope so. Get this over so everybody can get back to normal. I'll try not to cause you any trouble. Thank you for working with me." Ramon nodded and left the room.

Jesse chose a file from the box and flipped through it – mostly blank contracts apparently. He removed a legal pad from his briefcase, sat on the sofa and chose another file. This file contained what appeared to be closed contracts and Jesse began to list them on the legal pad, paying special attention to the real estate commissions due on closing. Once he was through all the files with contracts he totaled the amounts accruing to Mendez and, upon comparing that with the amount reported on the tax return, noted an under-reporting of $22,000. His heart skipped a beat. Although there possibly could be a logical explanation, this alone should be enough to keep the case open a while longer.

Jesse sorted the loose papers in the box into different categories, placed them on the table and quickly totaled the various paid invoices. He then compared them to the deductions taken on the return – not any difference of consequence. The loose papers, some of which were letters, he breezed through not expecting to find anything of importance. As he mechanically thumbed through these items his mind worked on the problem of keeping this case open. He knew that someone had tried to kill him and might try again. He suspected that same someone was responsible for Whitaker's automobile accident and his subsequent death. Someone was playing for keeps. It had to have something to do with the findings in the public records. Who owned this trust? *If I get the chance, I'll damn sure find out.* He'd probably need another subpoena, though.

He continued to skim through the miscellaneous papers, automatically tossing one short letter on the pile and reaching for another. Almost finished, something jogged his mind and he picked up the last tossed letter, not really able to discern the reason for doing so. The letter referred to two small checks apparently for completing some job, although the letter only said, "Per our telephone conversation today." Jesse scanned his list of amounts gleaned from the contracts and didn't find the two amounts. *How many more omissions has this guy made?* The signature on the letter meant nothing to Jesse and neither did the corporate name – Allied Paint Corporation.

After making a copy of the letter from Allied Paint on the taxpayer's fax-copier, Jesse gathered his files and notes, stuffed them in his briefcase and headed for the door, accompanied by the Personal Representative. "Thank you for your cooperation Mr. Mendez, I trust I wasn't too big of a pest."

"Is the examination over?"

"There will be tax due. I've made a rough calculation of about $6,000. I'll prepare my report, get it approved, and the Service will be in touch with you in a few weeks. Jesse stepped through the door and the knowledge hit him like a jolt from the blue – there'd been a large contribution thank-you letter. He pushed against the door as Mendez tried to close it. "Excuse me, sir. Was Mr. Mendez a Muslim?"

Mendez seemed taken aback by the question. "Uh. Uh. Why, yes. He converted to that religion sometime last year. How did you know that? Is that an issue?"

Jesse's mind ran wild as he moved back into the room looking toward the box on the coffee table. The vision of the Arabian man in the BMW loomed to the forefront. "No. No. It shouldn't produce any additional adjustments." He moved toward the table. "Can I take one more look at the bank statements. Just want to see the checks he wrote to the mosque." Jesse also wanted to copy the checks and the thank-you letter for future reference.

"Sure, go ahead."

Amy Turner shut her car door as Jesse pulled into the Revenue Service parking lot. He yelled at her, "Amy, can I see you a second?" Amy hesitated and Jesse parked the rental car next to hers.

She moved to the rear of Jesse's car while he gathered his things and closed the door. "Where've you been, Jesse? Haven't seen you in over a week. Not sick, I hope. Come on over here, out of the sun. New car, huh?" She looked back at him as she started walking toward the building. "Is that a bandage under your sleeve?"

They took advantage of the shade underneath a large Banyan tree next to the building. Amy, a slight brunette with soft brown eyes and enticing good-looks and body, was two years younger than Jesse, and they had become close friends after taking on another case during his brief stint with the Criminal Investigation Division. She was a thirteen-year veteran with the Service, and he had great respect for her insight and logical reasoning. Catching up with her, he said, "Yeah. Had a little accident." He pulled his shirtsleeve back to reveal the bandage that went almost to his elbow.

Her eyes widened and a slight frown appeared on her face. "What happened? Out in your boat?"

"Auto accident. What I wanted to talk with you about." He held his briefcase in both hands as he related the events of the past several days. He glanced toward the parking lot. "That's a rental. Need to go looking for another one soon."

"My heavens. I guess you're lucky to be walking around. What do you make of it? You figure Whitaker's situation is somehow connected to yours? Do you think these people killed him?" A pained look replaced the frown and she placed her hand on his arm. "Are they trying to kill you?"

"I definitely think so. Everything seems to point in that direction. I think it's connected somehow to this little TPC examination. Just how, I don't know, but I want to keep the case open until I can find out. I have some ideas but need more time."

"What's the problem there?"

"Danny's under pressure to close out these TPC cases. You know we're only given so much time to get them done and out. You remember how it was." Amy had only been with CID for three years and before that, a regular field agent like Jesse. Back then he had felt a slight attraction to her, but they were both married at the time, and he had simply flipped it off as he would with anyone else. After their divorces, both of which had occurred about the same time, they had grown steadily closer.

"How do you suppose I can help?" She glanced at her watch.

"I'd like you to review what I've found and see if you agree the case warrants transfer to CID. Or, at the very least, have the Division take a look at it and recommend a little more time to tie things together better. I have to meet with Danny tomorrow afternoon. I may be able to convince him on my own but it would be helpful if I had more backing. Can you swing it?"

Amy glanced at her watch again and began moving toward the door. "I'll sure try." She waited while he opened the door, then stepped through. "I'll talk to the boss right now." She headed down the hall. "Jesse, you will be careful, won't you?"

"Yes. I'll be on top alert." He trailed behind her and as she turned into her office, he said, "Maybe we can have lunch sometime soon."

She smiled. "Yes, I'd like that."

CHAPTER 9

Feldman's eyes were glued to papers on his desk and his face betrayed his irritation when Jesse entered the office Wednesday afternoon. Jesse's insides rumbled because of more information he'd gleaned at the courthouse this morning and the other information obtained from the taxpayer's data. He felt it was enough to get a few more days to tie the various ideas together. This was *the* case – he knew it.

Feldman laid the pencil on top of the papers, moved them to the side and looked up at Jesse. "Okay, Jesse, are you ready to close this case?"

An unwanted grin spread across Jesse's face as he laid his briefcase on the desk and placed his hand on the back of the chair. Feldman frowned but nodded for Jesse to sit.

"Well?" Feldman asked.

"I can close it today with a sizable adjustment if that's what you want." He extracted a file from the case. "I've completed the report but I . . . ."

Feldman reached across the desk, took the file from Jesse's hand and opened it. Almost to himself, he said, "Okay. Looks good, $6,300 adjustment." He grinned at Jesse. "This makes the delay worthwhile." He closed the file. "I accept your report and I'll rule on it tomorrow."

Jesse's mind raced. That ending was not supposed to be the way this played out. "Wait a minute, Danny. You've got to hear me out. You've—"

"Are you still toying with that crazy notion of yours – that terrorists have some sinister plot going and that they tried to kill you? Come on, Jesse, get real. You've done a good job. Let's leave it at that. That'll be all."

Jesse's face now reflected his growing anger that others refused to see the importance of what he'd found. Without considering his employment position, he glared down at Feldman. "Damn it, Danny, you've got to listen to what I have to say. If you still feel the same way afterwards, then I'll quit and get someone else to listen." He withdrew more papers from his briefcase.

Feldman's face revealed his disbelief at Jesse's outburst, but it quickly softened to some sort of understanding. He looked impatiently at his watch. "Okay, let's hear it. Better be good – you taking up my time with this craziness of yours. Sit down."

Jesse sat on the edge of the chair. The tenseness in his body would not ease up. "You'll remember I told you about the Arab-looking man in the BMW. He was at the scene the afternoon the taxpayer was murdered. He was parked near the courthouse when I came out the same day." Jesse paused and searched Feldman's eyes for understanding. "He was at the scene of my accident last week."

"Aw. Come on, Jesse. There goes that mind of yours again. You've got to—"

"Danny, the taxpayer is a Muslim. No different than those Arabs who flew into the Trade Center, the Pentagon and, would've gotten the White House had it not been for the brave souls on that airplane." Jesse noted the change on Feldman's face.

Feldman said, "Mendez is not an Arab name. I think it's probably Cuban. Don't you?"

"Mendez is a recent convert to the Muslim religion." Feldman's eyebrow raised but he didn't speak, and Jesse continued. "Mendez made sizable contributions to a local mosque," he paused to let that sink in. "I'm thinking the mosque may be the owner of the trust."

"What trust?"

"You'll remember that Mendez was the trustee of a trust that owned a large piece of real estate."

"How're you able to tie that to the mosque?"

"I can't yet." Jesse looked hard at Feldman. "That's why I need more time and the backing from the Service. I've got to somehow penetrate that trust. If my suspicions are correct, there will be others."

The unconvinced look returned to Feldman's face. "Is that all?"

"Not quite." He flipped the pages of the legal pad. "Mendez received two small checks from a Miami company. The amounts were unreported, and are part of the adjustments. I was curious so I called the company and told them I wanted copies of the checks." Jesse fished in his briefcase, extracted the letter and handed it to Feldman. "They told me I'd have to go down there in person and show I.D. With your permission, I plan to go down there tomorrow."

"I'm at a loss now to see just how those two checks will further your idea of some kind of conspiracy." Feldman flipped open the file and scanned the tax return. "Mendez was a real estate agent and likely did some small job for the company." He scanned the report. "You've made the adjustment, what else is there?"

"One thing. I wanted to be sure the amounts were taxable and not just perhaps a reimbursement of some sort. Note the letter and the reference to their telephone conference. Like I said, I was curious, so I researched real estate transactions for the company to see if maybe the payments were in fact commissions."

"And? You found another connection to the Muslims?" Feldman's face reflected a deepening disapproval.

Jesse continued unabated, "The company bought the house of Senator Martin Walker. I wondered about that so I—"

"Good grief, Jesse. I knew your mind ran rampant and that you deal a lot in fantasy, but what in the hell does that have to do with your Muslim theory?"

"Like you say, my mind does play weird tricks on me sometime. I can't help that. Again I was curious so I did a little more research and found out the company sold the house six months later at a huge loss." Jesse noted the awe register on Feldman's face. "Now just why would someone buy a piece of real estate and sell it so soon at such a large loss?"

"My God. That is interesting. Not sure I see the connection to your other theory, though. Do you have an idea? Who's the company?"

"The company is Allied Paint Corporation, headquartered in Miami. I don't have a clue how it ties in except through Mendez. He was involved with the company and the mosque. I'd like to pull their return." Jesse paused, knowing the likelihood of the mosque filing a return was slim. "I'd also like—"

"I don't know, Jesse. Let me—" There was a knock on the door and the secretary peeked in. "Excuse me, Mr. Feldman, but Mr. Singleton would like a word with you if you've a moment."

"I'll be just a moment more. Ask him to wait one minute."

"He knows Jesse is in here and he'd like to talk with both you and Jesse."

Feldman looked questioningly at Jesse and said, "Send him—"

Jesse held up his hand to cut Feldman off and turned to the secretary. "Give me one more minute alone with Danny,

Mrs. Morrison." He looked to Feldman who nodded okay to the secretary.

"What is it now, Jesse? And how did he know about this?"

"Yesterday I asked Amy Turner to talk with him about the case to see if they'd be interested in taking it. Considering what's gone on, I had second thoughts about discussing everything with him. I'm just not sure about him now."

"What ever do you mean? More and more I'm not understanding you, Jesse. Ready to quit the Service if I don't hear you out, and now, CID has some interest and you hesitate." Feldman ran his hand through his hair as if in desperation.

"I'm just very nervous being around people of Arab heritage – afraid I've lost trust in them. I'd rather hold up on revealing the information about Allied Paint and the senator to him. Let's just see what he wants at this time. Okay?"

Feldman abruptly stood, walked to the picture of his family, ran his hands through his hair again, turned and faced Jesse, a perplexed but consoling look gracing his face. "Jesse, maybe you ought to see a psychiatrist. I think you're getting way out of hand. Now you're accusing one of our own?" He moved back to the desk but continued standing. "I know Gerald favors the Mid-Eastern race some, but you can rest assured that he's as American as you and me. His mother came to this country as a young girl and married a man of Arab descent who was a second-generation American. Where do you think he got the English name Singleton?" Feldman ran his hand through his hair again and, with a concerned look at Jesse, sat in his chair. "What do you want me to do, Jesse?"

Jesse, now self-criticizing himself for possibly blowing his last chance of retaining the case, leaned back in his chair and looked mournfully at Feldman. "I know I'm too much on edge and probably am seeing terrorists in every shadow, but maybe you would be, too, if you'd been in my shoes during the last few days." He looked to Feldman for understanding. "All I want is the opportunity to follow up on my suspicions. I feel very strongly that there's a connection between all these loose pieces, and I know, if there is the slightest connection, I'm the guy to find it." Confidence soared through his body and he squared his shoulders and sat erect.

Feldman's face revealed his understanding. "I know you are, Jesse. If anybody can do it, it's you. But I don't see—"

"Look, let's just fill him in on all that happened before today and see where it goes. No harm done, and I'd feel a lot better."

Feldman nodded agreement, spoke into the intercom and when Mrs. Morrison showed the tall, broad-shouldered man of about forty-five in, they both stood and shook his hand. Singleton took the chair next to Jesse and said, "I trust you're discussing Jesse's case and that I'm not otherwise intruding."

Feldman said, "Yes, we were discussing the case, and no, you're not intruding." He glanced at Jesse. "We're very much interested in your opinion."

Jesse gladdened inside, the angst of a moment ago gone. He looked at Singleton. Although the man couldn't be called dark, he sure resembled some of the Arabic people he'd met, and he certainly had the heritage. If Mendez, a Cuban, could convert to Muslim beliefs, certainly Singleton could be influenced, too.

Singleton said, "Amy gave me the rudiments but I need to hear it in Jesse's own words." He turned to face Jesse, and Feldman nodded his consent.

Jesse filled him in on all the events of the past few days and Singleton looked at Jesse with respect for his enthusiasm and vigor for pursuing the case, but Jesse worried about the deepening frown.

Singleton spoke directly to Feldman. "Danny, it appears to me that the Mendez case is mostly complete and, even if there is fraud, the man is dead. The most you can get are penalties." He looked apologetically at Jesse.

Jesse's heart sank. He knew his chances were slim without the support of CID. He looked long at Feldman who looked equally long back. Maybe he was being too suspicious of Arabic people. He'd never felt that way before. He made his decision and spoke to Singleton. "Let me finish. Let me tell you what I found out today." He glanced at Feldman for his reaction and, when he saw the slight grin, proceeded to tell Singleton about Allied Paint, Senator Martin Walker and the mosque – and of his wish to pull the returns. All the time he stared deep into the dark eyes trying to determine how far removed the man was from his heritage and if there was the slightest chance he would choose the wrong side if it came to that. Jesse's hopes raised somewhat as Singleton's eyes flickered with interest.

Before Singleton could respond, Feldman spoke. "I agree with you, Gerry." Jesse's hopes plummeted. "I think the Mendez case has gone as far as necessary and that we ought to wrap it up here and now." His eyes probed Jesse's. "But, I think I ought to allow Jesse to pull those returns and give him the time to see if they're worth pursuing." Jesse's eyes flashed the excitement that built up in his body.

Singleton said, "I agree. If a connection can be built between the entities, it will be worth probing further." He looked at Jesse, who was working with all his might to contain himself. Singleton stood and moved away from the chair. "Got to run. Please keep me informed." He took Jesse's hand. "Good job, Jesse. I like the way your mind works." At the door, Singleton turned toward the men. "What will you do about Senator Walker?"

CHAPTER 10

Jesse sat in the parking lot and stared past the large, sprawling warehouse near the wharf, at the ship in the harbor maneuvering for a docking position. He was pleased with himself that he had been able to purchase a used car similar to the one wrecked at a decent price. He hadn't wanted to fly his plane such a short distance and have to rent another car in Miami. Despite, or perhaps because of, owning his own plane and boat, rentals were too expensive for his poor pocket book. As the ship neared the dock, men and equipment moved into position to unload.

He extracted a paper from his briefcase and noted the appointment with Allied Paint at one o'clock wasn't for another hour and a half. As he strolled toward the ship, a large crane stretched its arm high into the cloudless sky. Bells clanged and whistles blew as the ship edged in to the wharf. Seagulls, flying in erratic patterns, chattered endlessly. The din of voices rose as ropes thrown from the boat were quickly secured to stanchions. Men began to stir and the crane moved closer to the ship. Smells of the sea permeated the area and mixed with the smells of ropes and engine exhausts.

Apprehension of the upcoming appointment dissipated as Jesse thought of the coming weekend when he would have his two children on his own boat with all the sea smells and adventure. For him there was nothing more enjoyable than cruising the intra-coastal or fishing in the wide-open ocean – especially when the children could join him, which wasn't too often, since their mother disapproved. She said they were too young and might fall overboard without adequate supervision and attention. He understood her concerns, but

Billy, six and Betsy, four, both loved every chance to be on the boat with their father.

Jesse's mind jerked back to the present when the crane lifted a large metal container from the hold and slowly swung it onto a waiting flatbed truck. The truck sagged a bit and creaked as the load settled. There was no name on the container; Jesse wondered if it held paint and where it was manufactured. His active, inquisitive mind took control. The name, Allied Paint Corporation, girded by the shape of a five-pointed star, was displayed in cursive style on the truck driver's door. From Jesse's position he could not see a name on the ship, so he strolled casually to the bow where the large ropes came down to the dock. The name Crown Princess didn't ring with him as a likely American name. Where was Allied getting its paint? Surely they didn't have to go outside the country. Martin Walker, the senator, popped into his head as he stared at the name.

Jesse had, after his meeting with Feldman and Singleton, requested the tax returns of the Kahid Mosque and Allied Paint, but with the normal browbeating and admonitions, he'd been delayed in requesting the senator's return without approval of higher ups. It irked him that the brass were so cautious when dealing with the elite of society. In his mind, everyone should be treated the same. Something was surely going on between Allied and the senator, and it was Jesse's job to get to the bottom of it, and the man's position should not play a part in the decision making. Requesting a look at the return was not tantamount to an examination. If nothing was found the look would end. It was a distinct possibility there was nothing sinister in the house sale. Perhaps Allied had simply made a bad deal. Maybe he could find out when he examined Allied. Jesse looked at his watch and moved toward the four-story office building behind the warehouse.

Jesse glanced around the reception room of Allied Paint as he waited for someone from accounting to come for him. Large paintings of battleships at sea graced two walls, and the wall behind Jesse held a picture of a tall bridge spanning a river with land and buildings on both sides. The receptionist, a pleasant young lady with a charming smile and blonde hair held back in a ponytail, reminded him of Amy. The thought of Amy warmed his innards. The middle-aged woman walking toward him interrupted his train of thought and brought him back to the task at hand.

Jesse's penchant for quality and fairness in all his audits, the reason for his constant promotions ahead of many of the other agents, had led him to fend off Feldman's desire to close the Mendez case until he had the opportunity to assure himself Allied's payments to Mendez were in fact income. He could've waited until the actual audit of Allied to gather the information, but Feldman persisted – he wanted to close the case without further delay.

"Mr. Hawkins?" The woman shook Jesse's hand, then led him through the door and down a long hall into a room with cubicles clustered in the center – employees busy at their various tasks. "I have copies of the checks you requested." She removed an envelope from the top of her desk and handed it to Jesse. "Can I see your identification card, please?"

Jesse produced his card and, while she examined it, extracted the check copies from the envelope and noted that both were made payable to Julio Mendez. The reverse side showed the endorsement by Mendez. "Can you tell me what the payments were for? Is there an invoice?"

The woman produced the original of the letter to Mendez, which mentioned the amounts. "This is the only authorization in the file."

"What account were the amounts charged to?"

She scanned the ledger for a second. "Outside Service." She patiently waited further questions. "Will that be all?"

Jesse placed the envelope and the checks in the file in his briefcase. "Thank you very much Miss . . . ."

"Mrs. Dexter."

"Uh, Mrs. Dexter. Thanks again." He made a mental note of the name and turned to leave, then quickly turned back to Mrs. Dexter. "Perhaps you can answer one more question for me." He noted the dissatisfaction on her face. "Is Mr. Mendez a regular with the company? Has he been hired before?"

"I'm sorry, Mr. Hawkins, but you'll have to ask my supervisor that question."

"Could you get him for me?"

"Follow me." She walked toward the end of the room, knocked politely on a door and entered. "Mr. Milton. Mr. Hawkins from the Internal Revenue Service would like a word with you, if you please." At the man's nod she ushered Jesse into the room and quickly retreated.

The man stood when Jesse entered. "Mr. Hawkins." He extended his hand toward Jesse. "I trust you obtained what you came for. How can I help you?"

"Thank you for seeing me, Mr. Milton. Just have one question." Jesse noted the sparseness of the small room – not even a picture. "How did Allied Paint come into contact with Mr. Mendez, way up in West Palm Beach?"

Milton seemed to think long on that question. "I'm not absolutely sure, but when I learned of your appointment, I did a little research on Mr. Mendez and found he had performed a couple of routine property appraisals in that area for us." Milton seemed satisfied with his answer.

"How did the company learn of him?"

Milton seemed hesitant again and Jesse gave him his best professional stare.

Milton said, "I really can't say, Mr. Hawkins. I'd suggest you speak with someone in upper management. Would you like me to introduce you?"

Jesse glanced at his watch. "Guess not, better be going." He reached for Milton's hand and grasped it when it was extended. "Thanks for your time, sir. I won't trouble you more today." Jesse noted no change in Milton's face with the word *today*. He wanted to ask where Allied got its paint, but decided to wait until the audit.

It was four-thirty when Jesse arrived back at the office and frowned at the evil grin on Michael Gibson's face as he approached his desk. A little weary after the trying trip from Miami, he loosened his tie, removed his coat and hung it on the back of the chair. There were only a few other agents at their desks. "What now, Mike? You got a good one?" He moved the two files to the side, laid his briefcase on the desk and scanned the telephone messages.

"No, but I hear you've got a doozy. Want to tell me about it?"

Jesse turned toward Gibson, a slight frown returning. "Who told you that? You still talking about that 'urgent file'?" He retrieved the Mendez file from the briefcase. "This?" He held it up so Gibson could see the "urgent" still on the front of the file. "Report goes in this afternoon, typical Taxpayer Compliance Case. Little change – not much." Jesse took his chair and glanced at the other two files. His heart skipped a beat. He leaned over to read the labels, Allied Paint and Kahid Mosque. One file appeared empty. A moment of doubt coursed through his body. He opened the mosque file. His heart sank. The one piece of paper in the file read, in bold capital letters, "NO TAX RETURN ON RECORD." He glanced at the Allied return, felt reassured about that one, then placed both files in the desk drawer along with several other cases, both ongoing and not started, and stood with the Mendez file in hand.

Gibson, still eyeing Jesse suspiciously, said, "I got the word from CID. Seems you may've come across something of interest to them. What is it? You need help?"

Jesse gazed unbelieving at Gibson. Who would've told him that? Jesse knew that Gibson had worked several cases with CID and therefore had personal contacts in the department, but only Amy and Singleton knew of his findings and aspirations. How rumors travel so fast was hard for him to digest. "I've got a couple of ideas. I'll tell you about them, but right now I've got to see Danny and get this case off my list." He walked away from the desk and turned his head to face Gibson. "Who knows, maybe you *can* be of help."

CHAPTER 11

Mrs. Dexter, with a tolerant demeanor, led Jesse to a desk far across the room in the accounting department of Allied Paint. From that vantage point he could see the supervisor through the large glass window busy at some task. Several files lay on the desk, and Jesse grimaced at the thought of searching through the two cardboard boxes on the floor next to the desk.

Mrs. Dexter stood patiently by the desk. "You can work here. I've provided what you asked for. If you need additional information, I'll be at my desk." She pointed across the room.

Jesse, aware of the obvious distaste she held for him, smiled and loosened his tie. "Thank you very much. I appreciate your cooperation. Hopefully I won't be too much of a bother." Mrs. Dexter strode away and Jesse removed his coat and sat at the desk. The supervisor looked up, then back down to the material on his desk without acknowledging Jesse's presence.

Jesse quickly scanned the balance sheet to get a general feeling of the company's overall financial status and was astounded at the relatively small amount of cash on hand at the end of the prior year. The income statement proved the most interesting. The unusual thing, in addition to the net loss shown, was the extremely small gross profit. With his portable calculator, he quickly determined the gross profit percentage – eighteen percent of sales. Most companies showed no less than forty percent, and many, much more than that. No wonder the company showed a net loss – not enough gross to cover operating expenses. He compared the financials to the tax return and found general agreement between them.

Jesse's major interests were the source of paint and the connection to Senator Walker, and he vowed to himself that he would, to the best of his ability, limit the audit to those items. Another glimpse at the balance sheet noted few assets other than the small amount of cash, accounts receivable, inventory, and virtually no debt. The income statement revealed that the loss, for the most part, was caused by the small amount of depreciation, a non-cash expense. He thought of the payment to Mendez and, to his astonishment when he looked at the Outside Service expense, found it to be much higher than the paltry sum paid to Mendez.

He picked up the general ledger and turned to the page containing detailed information of the various payments contained there. There were two items that resembled the payments to Mendez. In addition to other rather small payments, there was a large one for $150,000. He made a mental note of the date, December 14, 2005. He opened the cardboard box labeled "Invoices" and began to search. There was no invoice for that amount. The other box contained more invoices of no importance to the question and, way at the bottom, bank statements still in their envelopes. He extracted the bank statement for December and scanned the cleared checks – no $150,000. Jesse didn't know what to think except that the amount was significant if paid to one person or group.

With the bank statement and general ledger in hand, Jesse strolled over to Mrs. Dexter's desk. She seemed consumed by her duties of the moment. He waited politely for a minute and when she didn't look up said, "Excuse me, ma'am. Can I ask you a question?"

Mrs. Dexter, with a disturbed look on her face, laid the pencil on the material she was working on, covered it with a legal pad and looked up at Jesse. "Yes, Mr. Hawkins. What can I do for you?"

Jesse placed the ledger on the desk, careful not to disturb her material, opened it to the desired page and pointed to the amount in question. "That amount didn't clear in December." He held the bank statement open for her perusal. "Do you have the statement and canceled checks for this year?"

She took the statement, studied it for a moment, handed it back to Jesse and stood. "Hold on, I'll get it." She went into a room off to the side and within five minutes was back with three envelopes, which she handed to Jesse. "January, February and March. Will that be all?"

Jesse didn't move, but opened the January statement, scanned it quickly, rifled through the canceled checks and withdrew one. His heart was trying to beat a path through his ribs. His face must have looked contorted as he fought to keep the glee from showing. He handed her the check. "Would you please make a copy of this for me?" Mrs. Dexter took the check and placed it in the copying machine near her desk. "Both sides please, Mrs. Dexter." He had all he needed to extend the examination. He glanced at his watch. Only two more items to go – purchase and sale of the senator's house and the source of Allied's paint. He thanked Mrs. Dexter for her help and went back to his working area. Jesse had to finish up so he could catch Feldman before he left for the day.

It was a quarter to five when Jesse marched into Feldman's office. His mind had been a jumble during the drive from Miami. All the arguments and possibilities for a major case fought to gain control. He was at a loss as to how it all fit but, somehow, knew it did. He was certain, in his own mind at least, the mosque or its people were involved, too – maybe something really sinister. Feldman was stuffing files into his briefcase to work on at home.

Jesse caught Feldman by surprise. "Danny, hold on a bit before you leave. You've got to hear what I found out today. You're not going to believe it." Before Feldman could respond one way or the other, Jesse emptied his briefcase onto the desk.

Feldman looked at the clock on the far wall and back to Jesse. "You were in Miami today, right? I want to hear what you found but you'll have to make it quick." He finished packing his briefcase and stood as if to emphasize the importance of his time. "Got to pick up my wife in ten minutes. Let's hear it."

"Okay, quickly. I verified the purchase and sale of Senator Walker's house. Haven't had time to compare market values at the different dates, but I'll lay odds the values were the same. Definitely a payoff of some sort." The immediate frown on Feldman's face didn't go unnoticed by Jesse. Feldman seemed ready to speak, but Jesse fished through the material on the desk, held up the copy of the check and passed it to Feldman. "Who's that made out to?" Raised eyebrows replaced the frown on Feldman's face. Jesse said, "Check the endorsement – on page two."

"All right, we've got the connection between Allied and the senator, but it still doesn't prove anything. What was the check for?"

"It was entered on the books as Outside Service, the same classification as the two payments to Mendez, who didn't report them on his tax return. Questions are, what service did the senator render to Allied for such a large fee, and did he report it on his return?" Feldman continued to study the check. Jesse said, "Danny, I want to pull the senator's return. I think this is justification to do so."

Feldman returned the papers to Jesse and glanced again at the clock. "I agree with you but if we do that, you can bet we're going to catch hell from the top. Let me sleep on it."

He picked up his briefcase and moved toward the door. "I've got to go right now. Are you going back to Miami tomorrow?"

Jesse followed. "Yes, first thing in the morning. But, Danny I've got more."

"Not now, Jesse, see me first thing when you get back."

CHAPTER 12

Jesse merged in with other cars on I-95 and settled into his seat for the hour and a half drive from Miami to West Palm Beach, his mind afire with decisions to be made. From his prior review of state records, which revealed a change of the registered agent, he suspected Allied's ownership had changed. Although his suspicions were confirmed from the search of corporate records today, he had been unable to determine the identities of the new owners. Only one stock certificate was issued – to a nameless trust. There had been only one prior owner, too – Bristol Ltd. A review of the corporate minutes indicated the transfer of ownership occurred on January 10, 2006, with a new board of directors installed that same day. There were three Arab names on the board, and of particular interest, a Syed Rabia of West Palm Beach.

Still unable to contain his excitement and eager to share this information with Feldman, Jesse pounded the steering wheel with the flat of his hand. That man, Syed, could be both the connection to Mendez and the referral source. The driver in the next car looked at Jesse as if he was crazy and sped out of reach.

Another car zipped by and gave Jesse a dirty look. The thought of the killings flashed across his mind. He wondered if all the killings and his accident were unrelated. He finally realized he was in the fast lane going slow. He sped up and merged in with the other cars.

After a while those thoughts faded and the current questions pulsed through Jesse's mind, each trying to gain the top spot. One was the intent of the new owners. Were they simply acquiring a going business, even though it obviously wasn't profitable? That didn't make much sense to

Jesse, although he recognized he wasn't much of a businessman and was unaware of future growth and other financial possibilities. Number two, and perhaps most important, certainly the most exciting for Jesse, was the fact the new owner was a trust, with Arab names on the board. Was this the same as the real estate trust with Mendez as trustee? This tied directly into his conspiracy theory. These new owners surely knew of Allied's prior dealings with Senator Walker. And, of course, just what is the purpose of those dealings – apparently some favoritism, perhaps the contract with the U.S. Navy? The company sold only a paltry amount to others – the Navy contract was the plum.

Another question had to do with the product itself. Allied, the company in Miami, simply purchased the paint from the Provident Paint Company in Nassau, Bahamas, and sold most of it to one customer. Allied's gross profit was definitely inadequate, resulting in net losses and, in Jesse's mind, conjured up concepts of tax evasion. The big questions for Jesse were, did the Nassau company manufacture the paint and what was the cost of doing so? He remembered the name of the prior owner, Bristol Ltd., and the name on the ship delivering paint in Miami, Crown Princess, and wondered if things didn't go further. He wondered, too, how the Nassau company acquired the products necessary to make paint.

Jesse's mind immediately jumped gears, and Allied's income statement appeared as if he held it in front of him. There was no loss from the sale of the senator's house. Where would that have been reported? *Wait a minute. The sale by Allied was in 2006!* He tried to recall the balance sheet and general ledger to see if the purchase showed as an asset. The image wouldn't appear. *Damn.* How could he have missed that? He'd verified the sale but only from the closing statements and deeds. Why hadn't he traced it to the financial statements? *Damn. Damn.* He'd have to do it when he returned next week. He continued to wrestle with the question. How could he have been so dumb? Was the transaction not on the statements? Surely he would've been drawn to something as big as that. The revelation hit him like a thunderbolt. *My God, that money was filtered through the company from someplace else but was not entered on the books.*

Jesse's mind was still on fire as he pulled in to the parking lot at the Revenue Service office. He had been toying with the idea of going to Nassau to see what he could learn about the paint company there. Now it was settled. If Feldman approved he would fly over there tomorrow.

CHAPTER 13

As the small plane cleared the runway Jesse eased back on the control, climbed steadily until he passed the coastline, then leveled off at five thousand feet and slowly turned south for the two-hour flight to Nassau. Dark clouds sitting far out on the horizon were edged in a golden glow from the rising sun. Excitement built gradually as he slowly turned southeast and moved away from the beautiful beaches stretching all the way to Miami. This was the first time he would cross such a vast expanse of water for an extended period of time. Thoughts of the Bermuda Triangle and the Air Force planes lost in this same area during World War II flashed across his mind. He had flown across the Gulf to Key West on several occasions, but land had always been in sight in case of an emergency. His confidence returned in full force when he saw the large fishing boat making its way north. If they could brave the seas, so could he.

In due time he switched air control from Miami to the control tower in Nassau and zeroed in on the approach radar there. Tufts of clouds, seemingly fixed permanently in the still atmosphere, periodically blocked the sun slowly rising in the east.

"Nassau tower, 8425 Delta request permission to land, runway two-two." Jesse listened to the response in his headset. "8425 Delta cleared for landing, runway two-two."

"Two-five Delta, roger, runway two-two." Jesse maneuvered the Piper Arrow into the downwind approach, made the crosswind turn and lined up on runway 22. The sun, ahead and off to his right, was now about eleven o'clock high. The landing was as perfect as any he'd ever made, with the landing gear not bouncing once. Good feelings always came when he performed professionally.

Jesse secured the plane and went into the small building where pilots filed their flight plans or took care of other flight needs. In a small room off to the left were two men, one apparently getting lessons. A sideways glimpse at the student sent cold chills racing down Jesse's spine. The man, light-brown colored, sported a close trimmed beard that went in a thin line from his sideburns down around his chin. Jesse immediately recalled a similar looking man he'd met five years ago when he, too, was taking instruction. The man later turned out to be one of the men identified as a pilot in the World Trade Center disaster. Jesse fought off a strong urge to go directly back to his plane and head for home. Instead, he went into another room and asked the young woman there if she would call him a taxi.

While awaiting the arrival of the taxi, Jesse strolled outside to enjoy the fresh, breezy air drifting in from the Atlantic Ocean off to the east, just beyond rising sand dunes. A small plane touched down on runway 22 and, with only a slight bounce, turned onto the taxiway and proceeded toward the parking area. Jesse's gaze took in the other planes of all sizes and finally settled on his own sleek airplane nestled in between two others with high wings and tail wheels. His looked so much more like a fighter plane, with low wings and nose wheel. He stood a little tall with the knowledge that he was a pilot and had mastered the trying learning sessions. He had just flown across the ocean to land on a small island – no small feat, the result of his instrument training. Out of the corner of his eye, he saw a car pull in next to the building, and he moved toward the taxi.

Jesse opened the back door and, as he was getting in, said, "Provident Paint Company."

Before he could settle onto the seat, the driver turned toward him and said, "Provident Paint Company? Where is it?"

Jesse stared at the man in disbelief. He'd expected the company, whose sales were monumental, would be well-known on such a small island, especially to the cabbies. "You don't know where it is?"

"No, sir. Never heard of it."

"Okay, hold on. I'll go look in a phone book." He exited the car. "Be right back."

Inside the building Jesse found a phone book dangling from a chain next to the phone booth. He quickly flipped through the few pages to P and, to his utter amazement, there was no Provident Paint Company listed. He looked again to make sure, scanning all the P's – no listing. *Now what?* He ran his hand through his hair in puzzlement. Could he have been wrong with the name? His mind brought forth a clear image of all the invoices he had reviewed – the name clear – Provident Paint Company. His mind in a blaze, he walked back to the taxi, handed the man a five-dollar bill and told him he wouldn't need him today. The man smiled, thanked Jesse and drove off.

Jesse walked around to the front of the building and absentmindedly watched a Lear-Jet taxi toward the end of the runway preparing for takeoff. The wind was building. His mind would not let go of the problem. Someone had to know about the company. He placed his hand on the doorknob to enter the building when something like a blast furnace went off in his head. *A bank account!!!*

CHAPTER 14

It was mid-afternoon Friday and Syed was eager to get home. He routinely scanned the contract, signed and dated it at the bottom, placed it into the out-basket, and reached for another. All in all it had been a good week – three new investment clients each with assets exceeding $1.5 million. He mentally calculated his fees, at one percent, to be over $45,000 per year. During the coming week the clients would sign the contracts and he'd begin managing the funds – all part of a growing business. It would be a busy week.

Elation was still wending through his body when the phone rang. He picked up the receiver and placed it to his ear as he continued scanning the contract he had in his hand. A slight frown creased his face as he listened and then responded, "All right, I'll speak with him." He punched the button for the other line. "Yes, Zack. How are things down south? Everything all right, I hope." As he listened to Zack Olsen, CEO of Allied Paint, the frown deepened and all elation disappeared.

"You're being audited by a revenue agent from here? What's going on?" Syed moved the receiver away from his ear to mitigate the loud voice that followed.

Zack seemed excited. "It apparently started from the agent's questioning the payment to a Julio Mendez. I believe it was you who recommended Mr. Mendez for the appraisal of Senator Walker's house. It seems the agent simply wanted to know the reason for the payments but his questions went further. He was curious as to why we hired someone from your area. When we told him it was for an appraisal he seemed to understand, yet he pressed for how Mendez was recommended to us. He never did learn that, but I thought it best to alert you that he has returned and has begun what appears to be a full-scale audit. This is new – we've never had an audit before." Zack paused as if waiting for questions or comments, and when none were forthcoming, he continued, "Any ideas? Suggestions?"

Syed felt faint. Words would not emerge from his mouth. Sweat began building on his neck. He loosened his tie and unbuttoned his shirt. Finally he managed to speak. "What is he looking for now? I've never experienced an audit from them either. Is the agent questioning anything in particular?" Syed mopped his brow and neck with his handkerchief.

"He seemed quite interested in the payment to the senator last year and to the source of our paint. I don't know why he'd be interested in that. You don't think he suspects anything do you?"

Syed forced himself to back away from the terror that had a strong hold on him, stood and ran his hand through his thinning hair. Probably just a routine audit. The government must do this sort of thing all the time. The thought that this had all started from a question about Mendez jumped suddenly into his mind and he almost dropped the phone. How would the agent have known about the payment from Allied to Mendez? My God! In a raspy, thin voice he asked, "Who is this agent?"

There was a rustling of papers on the other end of the line and then, "A Jesse Hawkins."

The name didn't bring a reaction in Syed. He remembered that Hamza had told him the agent's name but because he was so averse to killing innocents he had not paid careful attention – rather not know that part of the operation. He knew full well the necessity to take whatever steps needed to overcome the enemy of his people and religion, but it still didn't sit well with him. The doubts he harbored about his decision to take the side against the infidels in power gained prominence when it came to killing others. The slight cough coming through the phone brought him back to reality.

"I'm sorry, Zack. My mind was trying to determine if there was a connection between the agent at Allied and the audit of Mendez. I think—"

"I'd say they were one and the same. This Mr. Hawkins first came here with the sole question of the Mendez payments. I guess it was something he found while here that sent him into a full examination of Allied. The payment to the senator, I suppose."

"I tend to agree with you. Those agents are probably always looking for connections and leads." That thought was the big worry for Syed and he thought Hamza had taken care of that. If this man was, in fact, the same agent, he definitely was the real snoopy kind – and tough. Where would his nose lead him? Were there enough tangible connections to allow him to unravel the whole operation – even the ultimate goal?

Syed was sure Zack had no knowledge of the real purpose or the extent of the whole operation. He was only concerned with Allied Paint, its continued contract with the Navy, and the profits collecting tax-free in foreign accounts. Zack had been transferred from the mother company in England to head Allied in Miami. But beyond that he knew nothing and it was best to keep it that way. "I'd venture to say the agent's questions and probing are normal operating procedure. Probably nothing to worry about." Syed paused as his mind delved into the memory stored there. "The payment was shown as a legitimate expense wasn't it? I mean there's an invoice and other proof isn't there?"

"Yes. It was entered on the books as Outside Service. It's a legitimate expense for us. He helps us keep the Navy contracts active." Silence pervaded the phone line. "I'm not sure if he gave us an invoice. I'm trying to picture one in my mind, but can't bring one up." Zack hesitated again. "I'll see what we have and get back to you."

"Wait a minute, Zack. I thought we were talking about the payment to Mendez. What is this about the payment to the senator listed as an expense? That payment was supposed to be a campaign contribution. It was listed as an expense?"

After undue hesitation, Zack said, "Payments to the senator have always been treated as expense. They—"

"But it was my understanding the total was to have been treated as extra compensation to employees and that they would, in effect, make the contribution to the senator." Syed wrenched inside. *What have they done?*

Through the phone, Syed heard ringing in the background. Then he heard Zack's voice. "That's my private line. Got to go. I'll call you later on today."

"But . . . ." That payment charged to the senator as an expense could lead to a total unraveling of the operation. Syed wanted to get to the bottom of this problem now. How could this have happened?

The ringing in the background continued and Zack said, "Sorry, Syed. Have to go. I'll get back."

Syed, still agitated, said, "All right. Keep me informed."

Syed eyed his treasured books as he walked in their direction and extracted his cell phone. He placed a call to Abdullah Zacaari, received no answer, and left a message.

CHAPTER 15

Syed, from his perch on the cement bench in the mosque garden, stared at the myriad flowers and shrubs, his mind fighting to find solutions to the many troubling questions dwelling there. After fifteen minutes the mixture of smells had all merged into one. He looked at his watch. Had Abdullah received his message? He may be on his way back to the university. Syed had decided to place another call when Abdullah stepped into the garden and strolled across the patio. Syed stood, took the extended hand and indicated a place on the bench. When both were seated, he said, "Please forgive me, Abdullah. I know you were planning to return to your home today, but I hoped for a word with you before you left. I was about to give up hope."

"It is all right, Syed. Do not fret. I will arrive home in due time. You have important information?"

"I have heard disturbing news today." Syed glanced away from the piercing eyes to gather his thoughts. A small bird flitted among the bushes picking at morsels gathered there. "It involves the new company I was able to acquire, Allied Paint Corporation in Miami. You remember."

Abdullah smiled. "Oh, yes. A superb source of cash, and generated right here on American soil – supported by a member of the United States Senate." The smile broadened and he patted Syed on the knee. "I cannot congratulate you enough. A supreme coup. What do you have?"

"Do you remember the revenue agent investigating the member of our mosque who was cooperating with us in the money business?" Abdullah nodded. Syed continued, "You will also remember the agent was, to my utter dismay, eliminated through an automobile accident." Syed noted the changed expression on Abdullah's face. "I am sorry. You

71

know me. I simply cannot get accustomed to the killing – even though I know it may be necessary in our quest." He looked to Abdullah for continued understanding of his weakness.

Abdullah patted the knee again and said, "I understand better than you might realize. You see, I, too, deplore needless killing – in addition, it is against our laws. We must turn to Allah, praise be his name, for his guidance in situations like these. We are in a quest to rid our country of the infidels. Unfortunately, that means taking the battle to their home ground – the only way we can survive, they give no quarter. Please do not worry yourself. We will leave these matters to others. Now what is it about this agent that causes you consternation?"

"He apparently has survived." Syed noted the unbelieving look on Abdullah's face. "The agent, through his connection with our Mendez, is now investigating Allied Paint and has discovered the connection to the senator. My worry is that his continued probing will somehow lead to the operation."

"How can that be?"

"I am unsure, but he has questioned why Mendez was chosen for the small job and how he was referred in the first place. If the agent can tie Mendez to the mosque, it may lead to me." Syed fought to keep the alarm generated in his body from spreading to his face. What had he done? Had he now placed himself in jeopardy?

A confirming look did not appear on Abdullah's face. "You are much needed by the *mujahadeen*. Your operation must not be compromised. The money you have spread in this country has allowed us to move further ahead than would otherwise have been possible in such a short time. We are on the verge of the largest coup in the history of the world. Allah sanctions all acts necessary to spread his word. Allah be praised." Abdullah's voice began to rise with the zeal building in his body. He stood, glared at the sky and spread his arms wide as if to invoke the wrath of the Almighty God. "Allah will strike the infidel, the slaughterer of millions, the enemy of all Islam, in the heart. Millions will perish in the first wave to atone for all those killed and mutilated by the infidel. He will . . . ." His voice cut off abruptly and he turned to face Syed. In a much softer tone he addressed Syed. "Forgive me. I am not accustomed to allowing my emotions free rein, but it is important that your mission not be altered. We must act to prevent it. There is too much at stake."

Syed kept his face calm even while he sat aghast at such an outburst from a man who was always controlled and completely businesslike. His own fears had retreated during the tirade and he felt an important and necessary part of the operation. His patriotism for his mother country and loyalty to his religion grew in the moment, and he realized that he must do everything possible to overcome his weakness. The future of Islam was at stake. But the idea of Islam calling for the killing of millions didn't reconcile with the Islam he had grown up with. Something was wrong with all this. "You will contact Hamza Nagin?"

"Yes, I will call him."

CHAPTER 16

Abdullah took the ticket from the woman in the turnpike toll booth, made his way to the on-ramp, and gathered speed as he merged into traffic on his way north to Orlando. He grimaced at the thought of another killing. At first Hamza had sounded outraged upon hearing the revenue agent had not been killed in the auto pile-up, but then had seemed eager to do it again. He had vowed that this time he would take care of the problem himself.

Abdullah forced himself to think on other things as he glanced at the clock on the dashboard and noted the time. He had two lectures to present tomorrow at the university, but nothing else planned that would interfere with a nice weekend with his daughter and her family who were flying in from New York. In two hours he'd be home, with time to shower and dress for the evening planned with his beloved wife.

The thought of New York brought him back to the present and Syed's words of a few minutes ago. "If the agent can tie Mendez to the mosque, it may lead to me." Syed's face had barely registered the small misstep in his misuse of words, which could place him in danger, but it was enough to be noticed by Abdullah, who was a master at reading facial signals. Abdullah had mustered all his power and technique to keep his facial features and his tone of voice conciliatory upon hearing the news of the revenue agent now pursuing Allied Paint Corporation. If it could indeed lead to Syed, what effect would that have on the operation? The answer to that question was crucial since D-Day was fast approaching. The D-Day thought turned his thinking to his daughter and how he could convince her that she must relocate – perhaps move to Florida. New York City would soon be a wasteland.

Maybe Florida wasn't the right place either – the commanders had mentioned Miami, as well as several other major U.S. cities, in their planning. She must be ready for the "Hiroshima" of the western world.

Abdullah inserted a disc into the audio player, and hoped the soft classical tunes would palliate his troubled mind. It worked for a peaceful few minutes; then Syed re-emerged. Syed had become like a son to him – how he imagined a son would be. Syed was a good man. Honest. Kind, considerate, and fair. Abdullah was well aware of the side of Syed that rebelled against illegality and violence, and the effect that had on the operation. Abdullah fully understood since he, unlike foreign-born Syed, was a native born citizen of the United States. Even though he had found many faults with the American system of government over the years, he had initially rejected any suggestions to side with his father's mother-country and wage war on the so-called infidel. In time, Abdullah had been persuaded to raise money through mosque donations and publication of an Arabic newsletter and, through those activities had begun to understand the plight of his father's people. Even though he had become more vocal in his criticism of U.S. policy in the Mid-East, he had maintained his positive attitude toward the country of his birth. That was until government agencies swooped down on him after 9/11 and kept him locked up for a year and a half simply because he was of Mid-Eastern descent, before their methods almost ruined his way of life – his religion. Now he fully accepted the term *infidel* and the fact that the United States was preoccupied with taking over the entire Mid-East and spreading their religion throughout – proclaiming the Jews to the detriment of all else. His fingers tightened on the steering wheel. He realized he was beginning to boil at the injustices he imagined.

Back to the problem of Syed. How would Syed react to the knowledge that millions would be killed in the initial attack? Would it be necessary to take action against him if it came to that? Abdullah quickly forced such thoughts from his mind, but Syed's image remained. Abdullah remembered how impressed he had been when Syed's father first introduced them in 1999. An MBA graduate from Yale at twenty-five, Syed, a rather good looking, fair skinned Arab, had spent two years with a large brokerage house on Wall Street in New York City, and in 1999 had a fledgling financial consulting business progressing rapidly.

Abdullah had thought at the time that Syed was the ideal person to organize and head up the money raising efforts to gain a foothold in the American business community. Abdullah had been proven right. Syed had initially believed that the money he received from the mosque to purchase interests in strategic U.S. businesses came from wealthy donors throughout south Florida. He had believed that his participation was completely legal and that it would ultimately benefit people in Mid-Eastern countries. Over time Syed had come to accept the proposition that the aim of the United States was to alter the Mid-East by changing its governments and religion. By the time Syed finally learned the true nature of the operation, he had already devised an elaborate scheme to bring in untold amounts of money and effectively wash it before making legitimate investments. His success was celebrated in the highest echelons of the *Mujahadeen*, and one day soon he would be honored.

A contented smile broadened on Abdullah's face as he replaced the disc. Soft, pleasant music wafted in the still, cool air. Yes, Syed was quite a man – could easily be his son. *I could never harm him, but . . . .*

The smile quickly changed to a frown as his thoughts abruptly turned to the tax examination by the revenue agent, and the possible consequences that held for the operation. Hamza Nazim had reported that the agent was surely dead from the inferno following the car pile-up and that the other agent in the hospital had also been eliminated. What had gone wrong?

Hamza was not generally wrong in such matters. Maybe it was because he'd had to make it look like an accident rather than doing it himself.

Abdullah had first met Hamza while teaching high school in Miami. At the behest of the boy's mother, Abdullah had taken Hamza under his wing to try and bring to the surface the apparent genius residing deep within a very disturbed youth. The boy was known as a troublemaker and bully on the school campus and in his neighborhood. Even though Hamza continued to exhibit meanness to his peers, his academic prowess emerged under the guidance and urging of Abdullah and placed him in the top ten of his class in his senior year. When Abdullah transferred to the university, his only contact with the boy was through Hamza's mother. The boy graduated from high school, entered junior college and seemed on his way to a good life. Upon the death of his mother, he quickly reverted to his old, perhaps natural, ways. He dropped out of school, shaved his head, inserted an earring in the shape of a knife and began leading a gang in the neighborhood, exacting tribute from the citizens.

After Hamza's recent conversion to Islam and because of the occasional need for gang action, Abdullah reluctantly made Hamza a part of the operation. Even though Syed would have nothing to do with ordering such activities, it seemed necessary to expose Syed to the realities and to get him further involved. It was decided that Hamza would get his orders from Abdullah but report directly to Syed.

Abdullah ejected the disc and inserted another. His mind shifted again to the problem of Syed and the revenue agent.

How could the agent possibly make a connection between Allied Paint, Syed, and the operation? Even if he did examine Syed, he wouldn't find anything relevant. Syed ran his business and personal life above reproach. He felt it was his duty to contribute to the government's cash needs. Maybe trying to eliminate the agent had not been the wisest action to take. That kind of push apparently only deepened the government's resolve. He pounded the steering wheel with the heel of his hand, peeved with himself for ordering the killing of Mendez and the agents, and said to the road ahead, "Look where that has taken us." Abdullah was not one to chasten himself, but that decision was probably one of the worst he had ever made.

Abdullah entered Syed's number into his cell phone, tapped his finger on the steering wheel in tune to the music, and when the answering machine finished its spiel, said, "Syed this is Abdullah. I deem it wise to alter our plans. We should not harm the revenue agent. I will contact Hamza and deter him. Call me if you have questions." Deter him? At least for the moment.

Hamza knelt alone in the praying room of the mosque in Miami, serene and feeling the presence of Allah. The muscles in his shoulders and arms bulged as he bent his body forward, placed his head and outstretched hands on the tiled floor, and prayed in a low voice. He prayed for understanding and forgiveness from Allah for having to use violence against another person. Even though he personally enjoyed watching people squirm and suffer, and, for some unknown reason, used every opportunity to exact begging from his victims, he had vowed to follow the laws of Allah as set forth by his messenger, Mohammed. Hamza understood the law against killing but understood that it was acceptable to further the *Jihad*, and to spread the word of Islam.

He could not understand how he'd misread the fate of the revenue agent. The crash had been so well-planned. No one could possibly survive being buried under an exploding car. But the name rang true – it had to be the same agent. This time he would take care of the matter himself.

He ignored the muted signal from the cell phone and continued with his prayer.

CHAPTER 17

Martin Walker nodded to the senator to continue with her questioning of the Department of State representative and turned to the aide sitting behind him. The aide leaned forward and pointed to the remaining name on the paper. Martin sighed and returned his focus to the center of the room where the middle-aged representative, waiting patiently, adjusted the papers on the table in front of him. Martin glanced down the line of senators seated at the long, arched dais, and indicated to a senator four chairs to his left that he was the final questioner. Martin was ready for a break. The session thus far seemed long and arduous to him and he felt growing agitation. Yes, the war in Iraq was ill-gotten and was costing way too much, but he agreed with the President, they must stay the course. To Martin, there didn't seem to be any alternative, and they did seem to be making progress.

The emphatic voice seemed planned to provoke. "Mr. Blake, I want to thank you for your time and candor today and I want, if at all possible, to obtain an admission from this administration that the war in Iraq is ill-founded, and that a timetable for withdrawal of our troops be set without further procrastination. This war has, so far, claimed 2,500 of our bravest young men and women and has seriously maimed another 15,000 whose lives will be forever altered, some of whom will never fully recover." She looked at the file in front of her then back up to the official. "This horrible misuse of power has cost this country, during the last three years, a total of $400 billion and is expected to cost $1 billion each day we remain. You know, and everyone else knows, there was no valid reason for going into that country in the first place. The administration is attempting to blame the misstep on faulty intelligence, but you know, and I know, and most other caring people know that the president and his cohorts demanded the intelligence they got, even when it was definitely questionable. There were no weapons of mass destruction, no nuclear potential, and al Qaeda was not allowed in the country under Saddam Hussein."

She hesitated for a brief second, glanced furtively at Martin, then said, "Now I want you to forget your loyalty to the president and his henchmen for a moment and place your loyalty to the American people, where it belongs. During this hearing you have avoided the question like the true master you are, and now is the time to come clean." She stared directly at the man as if to dare him to defy her admonition. He kept his eyes locked onto hers as he waited for the question. The room remained silent. Martin looked at the small clock in front of him.

"Mr. Blake, I ask you, has a timetable been set to bring our young men home? How many more must be killed and maimed? How much more will our economy be allowed to deteriorate? When will this horrible war end? When, Mr. Blake? What is the plan?"

Norman Blake didn't make the slightest move except to keep his eyes focused on the questioner. The room remained hushed. Martin noted that most of the senators appeared subdued and ready to end the endless, repetitive questioning, the answers to which were also repetitive. He knew that something must be done to stop the continued bleeding of men and resources, but the available options produced no viable solutions.

Blake, his hands resting on each side of the file in front of him, apparently eager to end the two hours of grilling, said, "I sincerely respect your questions and concerns, Senator. Please believe me when I say that I share them." He gazed from left to right at the curved row of senators on the panel. "I have listened to all sides of this debate today, as I have in the past, and I have to say I agree with all of them. That is, we must find a solution to the problem as soon as possible. But I have to tell you, as I have throughout this session, the president and his Cabinet have thoroughly considered all options and have determined that staying the course is the only one that is viable. They are working continuously with the U.S. Military, the Iraqi government, and the Iraqi Army to develop a plan for withdrawal. They fully understand that removal of Coalition Forces from the area is required for the ultimate benefit of the Iraqi people and for the benefit of the United States." Again he removed his focus from the questioning senator to look into the eyes of each of the other senators. "Believe me, it is not in the best interests of either country to set a date for withdrawal."

The adamancy of the senator's voice hadn't changed. "I find it hard to understand why the president can't simply tell the American people when this war will end and when our young men and women will be coming home. I—"

Martin interjected, "The senator's time is up." He looked down the row and nodded to the next and final speaker.

The middle-aged senator fingered the knot on his tie. "Thank you, Senator Walker. I will just take a minute." He spoke directly to the visitor. "Mr. Blake, let me first thank you for devoting your valuable time to the questions of this panel. We all recognize the enormity of the situation and the extreme costs in lives and money. While we are all seriously concerned about the young men and women who daily place their lives in harm's way, our primary concern on this panel is the financial aspect. As my respected senator has noted, the costs have been astronomical and will continue to be so as long as we're engaged there. But, no matter the reason for this engagement, or judgment errors made in the past, the blunt fact is that we are at war – not only in Iraq where we're trying to liberate the people from tyranny, but here at home from those who would love to see this great country go down in defeat. We must not lose either battle." His voice quivered slightly and he paused to glance at the other senators along the dais. "We must, too, be ready to cede some of our liberties if necessary for ultimate victory. We must not lose." He choked up again and looked first to Blake, then to Walker. "That's all I have, sir."

Martin casually eyed the other patrons in the Senate cafeteria as he stirred cream and sugar into his coffee, half- hearing the conversation between the two senators sitting at his table. When there was a pause in the discussion, he said, "I was very touched with Will's sincerity. I was afraid for a minute that he might break down. I think his little speech had a like effect on most of the others – even some of the diehards. I'm afraid that I, too, get a wee bit emotional when I get to reflecting on this country and our system of freedoms, and the thought that we might not be up to the task of taking the necessary hard road to protect those freedoms. I abhor the thought of losing any of our rights – those initially adopted in the Constitution and all those we've fought to amass over the years." In deep thought about the country he loved so much, he lifted the coffee cup and stared into it for a second before he took a sip. "But, as Will so aptly said, it just may be necessary to give up some of them temporarily. We've never been in a war like the one we're in now. How're we to fight an enemy we can't see?" He again lifted his cup and stared over the rim at the two senators sitting across from him.

Gordon spoke. "I don't see the great problem of requiring that some freedoms of some people be curtailed for a period of time. We did it during World War II, and that was an enemy we could see. Today the enemy could be sitting right over there at the next table and we wouldn't know it." He motioned with his arm at others in the room. "Radical Muslims have vowed to take us down and if we don't get serious, they just may be able to pull it off. They're relentless. They're—"

The other senator butted in, "Question is, what liberties do you curtail? The president already, right after 9/11, began snooping on people's telephone conversations in contradiction to the procedures in place. Where does it end?"

Martin answered, "I know it's a tough proposition but it's one we must grapple with whether we like it or not. I think our agencies were asleep at the wheel before 9/11. As we've heard since, there were many clues available, but all too far-fetched to be deemed viable. They were pooh-poohed, and the result was the deaths of three thousand innocent people, and had a few brave souls not acted, the ultimate would've occurred – the destruction of the White House and, had he been in residence, our leader." He drank the rest of his coffee and signaled for the waiter. "Even though we have, during the last three years, reorganized the intelligence system, I have a hunch we're still pooh-poohing the facts." He took the bill from the waiter, calculated a generous tip, signed it and returned it to the waiter with a slight approving grin. He stood. "And this brings us to the immigration bill debate next week. I think our borders and ports-of-entry are all too lax and that enemy cells are pouring into the country and setting up for the ultimate attack. When you consider the rogue countries of Venezuela, with its oil and ease of entry, and North Korea and Iran with their nuclear capability and their hatred of this country, it's easy to consider the possibility of a nuclear attack of immense proportions. We must protect our borders and take steps to root out the plotting cells." The other senators stood also and they all began moving toward the door. Martin continued. "I don't know how we're to do it, but we must. It's our duty to control immigration."

Martin held the door and he and Senator McCormick stepped into the elevator. Martin said, "Gordie, this immigration bill is going to be a tough one to craft, what with the House version to contend with." He pressed the button for the fifth floor and looked straight at Gordon. "We've got to pull out the stops. The time is now if we're to get anything worthwhile that will have a chance against the persistent encroachers. I can feel it in my gut that the hard-liners are crossing our borders in droves . . . preparing for the next attack."

The elevator door opened and he waited for Gordon to exit and stepped out behind him. Martin said, "What do you think?" They walked down the hall toward their respective offices.

"I agree with you wholeheartedly. This is the time to call in the favors – the time for maximum effort. I'll do my share, count on it." He stopped as Martin reached for the doorknob to his office and placed his hand on Martin's arm. "But Martin, I have a greater concern. I wonder—"

"What kind of concern?" Martin turned to look directly at Gordon.

"I'm concerned for you . . . ." Gordon's facial expression tried to outdo the look of dismay and question on Martin's face. "There's a rumble arising among your strongest supporters in the Senate. They seem to be worried about your re-election, and the effect that will have not only on immigration issues but many others as well – even on their individual chances at the polls."

Martin recalled his recent meeting with his staff where they had discussed their deep concerns about financing the upcoming campaign. Potential fund sources were drying up at an ever-increasing rate. He had been unable at the time to account for his waning popularity. It seemed the press was picking at his weaknesses while touting his opponent's strong points; his youth, good looks, broad smile, and general charisma. "We're working on that. We've got ideas.

Count on me to be around for another term." He paused as he searched Gordon's face for understanding and backing. "You're still with me, aren't you Gordie?"

Gordon didn't hesitate and extended his hand. "You bet. I've always been with you and I always will be. And if you need any assistance, you call on me without hesitation."

Martin took the hand and squeezed, exuding his appreciation for Gordon's unwavering loyalty. "I knew I could count on you, Gordie. We've been through some rough times together, but we've always won out in the end. It'll be no different this time."

Gordon started to move away as Martin opened the door. He stopped and looked at Martin. "Have you heard any more about the Allied Paint issue? That reporter seems to be asking more questions throughout the building and all over town."

Martin, tired and weary from a long day, especially after the conversation with Gordon McCormick, made an attempt to sift through the various reports and memos on his desk. The thought of his loving wife for so many years trying to take most of his small estate would not depart from his mind. He was about to get up and head for home, maybe stopping at the local pub for a nightcap, when Thomas Benson, after a slight rap on the door, entered and walked quickly to the desk. "What is it, Tom?"

"Allied Paint Corporation is being audited by a revenue agent in your district."

CHAPTER 18

The children squealed and tugged to get released from their mother's hold as Jesse drove into the driveway. She allowed them to pull her toward the car, and when Jesse stopped and killed the engine, she let them loose. Jesse had to coax them away from the driver's door so he could exit. Over their excited voices Jesse edged out of the car and took them both in his arms. "Okay. Okay. Go get your things." They squirmed to get down. "Hurry now, or we may not get to go." They ran to the house and went inside.

He looked at the house that once was partially his, and as always, a certain sadness revisited even though it had now been over two years since the divorce. The sight of the children always brought into view that awful day when he'd backed out of the driveway, ending ten years of marriage, and the possible loss of his dearly loved children. "Hello, Thelma. Everything okay?" Thelma, looking peeved, hadn't moved from the small brick walkway to the front door.

"You know I don't like you taking them out on that boat. One of these days . . . ." She gazed to the clear blue sky as if calling on the Almighty for a vision, then directly at Jesse. "I just wish you would—"

"Don't worry, Thelma. We've been over this a hundred times. Nothing's going to happen. We're not going out to the ocean. Just a little fishing and a swim at Peanut Island – maybe search for shells there, have a picnic. You know they love—"

"I don't care what you say, Jesse. I don't like it and I can only hope and pray nothing goes wrong. I—"

The front door slammed against the wall as Billy and Betsy burst through it and ran to the car, yelling in unison, "Come on, Daddy. Come on. Hurry!" They both tried to get in the front passenger door and began to argue about whose turn it was to ride in front.

Jesse moved around to that side of the car and said, "Don't worry, Thelma. Everything will be all right. It always has, hasn't it?" Billy pouted but got into the back seat. It was Betsy's turn in front.

Jesse eased the sixteen-foot boat off the trailer, pushed it away from the dock and, with the rope, pulled it around and secured it to the dock next to the launching ramp. After parking the car and trailer and ensuring the boat and engine were in tip-top shape, he called to the children who had been playing on the slide. Watching them run toward the boat, each squealing and vying to be first on board, he again felt the loser in him rise to the top. How could he ever assure their future, not being involved in their daily lives. "Whoa." Jesse caught them both by the arm as they ran onto the dock. "Easy. Don't want to go for a swim now, do you?" He helped Betsy over the side.

Billy made it into the boat by himself and ran directly to the cockpit and placed his hands on the helm. "I get to steer first." He began turning the wheel back and forth. Betsy, with her doll in hand, sat on the cooler and watched as Jesse boarded, unlashed the rope and pushed off.

Jesse tossed a lifejacket to each of them. "Okay, you know the drill – lifejackets on." He slipped into one and latched it.

The outboard fired up on the fourth push of the starter button and Jesse took control of the steering wheel, shifted to reverse and backed out into the channel. As he shifted to the forward gear, he made a mental note to get the starter fixed and, while he was at it, get the motor overhauled – probably well overdue.

A sense of well-being and contentment took control as Jesse gazed past two lone, white tufts of clouds hanging unmoving above a hundred-foot yacht heading north toward the inlet. The rest of the sky was a magnificent blue in all directions. This day would definitely be one of the best yet. The waves cascading from the yacht's bow multiplied and diminished in strength as they made their way across the wide expanse of Lake Worth. Jesse turned north and easily rode what remained of the waves.

Betsy, tugging at his leg, pulled Jesse from his reverie. Billy stood entranced as a small boat rode the waves close to the yacht it was trying to pass. Betsy asked, "Daddy, can I get up there?" She pointed to the console and Jesse lifted her up so she could see through the windshield.

Billy yelled against the building wind as the boat sped forward, "Look, Daddy." He looked at Jesse, then pointed toward the small boat caught in the waves of the yacht. "They're going to turn over."

Jesse looked at the small boat being tossed by the waves. "No. They'll be all right. They know what they're doing – just having some fun."

Billy asked, "Can we do it, too, Daddy?"

"Not now. We'll probably get some waves when we get into the inlet." Jesse looked back at Billy. "You've done that before. Remember?"

The small boat turned toward Jesse, racing to outrun the tumultuous waves. Jesse's heart leapt. The two men in the boat, now facing directly toward him, had light-brown skin. Jesse's mind immediately conjured up the image of the man in the BMW and brought back the tax examination, which he had so hoped would be put to the background for this special day. His hands gripped the steering wheel. Was this the same man? Both men wore baseball caps and Jesse was unable to compare either man with the bald-headed image in the

BMW. The square, brutal-looking face of one man, however, did ring a bell. Were they going to try again? What to do?

In safe water again, the boat turned north and quickly sped away.

Billy moved next to Jesse. "Can I steer, Daddy?"

Jesse stared at the retreating boat, his mind recounting all the events of the past two weeks, the murders, the auto accident, the examination and its myriad problems and loose connections. He would have to concentrate all his resources if he were to solve the case. Simply no time left for relaxation on his cherished ocean. How was he to make the connection to the mosque? And where did it go from there? Was there a connection to the senator? Was he connected to a plot to bomb the United States? How absurd. *There goes my crazy mind again – always searching for that wild case.*

The small boat moved around a small island and out of sight. The large yacht was angling toward the inlet, heading for the ocean. The thought of going out there entered Jesse's mind – a great day for it. Maybe?

"Daddy." Billy tugged at Jesse's arm.

Jesse's hands relaxed. He took a deep breath and let it out slowly. He placed a hand on Billy's shoulder. "In a little while, son." He looked down at the little boy so eagerly wanting to be a grown-up so he could steer the boat. Jesse knew he would never devote all his time to his job, no matter how important the case was. He tousled Billy's hair. "Who wants to go fishing?"

"I do. I do." Billy ran to pick his rod off the deck. Betsy turned and looked at both as if they were daft.

Jesse reeled in his second fish, removed it from the hook and tossed it into the container in the middle of the boat. The inlet remained calm and the ocean farther out seemed flat as a pancake. He envied the people on the yacht. He wondered if they were just out for a ride or going to the Bahamas. His mind tried to carry him back to Nassau and the information gleaned there on his recent trip.

Billy looked glum. Betsy sat under the steering wheel playing with her doll. Jesse baited the hook and was ready to cast when Billy laid his rod on the deck and grabbed onto Jesse's.

"Let me use yours, Daddy." Billy tugged on the rod. "Yours is better than mine."

"This one's too big for you, son. Yours is as good as mine." He reached to get Billy's rod off the deck. "Here, let me show you."

Billy held onto the large rod. "I want to use this one. You throw it out for me."

Jesse gave a small smile of understanding, tousled Billy's hair and said, "Okay. I'll cast it. You hold on tight and reel them in at the first tug." Billy's face was determined and facing to where the cork gently bobbed.

The line had barely touched the water when a fish took the bait and yanked the rod out of Billy's hand. He squealed and Jesse grabbed the pole before it went over the side. He let the fish take the line for a bit, then jerked back and handed the rod back to Billy. "Reel him in. Feels like a big one."

Betsy ran to Billy as he, like the grown man he was, began to slowly reel in the line. Betsy said, "Wow! You caught one, Billy." She placed her hand on the rod. "Can I help?"

Billy moved the rod away from her. "No. I'm doing this." The line went taut and pulled Billy to the side of the boat. Jesse started to intercede but Billy regained control.

Betsy looked to Jesse. "Daddy. Make Billy let me do it, too."

Jesse consoled her. "Let Billy get this one, honey. You can get the next one. Okay?" Betsy pouted and went back to her place under the helm. Jesse helped Billy take the fish on board and had already removed the hook from its mouth when Billy's line, still in the water, started racing away. Jesse yelled to Betsy, "Come on Bet, come reel him in."

CHAPTER **19**

The blazing sun was tilted a little to the west when Jesse loaded the last of the gear onto the boat. Billy and Betsy ran along the westerly shore of Peanut Island, darting in and out of the water lapping at the edge of the beach. They squealed in unison as boats raced by, sending waves washing up on the beach. Invariably they would wait until the last minute to escape the rushing water and end up being drenched to their waists.

Jesse stared at them for a long moment, enjoying their glee as much as they. He loved these moments with his children and regretted that it could only be on weekends – the tragic story of divorce. He laughed out loud when Betsy tripped before she could escape from an incoming wave. The wave covered most of her body. With a pained look on her face as she scampered to safety, she looked as if she would cry, but instead, ran toward Jesse yelling. "Daddy. Daddy. Did you see that big wave? It got me all wet."

"Yes. I saw it." Jesse took a towel from the boat and handed it to her. "Here, dry yourself off." He whistled for Billy, who came running, kicking at the water as he did. "Okay. You both get dried off now. Time to go."

Billy said, "Is there anything else left to eat? Can I have another hotdog?" He crawled up on the side of the boat trying to pry the top off the ice chest.

"You'll have to eat it cold. Fire's out and we have to go." Jesse boosted Betsy into the boat and Billy pulled himself in. They all put their lifejackets on. Jesse dragged the anchor from the beach, shoved the boat into the water and climbed aboard. After five tries the motor coughed, then ran smooth. Jesse headed south toward the launch ramp. He lifted Betsy to her favorite spot on the console at the windshield.

With a wiener in his hand, Billy asked, "Can I steer, Daddy?"

Jesse looked admiringly at Billy and said, "Let's get out into the channel and you can steer us back to the dock. Okay?"

The yacht turned into Lake Worth from the inlet. Jesse could barely see the captain. The ship apparently had been on a trial run out on the ocean. That was customary after an overhaul or other substantial maintenance. Jesse did a double take when, out of the corner of his eye, he spotted the other small boat that had come toward them earlier, emerging from around the easterly edge of Peanut Island, a little behind the yacht. He fought off the emerging thought of danger. Everybody heading for home, he reckoned. Jesse was ready, too. The day, with the absolute best weather ever, had been as enjoyable as planned. Tonight he would take in a movie with Amy, dinner after and . . . who knows?

When they entered the main channel heading south, Jesse said to Billy, "Okay boy, your turn to steer." He placed the ice chest in front of the wheel and Billy stepped up and took control. Betsy looked on, pleased that Billy was able to direct the craft. All Billy had to do was keep the boat straight – nothing ahead to go around. Jesse set the speed at a rate he considered non-taxing for Billy but enough to stay well ahead of the yacht.

Three small boats raced to pass a fifty-foot yacht, all heading north in the calm water, making their way toward the inlet. After assessing how the waves would affect his boat, Jesse assured himself that Billy had control and moved to the back of the boat to prepare for unloading when they reached the dock. The small boat from the morning emerged from behind the incoming yacht, quickly overtook it, and raced toward Jesse. He determined the boat would pass to his right and the waves emitted would not seriously affect control of his own boat. The boat veered well to the right as Jesse had forecast. The waves appeared nominal but Jesse kept a keen eye on them, ready to assist Billy if necessary.

When the small boat passed, several boat lengths to the west, one of the men waved and Jesse automatically waved back. As the boat sped away, the square-faced man removed his cap and Jesse gasped. His insides tightened almost out of control and his hair felt like it was standing straight up. Sunlight glanced off the brown, bald head and instantly entered Jesse's eyes. My God. That was the man in the BMW. *I'm sure of it.* The yacht had suddenly gained speed and was fast approaching Jesse's boat. It finally dawned on him that his own boat had slowed. *I've got to get out of here.*

When Jesse yelled, Billy jumped, and when he turned to see Jesse, the force of his hand on the steering wheel caused the boat to head west, causing it to slow more due to the waves coming from the small boat. Jesse helped Billy from the ice chest. "I'll take over from here. You get to the back and sit on the floor." He removed Betsy from the console and told her to do the same. Both children looked shocked at Jesse's sudden, unusual action.

To the west, Jesse could clearly see the small boat moving south but at a slower pace. The yacht was plowing dead ahead. Jesse knew he couldn't put in to the westerly dock if those people were after him. He'd have to go east and that meant cutting in front of the fast moving yacht. He looked to the children cowering against the bulkhead in the rear. He made the decision and turned to the left and plunged the throttle forward. The boat lunged and when the boat was directly in front of the yacht, the unbelievable happened – the motor quit. The absence of sound was deafening. Time stood still.

Jesse pushed the starter button – no sound. The yacht was almost on them. Didn't they see him?

Billy screamed, "Daddy, the boat's going to run over us."

Jesse could almost reach out and touch the yacht. After the third time at the starter with no luck, Jesse, heart pumping overtime and mind running ahead of normal, sprang for the motor. Turbulent wake was forced to each side as the yacht's bow sliced through the water. Thelma's words echoed in his head. "You know I don't like them out on that boat. One of these days . . . ."

Jesse grabbed Billy and Betsy by the hand and directed them to the front. "You all get on the deck next to the steering wheel."

After the first pull, the motor purred like a kitten and was music to his ears. The yacht, its hulk towering above, would ram them in the next instant. Jesse jumped to the front, took hold of the steering wheel, eased the throttle forward and when the motor held, advanced it full throttle. The bow of the yacht touched the rear side of the boat and pushed it forward as Jesse fought to keep from capsizing. The sound of the boat scraping against the yacht was deafening as Jesse turned the boat and ran full speed in the opposite direction, all the time fighting to get through the tumultuous wake and away from the yacht. Jesse felt relief for a moment, then uncontrolled fear and dread as his boat tilted to its side, riding the crest of the yacht's wake. Jesse clung tightly to the steering wheel to avoid being tossed overboard. The propeller, now out of the water, sounded as if it would fly off. Jesse feared the boat would capsize. Both children were compressed against the side. *"My children will be killed!"*

Hamza watched the drama play out and experienced shock when the yacht proceeded south and Jesse's boat was not to be seen. Had it been pushed along with the yacht? He looked beyond the other boats moored on the east side of the lake.

To his crony he said, "Okay, let's go find them." He would not fail again.

As their boat started to move, the vibration against Hamza's leg and the soft tone of the cell phone interrupted his avid lust to kill, a small frown formed on the square, savage face. He removed the phone from his pocket, flicked it open and spoke into it. "Yes?"

The frown broadened as he listened to the voice on the other end. Then he spoke again, "What? I can't hear you well." Hamza motioned for his assistant to cut the engine and when it was quiet spoke into the phone. "Did I hear you right?"

CHAPTER **20**

Jesse, with his elbows on the desk and a hand covering each side of his head, stared straight ahead, seeing nothing. He couldn't hear the other agents in the room even if he wanted to. Mondays were usually tough but this one was like no other he'd ever experienced. His mind simply refused to cooperate and move ahead. The unopened files on his desk bore mute testimony to his inability to function normally. He had been in that stupor since the boating accident Saturday. No matter how hard he tried to focus on other things, the image of his two children jammed against the side of the boat, sheer terror on their faces, remained preeminent. Would it ever fade? The meeting with his ex-wife Saturday afternoon jumped ahead of other thoughts trying to enter.

When Jesse had parked in the driveway Saturday afternoon, Thelma came out the door and was immediately taken aback as Billy and Betsy bolted from the car and ran to her, both trying to tell her what happened. "Mama, Mama. The big boat—" They grabbed her around the waist and held on tight.

"Hold on, hold on. One at a time." Thelma cuddled them. They both tried again to tell her. "Wait." She backed them off a bit, glanced at Jesse with a look of wonder, then back at them. "Hold on, Betsy. Let Billy tell it."

Jesse opened the car door but remained seated, knowing full well he was going to be in for it from Thelma.

Billy blurted out, "Mama, the big boat almost ran over us. I was scared. I . . . ." He again buried his head against her.

"What?" Thelma cuddled him again and looked to Jesse for an explanation, then quickly back at Billy. She held Billy away from her. "What did you say? A boat almost ran over you?"

Becky joined in again and they both said, "Yes, Mama. A big boat ran right into us and we were scared to death." Billy looked to Jesse. "Ask Daddy."

Jesse stepped out of the car. "Let me explain, Thelma. The boat—"

"Am I hearing this right? You were almost run over? What happened?" Thelma stared incredulously at Jesse as he walked toward them. "I told you . . . ." She stooped down and cuddled the children to her again. With a voice quivering from a stifled cry, she exclaimed, "My God. My children were almost killed. I can't believe it." She stood and glared at Jesse, and after Jesse explained what happened, she said, "I told you this would happen and you wouldn't listen. I'll see to it that you never get a chance to do that again. Now you get out of here." She pointed to the road and led the children into the house.

The files on the desk came back into view, but the image of Billy and Betsy both looking mournfully at him as they were hurried into the house that day would haunt Jesse forever. How would he ever be able to change that image, and the image of them pressed against the bulkhead of the boat? In another second they would've been dead. How could it have happened? Would Thelma try to keep him from his children? The thoughts kept tumbling in his head as he tried to put them in order. The contents of the file he opened were meaningless. The chair next to him was empty and he was thankful Mike hadn't been in this morning. *Of course his yakking might get me out of my stupor.* He glanced around the room again and thought of going in to see Feldman. Maybe Amy was in. He needed to explain things to her anyway.

CHAPTER 21

Amy didn't press for answers as she and Jesse walked toward the park fronting Lake Worth even though questions were prominent in her mind. She had seen the anguish plainly exhibited on his face when he entered her office asking for a few moments alone with her. Her only thought at the time was that something terrible was bothering him and that she must somehow help.

They took a bench facing the waterway and Jesse looked deep into her eyes. A tear formed in the corner of his eye and he quickly looked out over the water.

Amy waited an appropriate time for him to collect himself, rubbed her hand gently across his back, and when he turned back to her, said, "Something bad has happened, I know . . . but you've got to get it out, Jesse. This isn't like you." She waited a moment, but Jesse said nothing and continued to look into her eyes as if searching for a cure. She placed her hands on both sides of his face and he immediately pressed his face against her breast. "What is it, Jesse? Get it out." She caressed his back.

Jesse backed away and swabbed the tears with his handkerchief. He looked out over the water and when he turned back, the anguished look was almost gone – he seemed more collected. He took her hands and rubbed them softly. "First let me apologize for not keeping our date Saturday and for not even calling, but I was so out of it after losing my children that I—"

"Losing your children? What are you talking about?" Amy was aghast. "You mean your ex-wife is taking them away? What are you saying?"

Jesse stood and looked again out over the water, walked to the edge and tossed a rock far out. Amy followed, but waited until he was ready to talk. He turned to her and said, "That may happen, but it was more than that. It—"

"More than that? What—"

"Hear me out." He took her hands in his.

"I'm sorry, Jesse. I didn't mean . . . ." She led him back to the bench. "Go ahead, tell me what happened."

"The tangled thoughts won't stay clear in my mind. As you know, I took the kids out on the boat Saturday and we had a good time as usual. They enjoyed every minute of it." Jesse's voice quivered and he paused. "Until the end." He seemed to be trying to clear the web in his brain.

"What tangled thoughts? What happened, Jesse?" Amy saw the pained look in Jesse's face and backed off.

Jesse continued as if Amy hadn't spoken. "Early on, a small boat trying to get out of the wake of a large yacht came straight for us. One of the occupants seemed familiar – like the Arab guy I saw at the scene of my auto accident."

Amy's brow arched and she started to ask a question, but thought better of it.

"But the boat sped away and the thought left me. We fished, had a swim, ate lunch, had a great time, then headed for home – Billy steering." Jesse paused again. Amy thought he was regaining his old self. He continued, "Then somehow, the small boat was back and so was the yacht. This time when I saw the dark, bald head, I knew it was the same guy that tried to kill me before. I decided not to put in at the regular dock. As I took the wheel from Billy and turned to head east, the motor quit. I barely got it started when the yacht was right on us. As I tried to pull away the yacht touched us in the rear and we scraped along the side and then got caught in its wake. We rose with the crest and tilted over. The prop came out of the water. The children were thrown against the bulkhead."

Amy's gut churned. She hoped it didn't show on her face. Jesse needed strength, she knew that. She must remain strong for him.

"I knew without a doubt we were going over. My children were about to die." Jesse paused and looked ready to lose it again. His lip curled up as if he was ready to cry. He took a deep breath, looked out over the water, and when he turned back was again in control. "I've never tasted fear like that before. I had no idea what kind of forces I was up against." He paused again. "Then suddenly the crest leveled off and the boat reversed its tilt. The propeller submerged and the boat eased farther away from the yacht. We were safe; my children weren't going to die."

Amy interjected, "Thank God for that but . . . where was the small boat with the Arabs? Do you think the yacht was part of a plot to kill you, or was this all just one great big unfortunate accident?"

"When we got away from the yacht, I felt an immediate sense of peace – we'd made it. Then I remembered the Arabs and my reason for going east in front of the yacht."

Amy marveled at Jesse. This talking was definitely getting it out of him.

"While we were hidden from the Arabs by the yacht, I parked my boat between other boats moored on the east side of Lake Worth. I cuddled the frightened children to me and coaxed them to be quiet. When the yacht passed completely, I saw the Arab boat start towards us, then for some reason stop and head in the opposite direction. I breathed a sigh of relief, happy that my children were still alive."

Amy stood and took Jesse in her arms. "Oh, Jesse. I'm so glad." After a moment, the investigator in her took command again, and she pushed back and asked, "So, do you think this was definitely a plot to kill you? You think the boat and the yacht were in on it?"

"I'm sure there was a plot to kill me. I'd know that Arab anywhere. Why else was he watching me? I don't know if the yacht was part of it, but when I think back on it, they were both close together early in the day, and there again at the end. A coincidence? I don't think so. That yacht was coming mighty fast and they should've seen me before my motor quit."

"Are you going to follow through? Examine the mosque? The senator?"

"That's one of the reasons I wanted to talk to you. On Saturday, right after the accident, I was in a total rage against anybody connected with that baldheaded Arab. If I could've found him, I'd have taken him out by myself. But after the meeting with Thelma on Saturday, and right on in to this morning, I've been at a complete loss. Still concerned with the kids and what psychological damage may have been done to them and, of course, worried that Thelma may try to keep me from seeing them. But now I'm ready to tackle those buzzards again. I've got to convince Danny to let me audit that mosque even though they didn't file a return." Jesse took Amy by the arm. "Come on; let's go back to the office. Got a million things to do. Want to pull the senator's return, too . . . and I haven't given up on getting the examinations transferred to CID." He looked at her and smiled. "Maybe we can work on it together."

As they walked toward the office, Amy, struggling to keep up, felt a warm feeling making its way through her body when Jesse placed his arm around her waist. She looked up into his face.

He said, "Amy, thank you so much for listening. I don't know if I could've gotten through this without you." His fingers massaged her side and he grinned. "Let's have that Saturday dinner tonight."

"At my apartment. It's the most relaxing, and . . . ." She laid her head against his shoulder and smiled.

Without taking his hand from her waist, Jesse turned to face her and stopped. He peered solemnly into her eyes and pulled her close to him and they kissed. She didn't want it to end. He whispered, "I'm nuts about you Amy. Why don't we—?" Another agent came through the door and the exhilaration ended.

Jesse didn't seem to notice her weak smile as he held the door for her. Something nagged at her senses. At the entrance to her office, she caressed his arm and, as he moved away said, "Jesse, you will be careful, won't you?"

CHAPTER 22

When Martin entered the lawyer's waiting room, he immediately saw his wife sitting by an end table engrossed in a magazine. She looked up at him as he spoke to the receptionist. "I'm Martin Walker, I have an appointment with Ms. Langton." He met Roberta's eyes momentarily then looked back at the pretty clerk.

The receptionist looked down at the day calendar. "Yes, sir, two o'clock. I'll let her know you're here." The young girl flicked her eyelash and glanced at Roberta Walker, now holding the magazine on her lap.

Martin forced his eyes away from the girl and made his way across the room. He mentally compared the two women. While the girl was certainly younger, his wife at fifty-six, a beauty in her own right, still stirred up strong emotions whenever he chanced to meet her. They had been married twenty-one years this month and now it was close to being over. Maybe they would come to an agreement today. Roberta crossed her legs and motioned for him to take the chair next to hers. Even in his seventy-fourth year his passion for her reared its head at the sight of her thigh.

The reason for her leaving was still unclear, but he suspected it had something to do with the mysterious disappearance of the young female aide on his staff. Roberta had been curious about his relationship with the girl but accepted his explanation and hadn't pressed it even after all the newspaper coverage. The police had investigated and suspected a tie between him and the aide, but could find no evidence to support their case, especially when the girl could not be found. The media wouldn't drop it, and the incident stayed in the news for months – tarnishing not only his marriage but his political career as well.

They had no children and Roberta constantly maintained that there wasn't another man. She said simply that the relationship had grown old, that she needed to get on with her life. He knew he had always worked too many hours and days, and he never could seem to control the impulse to serve, to serve the country he so loved; to serve his constituents – they relied on him.

He forced a smile as he eased into the chair. "How've you been, Robbie?

Roberta laid the magazine on the table next to her, smiled and placed her hand on his. "I've been as well as possible, I guess. And you?"

"Frankly, I'm burdened at the moment. Tired. But most of all I'm burdened by your absence. I need you, Robbie." He placed his hand on top of hers. After a long second, she removed her hand.

"Oh, Martin. Let's don't go there again. It's over between us. I'm so sorry. Please forgive me." She looked pleadingly into his eyes. He started to speak when the door opened and in walked his attorney.

Bruce McDonald stepped into the room, received acknowledgment from the receptionist, and moved directly toward the couple. "Martin, Mrs. Walker." He reached to take each of their hands in turn while holding his briefcase in his left hand. "Are we about ready?"

Esther Langton emerged from her office, beckoned them to come in, and directed them to the conference table at the far side of the room. She picked a paper from the stack in front of her, scanned it for a second, glanced briefly at Martin and Roberta, then fixed her eyes on McDonald, who was extracting papers from his briefcase. "Bruce, let's cut to the chase. This is the list of Mrs. Walker's requirements, which if met, will allow us to avoid a contentious, time-consuming, and . . ." she looked into Martin's eyes as if to drive home the point . . . "a very costly court battle. We're all familiar with the list and it's a simple matter to accept and walk away from here without further ado."

Martin took the paper from McDonald and spent a moment reading it. He looked at Roberta, then at Ms. Langton. "I still can't understand why I must give more than two-thirds of what we own, including the house and, in addition, pay alimony for the rest of my life. Already, she has a piece of property I bought in her name alone, and on which, an offer has been made for 1.3 million dollars." He looked to Roberta for an explanation of why she was being so hard. Her expression remained blank and she looked straight at Ms. Langton.

He and Roberta had, on numerous occasions, discussed this issue in private, and she seemed to have understood his position. Now here she was back at the same old approach – wanting virtually everything. "You're leaving me with nothing, Robbie." He thought about his earlier meeting with his aide and the problem of re-election and the effect that could have on his retirement benefits. "I'm an old man with not much chance to recoup." She didn't look at him and he started to boil inside. *By God, if she wants a fight.*

To McDonald he said, "What the hell's she got that could let her demand that much of the estate?" McDonald's furtive glance at Ms. Langton didn't go unnoticed by Martin. "Does this have to do with all that media hoopla two years ago?" He quickly glanced at the others then back to McDonald. "I was cleared of all that." He now turned directly to Roberta. "If this was a problem with you, why didn't you talk with me about it then? You think I had an affair with her? Is that what this is all about?" Roberta didn't respond or look at him.

McDonald placed his hand on Martin's arm. "Martin, unfortunately, this is an issue that won't easily go away. I know, from previous conversations, you don't want to believe that, but I'm afraid it's come to this. A civil—"

Martin interrupted, "But I was cleared of any wrong doing in that case. I—"

"I know. I know. But a civil case is different. The investigation brought out that you had a close, personal relationship with the young woman and that she disappeared under rather mysterious circumstances. Although the state didn't have enough evidence to prosecute, a lesser degree of certainty is required in a civil case." Martin tried to override him, but he continued. "If Mrs. Walker chooses to use that incident in her case against you, the jury will likely be sympathetic. Even if she doesn't, the issue will surface and therefore affect the jury. There must . . . ."

Bull. This was no damn different than the last meeting. Martin abruptly stood and backed away from the table. His emotions took control and his anger flared. He looked at Roberta. "I can't believe you'd do this. I . . . ." She refused to look at him. "Well I don't give a damn. I'm not going to agree to what's on that paper. I don't give a damn what it costs. We'll both be on the dole." He turned and stormed out of the office.

CHAPTER 23

Martin shuffled papers on his desk, looking for something of interest to distract him from the disagreeable moments with his wife. He had to get on with the many items of concern needing immediate attention. Why was Roberta being like this? She had agreed on a settlement, and now she wanted more – wanted it all – even after the sweetheart real estate deal he had purchased in her name.

Two years ago, simply because of a choice introduction provided to a large developer, Martin had been given the opportunity to purchase a small parcel of a large tract of land, which he had chosen to title in his wife's name. They had been on good terms at the time, and he figured it would be good politics to be separated from the deal. He recognized that his presence at the meeting with the county zoning department might have affected the ultimate zoning guarantee, but he had applied no political pressure – simply an introduction.

Through the closed door to the outer office, he heard the soft ringing of the telephone. A moment later, the door opened slightly and Sylvia Bauer poked her head around the edge. "I'm sorry, Senator, but I must speak with you for a moment, if I may." Her face conveyed concern about something, but she remained behind the door.

Martin cornered his agitation and kept his face blank. "Yes, come on in, Sylvia. I can't seem to get into this pile anyway. What've you got?"

Sylvia left the door open and moved toward the desk. "Please forgive me. I know you have a full agenda, but do you remember the young lady who has been ordered deported?"

Martin was unable to control the frown that appeared out of nowhere. "Yes. I haven't forgotten her plight. Has she received news?"

"No, sir, but she calls every other day. She seems very concerned that deportation is imminent. Do you have any comforting news I can relay to her?"

"I have discussed her case with colleagues on the immigration committee, and they agree with me that changes to the law are necessary. The committee meets in two weeks and we should have something positive hammered out soon after that. Tell her not to worry and . . . if she gets orders from Immigration, have her call me at once. I will intercede personally and delay deportation until the committee acts."

"Oh, thank you, Senator." Sylvia retreated toward the door. "I will relay your thoughts immediately."

Martin watched her retreat. His mind moved back to dealing with Senate problems and away from the personal. He deeply regretted that he had been unable to have the immigration law changed sooner to help that young woman. Just a matter of time, though. He sifted through the various papers, made necessary decisions and soon had all the problems sorted and catalogued in his mind. The office phone rang again in the lobby. The intercom light flashed on. He wrinkled his brow as he pushed the talk button. "Yes, Sylvia?"

"There's a Mr. Edward Buchanan from the Internal Revenue Service on the line."

The wrinkled brow spread to the forehead and he hesitated, considering whether he should accept the call. The news could go either way. Benson had been in contact with the agency. He picked up the phone receiver and said, "Hello, Eddie. How've you been? This about Allied Paint? Good news, I hope."

"Hi, Marty. I guess you can say I'm in pretty good shape – have been better. No, it's not about Allied. The agent is already auditing that." Buchanan's hesitation caused a tingle in Martin's chest. He continued, "The office in your hometown has requested your personal return. Just wanted to let you know."

Martin quickly removed the phone away from his mouth to mask the audible sigh emanating from his throat. He collected himself. "What does it mean, Eddie? Why would they want to look at my return? Somehow connected to the Allied audit?"

"I guess it could, but I don't really understand why. I know you asked to have that audit squelched, and I'm sorry we were unable to do anything about it. Your aide called in too late. Not sure I could've done anything anyway, but could've tried. You never did say what the problem was."

"Well, that doesn't make any difference now; the audit is already in progress. Allied's employees are big contributors to my campaign – always have been. Is there anything you can do to deter the audit of my return? I don't need that now – too many other irons in the fire."

"That's why I called. Wanted to get your permission to call the local office manager and see just what their interest is. May be able to nip it in the bud."

"I would certainly appreciate that. Do you think you can have it called off?"

"There's a good possibility. Auditing those in power can sometimes turn out to be a black mark on an agent's record – not good for one's progress."

"I get your meaning. I don't want anyone to be hurt in this process, but, like I say, I don't need the hassle of a revenue agent at this time. When does your term end?"

"Next year." Buchanan paused long enough for that fact to settle in on Martin. "Okay, I'll hang up now and put in a call to the local office. I'll be in touch. Have a good week, Marty." The phone went dead.

CHAPTER 24

After leaving Amy, Jesse went directly to the courthouse and found the solid link he'd been searching for. Syed Rabia, a new board member of Allied Paint, *and* the referral contact between Mendez and Allied, had been named trustee for the land previously owned by Mendez as trustee. Because of the Mendez connection to the local mosque, Jesse was certain the mosque was involved in money laundering – likely through Allied.

Jesse, almost breathless when he brushed aside the secretary's frantic gestures to stop him, barged headlong into Feldman's office with a triumphant grin on his face. Feldman was on the phone and his face immediately changed to reflect his extreme displeasure at Jesse's abrupt entrance. Feldman cupped the phone mouthpiece and said in a low voice, "What the hell are you . . . ?" His attention was redirected to the caller and spoke into the telephone. "Yes, sir. I understand. I will take personal responsibility and won't make any moves without first discussing it with you." Feldman frowned at Jesse, and spoke again into the phone. "Yes, sir. I will, I will." Jesse's grin was long gone.

Feldman placed the phone in its holder, glared at Jesse and ran both hands through his hair. "Jesse, what the hell am I going to do with you? Have you gone absolutely mad?" He stood, walked to the window and, looking out, said, "You know who that was?" He turned toward the desk and before Jesse could respond, said, "That was the top brass in Atlanta. You have any idea why they'd be calling me?" He walked to the desk and stood behind his chair.

Jesse blurted, "Top brass . . . in Atlanta? My God, no. I have no idea." It finally dawned on him why Atlanta would be calling. He looked sheepishly at Feldman. "The senator's return?"

Feldman simply stared at Jesse and took his chair. "I don't know why I let you talk me into requesting his return. I knew it would be trouble." He ran one hand through his hair and looked at the ceiling. "This could cost me my job. Twenty-three years gone to hell and . . . all because of . . . ." He looked mournfully at Jesse. "You understand what I'm saying, Jesse? Do you really understand?" The angry look returned. "Now tell me what the hell you mean barging in here the way you did. Have you lost all respect for protocol? You ready to lose your job, too?"

Jesse, his stupid move finally sinking in far enough to have serious meaning, and with a pleading look at Feldman said, "Danny, please forgive me. I was just so excited I threw all caution to the wind. Mrs. Morrison tried to stop me, but I just had to share the new information with you." Elation began to build again and a grin tried to form on Jesse's face. He forced it away. "But what are they saying about the senator's return? We have the right to look at it . . . don't we? I don't see why—"

"Senator Walker is a powerful man. Through his position and connections, he controls the fate of many . . . including mine . . . and . . . yours . . . ." Feldman peered into Jesse's eyes. "Don't you understand that, Jesse?"

Jesse thought about the attempts on his life and what he'd have to do to avoid losing it. He'd heard many stories about political abuse by the powerful but had never experienced it first hand. "Yeah. I think I understand." The image of his two children crushed against the side of the boat flashed, quickly replaced with the square, dark face of his sworn enemy. Jesse's fortitude bolstered, and he looked straight and hard into Feldman's eyes. "I know, too, Danny, that we have a job to do, and I say we can't back away every time somebody offers a threat. If we believe in what we're doing, then we must be willing to stand up to outside threats. Otherwise, we ought to quit." Jesse loosened his grip on the back of the chair.

Feldman's facial expression seemed to convey understanding, but he said, "I know what you're saying, and I agree with it, in general, but we've got to be practical, too. We can't go running off on every wild goose chase . . . in search of the case that's going to change the world. We've got to—"

"I know I sometimes give the impression that I'm chasing a far-reaching dream. I have to admit my mind does go off the radar sometime, but reason has always won out. Certainly I follow my nose, but I never let it take me beyond the facts and logic . . . and reality." Jesse moved away from the chair and stood straight up, now in his most serious mood. "Danny, all along I've tried to lay out all the facts and questions to you. I continue to gather more, and they continue to lead toward the fantasy – the big case. The Mendez case is long gone. We're now into something much, much larger, the end result of which, I do not know . . . at this time. I can't tell you what will come of Senator Walker's case until I get his return and see if he reported the money received from Allied Paint. If it hasn't been reported, then I think we should start a full-scale examination. He is definitely connected to Allied, who by all counts, at this time, is evading tax and likely laundering money for some unknown reason. He—"

"That's the kind of thinking and logic I'm afraid of. Because the source in Nassau appears to be just a bank account, you jump to that conclusion. You don't know that for a fact. How much of the rest of your so-called facts are similar? You see where I'm coming from, Jesse?" Before Jesse could respond, Feldman added an additional question.

"What was it you were so fired up about that sent you barging into my office? More facts?"

"You may remember that Allied Paint was bought out early this year. Several of the new board members are of Arab descent, one, a Syed Rabia resides in West Palm Beach. This is the same Syed who recommended Mendez to Allied Paint for the appraisal of Senator Walker's house, and—"

"Now see here, Jesse. I remember the fact that Mendez was paid by Allied for some task in this city. I don't remember that it was for the appraisal of the senator's house. Did you establish that as fact?" Feldman gazed at Jesse, as if sorry for throwing mud at him.

"I agree I can't pinpoint the job performed by Mendez, but it was performed in this city and Allied never used him again, and, to the best of my knowledge, the purchase and sale of the senator's house is the only transaction by Allied in this area." Jesse held his own with Feldman. "Sometimes logic alone allows one to span the gap. But anyway, that small item doesn't alter my premise in the least. The idea is that I was able to link the Kihad Mosque to both Mendez and Rabia, and that in turn leads to Allied and the senator and . . . the possibility of tax evasion and laundered money."

"Oh, Jesse. What—?"

"Hear me out, Danny. One of the things that first got me interested in the Mendez case was the real estate bought in his name as trustee. I always wondered who the real owner was since Mendez obviously didn't have that kind of money." Feldman's impatience was displayed on his face but he didn't utter a sound.

Jesse continued, "Since his death, I've been wondering whose name the property would be titled to. This morning I found out." He watched Feldman's face for any change of expression and seeing none, said, "Syed Rabia."

Feldman's brow arched slightly. "And you're saying that because Mendez was a member of the Kihad Mosque and Rabia was connected to Mendez, the mosque must be the owner? Isn't that quite a leap?"

Jesse leaned on the chair again and stared hard into Feldman's eyes. "Yes, it is a leap, and yes, I am saying the mosque is the likely owner. And, Danny, I'm asking you here and now to allow me the authority to examine the Kihad Mosque. And before you say no, take a while and consider all the facts . . . and leaps, and consider that a look will not prove detrimental to the mosque unless we find facts to take further. All I ask is that you give it your best consideration. And, Danny . . . remember that we have a job to do." Jesse turned to leave. "Sleep on it, Danny."

Jesse opened the door and was about to step through when he turned to face Feldman. "Almost forgot to tell you. The bastards tried to kill me again Saturday." Jesse stepped through the doorway.

CHAPTER **25**

Jesse maneuvered through the busy intersection, his eyes analyzing the occupants of each car, searching for that now familiar square, dark face. Amy's words had struck a chord, and he knew he must remain on high alert at all times. There was no question that they were after him, and may even try to hit his children as a way to get at him. He had thought about turning the examination over to someone else. The idea of retiring from the service held a certain appeal – in a few months he would be eligible. That idea came into full view now, and a good feeling ran through his body. The image of living his life as he wished; his boat, airplane, children and . . . Amy, displayed vividly in his mind. Peace engulfed him. He relaxed his grip on the steering wheel and nestled into the seat. A blue BMW passed to his right and he tensed – the peaceful vision gone in a flash. His hands gripped the wheel again and his blood surged. The driver's face was not recognizable, but the realization that a similar man had tried to kill him and his children resurfaced, and Jesse immediately renewed his vow to put a stop to whatever these people were trying to do. He would remain on alert and would pursue the case as long as the higher-ups gave him the okay.

He turned onto Magnolia Street and was immediately impressed with the tall spire and minaret of the mosque. How could a religion with such an impressive building be involved in such deviousness as he imagined? Doubts began building in his mind. Was this examination another wild goose chase? A product of his over-active imagination? He questioned his motives and eased up on the accelerator as he turned into the mosque parking lot. He had to retain his resolve to get to whatever end there was, starting with the meeting today. He had been lucky to arrange it with the bookkeeper who was going out of town this afternoon for the weekend. Negative thoughts re-emerged. *Is this the end of the quest?*

Hamza watched from the far end of the street as the revenue agent parked in front of the mosque. He clinched the steering wheel until his fists began to hurt. Think boy. He reached for the pistol lying on the passenger seat and opened the door. This time he wouldn't fail. You're a dead man, sucker.

A car turned onto the street and drove toward where the agent parked. Hamza paused and remained seated in the car. His growing anger was getting the best of him again. All he knew for sure was that he had failed twice and failure was something he couldn't live with. He had never accepted failure and he never would. But, if he was to avoid failure again, he must control himself. He relaxed his hold on the gun. Through his teacher he had made great strides in controlling his emotions but they still ran rampant when things didn't go just right. He must act wisely.

The last words of Abdullah surfaced in his mind. "The revenue agent is not the important thing now. What is important is that you maintain your temper and seek the blessing of Allah. The time is fast approaching when you will likely be chosen by Allah for a task that will be sought my many. Self discipline is crucial. Don't let me down, son."

CHAPTER 26

Jesse was in awe as he walked around the mosque to the small, wooden building attached by a covered walkway to the rear of the mosque. A mixture of aromatic scents emanated from the many plants and flowers covering the large grounds. The magnificence of the building tugged at his eyes, and he promised himself he would arrange a tour of the entire building before he finished the audit. He looked at his watch – five minutes to nine – a tad early.

The bookkeeper, a short, clean-shaven, pudgy man of about thirty-five, wearing the same complexion as other Mid-Easterners, opened the door as Jesse reached to knock, and asked, "Mr. Hawkins?" He paused as Jesse nodded, then added, "I'm Khaled Sadequee. I spoke with you on the telephone." He stood back from the door. "Won't you come in please?"

Jesse took the extended hand and entered the building. "Thank you, Mr. Sadequee."

"Please call me, Khaled."

"Thank you, Khaled. I'm Jesse." He tightened his grip on Khaled's hand. "Hope I won't be much of a bother and take up too much of your time."

Khaled withdrew his hand, halfway turned and backed farther into the room. "No problem, but I do have a small question."

Jesse took that brief moment away from the probing eyes to size up the room. It was wide but shallow with a sofa at one end, desk about midway and a door to the left leading down a long hallway. The room was drab except for a very large mural of an elaborate mosque covering most of the wall behind the sofa. Jesse felt tempted to go closer to examine it in more detail but his thoughts were interrupted by the voice of Khaled.

"Mr. Hawk . . . er, Jesse, please follow me. The accounting records are this way." Khaled held his arm outstretched in a beckoning mode.

Jesse followed, and was soon led into a small, bleak room with no windows. The light over a small conference table was already on. A small stack of papers was arranged to the left of a chair at the table.

Khaled placed his hand on the papers. "Here is the information for 2005 as you requested. I think it's complete." He pulled the chair away from the table and stood behind it. "Jesse, why is the government auditing this mosque? I've been doing these books for ten years and can't recall anything out of the ordinary. I just can't figure out why the audit."

Jesse leafed through the pile of papers and immediately regretted not having asked for the normal three years. The fear of not finding anything of importance returned. When he finally looked at Khaled, he detected a tinge of worry that the examination would uncover something wrong with Khaled's accounting abilities and diligence. Jesse sought to ease that fear – he needed this fellow's utmost cooperation if he was to discover the sought-after plot. "The examination is routine, I assure you. The government periodically takes a look at tax-exempt organizations to ensure their compliance with the regulations." He thumbed through the papers again while still looking at Khaled. "I may need to look at a few more years." He noted the eyebrow movement. "Will that be a problem?"

"No. I don't think so. Of course I'll have to clear it with the imam. But I don't think he'll have any objections. Like I said, I feel quite certain that you'll find everything in order."

Jesse adjusted the chair for occupancy. "By the way, Khaled, do you work for a CPA firm in town?" Jesse sat in the chair as if the question was not important and began to separate the papers.

Khaled, with a touch of pride, said, "No. I work for myself. I have a bookkeeping office downtown. Been in business for ten years. The mosque was my first customer. Now I have two bookkeepers working for me."

Jesse turned to face Kahled. "That's great. I've often thought about opening a tax office when I retire. Who knows, maybe . . . . Do you do taxes?"

"Yes, we do, but specialize in accounting. There are enough problems there."

"Are you a CPA?" Jesse thought of his recent passing of three parts of the exam. When he passed the fourth part he would be eligible for the certificate. If he was to quit the Service, he would need to be a CPA if he was to have his own tax firm.

"No. I never took the additional step to attain the certificate, but I am qualified if I ever wanted to. I never saw the need."

"Were you born here?"

"Born in Philadelphia, but came here as a baby."

"Well, I guess that makes you a Florida native. You've got enough sand in your shoes." Jesse thought of the sand in his own shoes – four generations of sand, real sand – all of his folks had been fishermen on the west coast of Florida. He had managed to break with the past through good grades in high school and a scholarship to the University of Florida. His mind tried to take him back to those earlier days and the little boy playing in the surf, but he fought against it. He smiled broadly and turned back to the pile of papers. "Will you be here all day?"

"For the most part, I'm committed for the day. I'll be within touch of my cell phone." Khaled moved toward the door, and over his shoulder he said, "When you leave for lunch, just close the door. I'll be back to lock up."

The word "lunch" brought to mind his date with Amy today. Jesse glanced at his watch. "Thanks a lot, Khaled. I really appreciate your cooperation." He gave a thumbs-up as Khaled stepped through the door. "Hopefully I can be finished today."

Jesse turned his full attention to the papers. His eye had been zeroing in on the Balance Sheet, which lay on top of the pile. Property & Equipment, the account he was here for, stood out plain and clear, and the amount was significant. Here he would prove the trust real estate really belonged to the mosque – proof that the mosque was laundering money – proof that he was on to something big.

He flipped through the papers until he came to the General Ledger and slowed his search until he found the Property & Equipment page. The page contained numerous entries but the total corresponded with the amount on the Balance Sheet. His heart skipped a beat as his eyes sorted through the various entries and settled on a particular item. The entry, dated December 13, was titled simply, Real Estate Trust $546,489.15. Jesse sat back in the chair and took a deep breath. He could hardly believe his eyes. They hadn't even attempted to cover up the purchase. He looked around, halfway expecting Khaled to walk through the door. This was too much to hope for. The excitement running rampant through his body forbade settling down. He held the General Ledger page in his hand, looked again toward the door, back again at the stack of papers, finally stood and paced around the room. He had to contain himself. *Get hold of yourself, Jesse.* He walked back to the table. Where had the money come from to buy this property?

Jesse turned the General Ledger pages back until he came to the one marked Cash. He scanned the entries looking for a large deposit, and seeing none, compared the balance for January 1, with the balance at December 31, which showed $236,789.63 even after deducting the land purchase. He scratched his head in wonderment. They carried a lot of cash on the books. The monthly deposits averaged about $90,000 and Jesse thought that kind of high for normal contributions from members. He wondered if they'd received contributions from overseas. *Better look at the prior year.*

On his cell phone he dialed the number given him by Khaled, and on contact said, "Khaled, Jesse Hawkins here. I've got a bit of a problem and I wonder if you could provide me with the books for 2004?"

"What kind of problem? Maybe I can answer it on the phone."

"Has to do with cash balances. I see that a significant amount was used to purchase real estate in 2005 and wondered where the money came from. I need to—"

"Oh, yes. I remember that purchase. Let me think. I believe that was from a buildup of cash over the years, but let me get the ledger. I'll be right in. You need anything else while I'm at it?"

"No. I don't think so . . . not right now anyway. Thanks, Kahled." Jesse looked at his watch. He didn't want to be late for lunch with Amy.

Jesse stood and held the chair for Amy and motioned for the waitress. Amy was right on time, but Jesse had already had one cup of coffee. After reviewing the ledger for 2004, he'd been in a complete stew. There had been no unusual deposits in that year, and the balance at the end of 2003 was a large amount. Khaled had been right about the buildup of cash. The mosque, at someone's advice, was simply trying to diversify investments – reduce the large cash balance. This turn of events shot his off-shore money plot all to hell.

After Amy sat, Jesse did likewise and said, "What will you have to drink?" The waitress walked up and placed a menu in front of her.

"I'm ready for a cup of coffee." She picked up the menu but looked at Jesse. "I see you've got problems. The mosque audit not going well?" She opened the menu but kept her eyes on Jesse.

"You read me pretty well." Jesse tried to smile but his lips felt like they'd crack if he did. "I was hoping I would have good news for this meeting, but it didn't turn out that way." He toyed with the menu, already knowing what he wanted. "This may be the end, Amy." He hesitated so he could fully collect himself. Most cases he had high hopes for ended without anything of importance other than the collection of taxes. He had been so sure this one was different – *the case of a life time.*

"It looks like I ran out of leads. Back to the compliance audits."

Amy placed her hands over his. "I'm so sorry, Jesse. I know how much this meant to you." She massaged his hands and peered deep into his eyes. "Are you sure it's over? Nothing else you can do?"

After they placed their orders and the waitress walked away, Jesse said, "I've asked the bookkeeper to get me another two years of accounting records. I'll see if there's any connection to my theory and, if not . . . so be it, move on to better things." He finally allowed himself a laugh, which brought a large grin from Amy. "We're on for this weekend, huh?"

Amy again took his hands in hers. "I'm looking forward to it."

Jesse was finishing the afternoon examination of the additional two years he'd asked for, and jumped involuntarily when Khaled opened the door and stepped into the workroom.

Khaled asked, "Are you getting close, Jesse? It's after four and I've got to be going. Did you find all you were looking for? Do you have any more questions about that land purchase?"

Jesse turned in the chair. "No. It looks like the money had accumulated pretty much as you said. Just have a couple of questions for you and I'll be finished. I sure want to thank you for your cooperation, Khaled. I couldn't have made so much progress if it hadn't been for your help." He looked at the papers he'd been working on, then back at Khaled.

"Are all the receipts member contributions? Are they normal, average? Any from overseas sources?"

"To my knowledge all the receipts are from local members. In the early days the mosque received help from overseas to help support a fledgling organization, but it is now self-supporting. I don't recall any receipts from overseas sources during the past few years." Khaled stepped back as Jesse pushed the chair and rose. He continued, "So we get a clean bill of health?"

"Yes, I think so. Based on what you just said, income seems to be normal. Have a couple of questions about expenditures, if you'll give me a couple more minutes."

Khaled looked at his watch. "Sure. What's the issue with income and expenses, if they've all been reported?"

"Oh. I just need to satisfy myself that all income and expenses are related to the reason for the tax-exempt status and ensure a tax return wasn't necessary. Part of the audit of these types of organizations, all pretty routine stuff."

Khaled looked again at his watch. "What was your question about expenses? Is there a particular expenditure you're interested in?"

"Yes. In 2002 there were two payments to a 'Farouk' mosque. Both fairly large payments – $125,000 each. What were those payments for and where is the mosque located? Again, I'm concerned that they are qualified expenditures."

Khaled seemed a bit perplexed. "Was that the only year of payments? None in the other years?"

"Right. Only in 2002. If you can help me with this today, I'll be out of your hair." Jesse's face reflected his sincerity and eagerness to be finished with the project.

"Hold on. I'll be right back." Khaled went through the door.

Jesse was relieved when Khaled left, and let out a long, audible sigh of relief. When he had first noted these payments to another mosque it had been all he could do to rein in his emotions. Was it possible that he had been looking at the wrong mosque? He was unaware of another mosque in the area. Yet this mosque he was now working on was the owner of the trust property that had sent him out on this quest. Where did it all lead? Another dead-end? He stacked the papers in preparation for departure.

Khaled entered and handed Jesse two pieces of paper. "Here is the paperwork regarding those transfers you wanted."

The two papers were receipts for the expenditure amounts. When Jesse saw the receiving signature on both copies, he had to fight with all his might to control his exploding emotions. *Syed Rabia.*

CHAPTER 27

Syed paced back and forth in front of the park bench on the campus of the University of Central Florida in Orlando. The drive had been a frantic, non-stop, two-and-a-half hour trip after making the appointment with Abdullah. Ever since agreeing to meet with the revenue agent, his mind had vacillated with the alternatives – meet with the agent then talk with Abdullah, talk with Abdullah before or, don't talk with Abdullah at all until it could be determined just what the agent had in mind. None of the options were good. He remembered his words of consternation when he'd last met with Abdullah, that the agent's probing could lead to him, knowing immediately that was a dangerous thing to say. But what to do? Would Abdullah re-order the killing of the agent? *Will he turn against me?*

He sat on the bench for a minute and was back up pacing again. *My God! My God! What have I got myself into?* How could he have been so stupid to not give any consideration to government probing? Two birds twittered and frolicked at the edge of an isle of bushes off to the right, occasionally nipping at the abundance of white flowers there. The unmistakable, pleasant aroma of gardenias wafted in the soft breeze and entered his senses.

The image of his adoring, loving, smiling wife took dominance, and the serenity he enjoyed when with her or at his coveted occupation replaced the fear and agitation that had prevailed. That serene life was the ideal he had imagined when he first came to this country – education, business, marriage, children. What had gone wrong? Activism was not a part of his natural makeup. Nowhere in his life could he remember being involved in such things, even though he had been exposed to a lot of it in his mother country.

He tore his eyes away from the birds, now close together with feathers flapping excitedly, and walked back to the bench and the reality facing him. He would ask Abdullah to replace him.

The confused sounds of many voices broke into his thoughts and he turned to see hordes of students emerging from buildings along the eastern edge of the campus. The sun, still favoring the east, was almost straight up. He strained his eyes to focus on the students, expecting to see Abdullah among them. Shortly after the students dispersed, he recognized Abdullah making his way across the plaza.

Syed stood. Abdullah hugged him and said, "It is good to see you again, Syed. You look well." Abdullah paused, motioned for Syed to sit on the bench, and sat beside him. "I am sorry, though, that you are disturbed. I trust that I can allay those feelings." He patted Syed's knee in a comforting gesture. "Is Mary well?"

Syed's emotions eased a bit with Abdullah's gentle, calming voice. "Yes. Mary is well. She sends her greetings and looks forward to visiting with you during your trip to Miami next month."

"I am glad she is well." Abdullah adjusted himself on the bench and looked at his watch. "Unfortunately, my time is limited today – three more classes and a forum later in the afternoon. You sounded very distressed when you called. Something about the revenue agent examining Kihad Mosque, and now examining Farouk Mosque?" Abdullah's eyes seemed to plead for understanding for his lack of details of Syed's call. "You must forgive me for my apparent ignorance. I was in the midst of an important discussion when I took your call. Go ahead with your concern."

"I have agreed to meet the agent next Monday. He wanted to come earlier in the week, but I was able to deter him. I wanted the opportunity to speak with you first."

Abdullah's brow rose as if considering a very important issue. "Is he the same agent that examined Allied and Mendez?"

"As I understand it, yes, a Jesse Hawkins."

"Did he indicate the nature of his visit? How did he find out about Farouk Mosque? The mosque hasn't filed tax returns, has it?" Abdullah's face reflected a deepening concern.

"Neither of the mosques have filed returns. The bookkeeper for Kihad Mosque told me the examination was routine and that the agent gave them a clean bill of health. A search of the records by the agent reflected the first two payments to me at Farouk Mosque in 2002. I guess that is what pointed him toward me." Syed's gasp was internal and he hoped it didn't show on his face. He quickly looked toward the twittering birds to mask anything that might try to show. These people, and perhaps Abdullah as well, are capable of doing anything to accomplish their objective. *Even to me!* "The agent told the bookkeeper the government routinely checked on tax-free organizations to ensure compliance with the special, pertinent regulations. Maybe it is the same for Farouk Mosque. Do you think?"

Abdullah seemed to be looking at the birds, but Syed knew the wheels were turning in that brilliant mind. Abdullah said, "It is possible but . . . I doubt it. Kahid Mosque is different from Farouk Mosque." He paused, looked up at the still rising sun and compared its position with his watch. He seemed to be talking to himself. "But what can he find that will be a detriment to our cause? Money comes in from religious, Islamic businessmen abroad and is used to purchase interests in legitimate American businesses." He finally included Syed in his conversation. "What is wrong with that? It is not illegal for foreigners to buy into American companies, is it?" He smiled and patted

Syed's knee. "That is the approach to take. Let him determine differently . . . if he can." Abdullah eased to the edge of the bench as if ready to leave, apparently happy with his conclusion. "Our operation has changed. We must deter the agent without directing more attention to ourselves, while continuing with the money operation, except now it will be increased substantially, and . . . channeled differently. It will be used entirely for . . . . He stood. "I rely on you one hundred percent, Syed."

Syed, seeing the opportunity to explain his position slip away, stood and faced Abdullah. "I wanted to talk with you about that." Syed, deeply perplexed, fought hard to keep focused on Abdullah. He adored the man and would go to the ends of the earth to avoid anything that might destroy their relationship. He gazed into those dark, hazel eyes. "I wanted to talk with you about . . . resigning my position." The negative reaction, not unexpected, rapidly spread across Abdullah's face. "Mary would like to—"

"What? No!" Abdullah stared dumbfounded, as if not comprehending the words he heard. "What are you saying, Syed?"

It appeared that Abdullah was about to explode. Syed recalled the blustering scene on the mosque patio two weeks ago and his own fear resulting from the unfamiliar demonstration. Before he could begin his explanation, Abdullah seemed to control himself and placed his hand on Syed's arm.

Abdullah glanced at his watch and said, "Come, let us sit for a minute so I may digest what it is you have on your mind." They both sat and turned to look at each other. Abdullah's face was relaxed and apparently ready to analyze anything he was about to hear. "Please, Syed, tell me what is bothering you so deeply – why you wish to resign your position."

Syed's insides were churning fast enough to erupt at any minute. He fought hard to control himself so he could logically enter this man's exacting mind. "First . . . and foremost, I want you to know that you are more revered by me than my own father . . . if that is possible." There was no change on Abdullah's face, and his eyes didn't waver. "I know you trust me and have a lot of faith in me. I will go to all extremes to maintain that. I assure you that I will operate counter to my well-imbedded beliefs, if that is your desire." The turmoil eased with the light, softening of Abdullah's face – understanding?

"When my father first asked me to help arrange the importation of money to assist in the purchase of American businesses, I was reluctant. I had just gained citizenship in this country and was well on the way to establishing my own business, which I hoped to one day take public. That was the momentous day that I first met you, an introduction that proved to have positive, lasting effects in my life." Emotions stirred and Syed felt his lip quiver. Abdullah's face reflected a growing serenity.

"After listening to both you and Father, and after much thought, I felt a certain gladness at the opportunity to help my mother country gain a foothold in economic production and thus become industrially self-sufficient to the benefit of all its citizens. I worked faithfully with others to channel funds into the companies of choice. Then things began to change – toward the somewhat devious."

Abdullah peeked at his watch but continued to listen intently.

"It was decided, for some reason beyond my knowledge, that money coming into the country, through me, had to be hidden from view – laundered, in the words of some. That is the point where I became extremely agitated. I came to have doubts as to the real reason for bringing money into the country. Through you, my father, and others, I was convinced to continue with the operation and devise a scheme to hide the money. All of a sudden, I was part of an operation that I didn't fully understand – a dupe." Syed was immediately sorry for using that word, which might convey a different meaning to Abdullah, and he wanted, in the worst way, not to offend Abdullah in the least. He searched the face and there appeared to be a tinge of understanding.

"My world was almost destroyed when those people were attacked – some killed. Those acts were definitely over my head, but again, I was convinced by others and my religion to continue.

"All I ever wanted was to live a peaceful life with my wife and to be successful in business in this country I adopted as my own. During the past several years I have lived two lives, and what has disturbed me more than anything else is that I have been less than truthful to my wife. Abdullah, please understand me. I don't know what your part in all this is and how much of the operation you are aware of. I don't fully understand the operation, but . . . I suspect that it is something sinister – something beyond my capability to understand. I do not know what else to say. I need a different life, Abdullah."

Abdullah's face softened with understanding. He placed his hand on Syed's knee in a fatherly touch. "Syed, believe me, I understand your feelings. I have had many of the same during the past several years, but I, too, have been encouraged to stay the course, and now that we are approaching the end of the beginning, it is important that I continue. Others rely on me to finish what was started, and my religion requires me to continue. It is important for all Muslims in the mother country. I know how much you want to return to the normal life you seek, as do I, and the time is near for that to occur. Syed, I look upon you as the son I never had. If I could choose a son . . . it would be you." Abdullah's voice quivered and he hesitated. "I now humbly ask you, as a friend, a father, and a Muslim, to stay with me for one more month. It will all make perfect sense then." He looked at his watch and stood. "It grieves me to ask, but will you do it? I guarantee it will be no longer than one month." His eyes were plaintive. "I need you, Syed. I need you to complete my mission – our mission."

CHAPTER 28

Abdullah did not look back as he walked across the plaza toward the university building for his next appointment, his mind racing and fighting to sort through the many questions seeking solutions. As he opened the door to the building, he glanced back across the plaza – Syed was not in view. He felt a deep sense of remorse and allowed the door to close without going in. Staring blankly at the wide, serene expanse where students and faculty spent their free time relaxing and studying. He could not let go of the tough decisions he would have to make in the next few weeks. He recalled the meeting yesterday with Ayman Shurasi.

Abdullah had been taken aback as he stepped through the doorway to his office after his last class for the day. He glanced first at the lovely Arab woman on the sofa, and then to his secretary, who smiled as if there was some sort of conspiracy going on. He had hired Kakim Samra soon after relocating to the university, choosing her while still editor of the campus newsmagazine used to collect funds for al Qaeda. She, too, had become increasingly against the policies of the United States and was now a close confidant in the war against the Great Satan.

The thing that caused his astonishment, though, was not the beautiful woman on the sofa but rather the handbag lying on her lap. A simple, ordinary black bag, but with the number 9999 embroidered in the right upper corner. He had been expecting orders, but not like this. The time was now.

Mrs. Samra broke the momentary silence. "Mr. Zacaari," She shifted her gaze to the woman. "Ms. Ayman Shurasi has requested a meeting with you. She said you would be expecting her." Kakim's look returned to Abdullah for his approval.

"Yes, I will see her." Abdullah strolled to the sofa and the woman stood to greet him. She was a trim five-foot-five, dressed in a modest, gray, western-style pants suit. Her dark hair, hanging on both sides of her beautifully sculpted face, reached just above her shoulders. She looked like she belonged in this country, but he knew better.

Before he could speak, she said, "Mr. Zacaari. It is so nice to make your acquaintance. I adore your office décor." She motioned with her arm at the large paintings on three walls depicting scenes from the Mid-East. "I dearly love the scenes at Mecca and Medina. I miss them already."

Abdullah took the extended hand, glanced at the paintings, then back to her. "It is my pleasure to meet with you, Ms. Shurasi. I have been anticipating your visit." Still holding her hand, he led her toward his office. "Come, shall we go into my office?"

He noted the perplexed look on the secretary's face, and said to her, "Kakim, hold my calls." He and Ms. Shurasi entered his office and he led her to a chair in front of the desk. She glanced at more paintings of the Mid-East on each wall before taking her seat.

"Mr. Zacaari, I understand that you are an American citizen . . . born in this country. Yet you have so many beautiful paintings of the homeland. She looked again at the many paintings. "Is there an explanation?"

"Most certainly." He swept his arm around at the paintings. "We have no say in where we are born. These paintings are a reflection of my religion – of my true roots. All of my gains in this country are for the benefit of my ancestors and the beliefs they lived and died for. Does that make sense?"

"Yes, it does. I am very impressed. The *mujahadeen* are much impressed with you as well." She removed a sheaf of papers from her handbag. "They have honored you with a position of ultimate trust. We will talk of it. Time is of the essence."

"I was told to expect you. Please forgive me, but I did not expect a—"

"A woman?" She laid the papers on the desk and placed her bag on the floor next to her feet.

"I am sorry. But yes, I did not expect a woman, especially one dressed as you are." Abdullah smiled to indicate his acceptance of her. "You are to be much esteemed for this position to which you have been entrusted. My only hope is that I can attain such a position."

She removed the top sheet. "Please do not berate yourself. I find this attitude wherever I travel. I am very fortunate, and my attainment of this position will be a benefit and lesson to all women and provide them with hope, by the grace of Allah. Now let us get on with the message."

"I am sorry, but I must learn how you managed to get into this country? Did you arrive by air? You experienced no trouble with immigration authorities?"

"I literally walked across the border into the United States, after taking a boat from Venezuela to Mexico. Simple as that." Her face questioned the incredulous look on Abdullah's face. "Is there something wrong?"

"You mean no one tried to stop you?"

"If you possess proper passports from countries that are accepted by other countries, there are few questions. Many are entering in a like manner, which is part of the subject matter to be discussed."Abdullah had learned of the illegal traffic in passports and of the laws of some countries which allow persons from certain countries to enter without much questioning. It was a simple matter to begin one's journey from a country of acceptance if one was to avoid stringent questioning.

"Now if we may." She continued, picking up a paper. "I noticed from your facial expression in the lobby that you recognized the numbers on my handbag, and the meaning thereof."

"Yes. I have been taught to look for those numbers. I am aware that they have a greater significance as well." He noted the slight movement of her eyebrow and was a little amazed that she apparently hadn't thought that he knew. But maybe *she* didn't know. *Maybe I had just better listen.*

Her face calmed and she gathered several of the top sheets and held them in one hand. "The main purpose of this meeting is to inform you that the operation has been accelerated. I know you have not been using all the money received for the purchase of businesses, and that a portion has been used to aid various cells." She paused to see his reaction to her knowledge of his particular operation. Abdullah's facial expression didn't alter. "From this day forward, all money entering the country is to be channeled to these cells throughout the country." She waved the papers she held. "You are to visit the cells listed here," she again waved the papers in her hand, "to determine the individual needs." She placed her hand on the remaining sheets of paper on the desk. "It is important that they are well-funded in order to meet their deadlines."

Abdullah's heartbeat quickened as he listened to her speak in roundabout terms of the coming holocaust. "That doesn't leave much time. How much funding is required? What are the deadlines? When is the end?"

"The exact date is unknown by me, but the cells are to be prepared well before the sixth of June. Funds now held in reserve, as well as new funds, are to be used for that purpose. It is imperative to use whatever means necessary for

adequate funding and delivery. This includes everything."
She gazed directly into his eyes.

She really did know the other meaning of 9999. His respect for her increased dramatically. This was some woman to have been entrusted with such information and responsibility. He locked his eyes to hers and waited.

She asked, "You will be visiting the port in the near future?"

"I am scheduled to be in Miami in two weeks."

Abdullah's focus shifted to the couple walking slowly across the park toward him. He had been in a daze, staring unseeing, unaware of his surroundings. He acknowledged the couple and stepped to the side as they mounted the steps and moved to the door. Abdullah's thoughts turned again to Syed and the absolute necessity to keep him in the loop to ensure proper funding. At this late date, no one could match the effectiveness of Syed. If there wasn't enough money, Syed would find a way to obtain it. Abdullah trusted Syed implicitly and vowed he would use whatever resources he had to retain Syed's services.

CHAPTER **29**

Jesse, struggling to keep his inner pleasure from radiating throughout the agents' room, smiled and waved at Mrs. Morrison as he passed Feldman's office and made his way outside to the scheduled appointment with Syed Rabia. It had taken a whole week to arrange. Syed had seemed overly concerned, more so than normal, he thought. Everyone was always saying how bad Mondays were, and he generally agreed, especially after a long weekend on the ocean. But this one had to be the absolute best. This week would prove his theory of deep conspiracy – including the senator. The smile was still on his face when he waved to the office auditor and pushed through the front door. Even Feldman's admonition to be on the lookout for lurking dangers could not dampen the expanding elation. Jesse's conversation with Feldman last Monday afternoon, after a preliminary review of the senator's return, had been short and to the point.

"Jesse, I told you that you were chasing demons when I allowed the audit of Kahid Mosque. You found their operation to be perfectly legitimate – like I figured. And now, because that mosque transferred funds to another mosque, your case is somehow proved – money is being washed for devious reasons – terrorists lurk in every shadow. You say that because this Syed Rabia knew Mendez, heads up Farouk Mosque, and is on the board of Allied Paint, who you suspect of tax evasion, you somehow leap to the conclusion that it all connects together in a sinister plot.

"That bothers me some, but what you said before you left here two weeks ago stayed with me. That boating accident together with the auto accident and the death of Whittaker has to have more meaning than I've given it. I don't know about this mosque business, but I agree with you that something is definitely going on between Allied Paint and Senator Walker. Just how we handle that with the higher-ups, I'm not yet certain, but omission of income could be a criminal offense and warrants further investigation. As you so aptly put it, 'that's our job – what we're hired for'. So . . . ." Feldman paused and looked straight into Jesse's eyes. "I'm going to authorize this one last try with the audit of Farouk Mosque, and . . ." he paused again. "You go ahead with the senator's return. You—"

"Thanks a lot, Danny. I promise this is the end of the mosque thing if I find nothing. The senator is another matter."

"You be careful, Jesse. Stay alert."

Jesse, once outside, immediately scoured the parking lot and the neighborhood in general for sinister-looking cars, faces, or any other suspicious activity. He knew people were after him and could strike at any moment. Seeing no one, he almost bounced along to his car in the parking lot.

Everything seemed to be falling into place. A review of the senator's return after receiving it last Monday had proved him right – the senator had not reported the $150,000 on his return for 2005. Jesse knew Feldman, with that information, would allow the audit, no matter what the higher-ups had to say. Once the return reached the local office, Atlanta generally had no authority. It then remained with the agent to determine if and when to audit. Jesse had managed to arrange a meeting for Tuesday, May 9 with the senator's accountant and planned to fly to Washington D.C. if necessary. He may still have to do that if the audit was protracted. Key in the examination was determining the senator's connection to Allied and the apparent tax evasion and possible money laundering – a connection to Arabs.

Jesse could not fully comprehend Farouk Mosque's purchase of the real estate in Ft. Pierce and how that would ultimately play out in the big picture. The property, about two acres with a small, dingy, wooden house, had been purchased for $235,000 in 2002. That amount corresponded somewhat with the amount received from Kahid Mosque, and the property could have been purchased with the idea of eventually building a mosque there. His visit to the area last Monday, and his conversations with neighbors, confirmed his suspicions that the property had been vacant since purchase.

A small amount of anticipation tempered his otherwise still rising elation. He stared blankly at the wooden fence separating the government property from the adjoining office building. Was this mosque, like Kahid Mosque, completely on the up and up? Could he have been so wrong adding up all the pieces? *Well, whatever. Either we have something, or we don't. Can't dwell on might've beens.*

Jesse turned the ignition and the engine came to life. He entered the street, alert for car types and drivers, and proceeded toward his destiny.

CHAPTER **30**

Jesse, with briefcase in hand, shut the car door and turned to gaze at the sixty-foot yacht making its way north out on Lake Worth, waves from the bow gently rocking the boats moored along Flagler Drive. The drawbridge span continued to lower as traffic waited patiently. He thought of that moment two weeks ago when he was about to be crunched by just such a vessel. He shuddered at the now-familiar image of his children clinging to the side of his small boat. He glanced around, halfway expecting to see killers charging toward him. He wondered why they hadn't been back. Was it all just a strange coincidence? His rampant mind? He didn't think so and glanced around again.

The breeze was slight and the sun hung high in the sky out over the ocean beyond the treetops. He glanced at his watch, shook the prior images from his mind and moved toward the impressive twelve-story, black-glass building facing the Intracoastal Waterway.

Jesse exited the elevator on the tenth floor and strolled down the hall to Suite 1003. The window at the end provided an exemplary view of the ocean out beyond the island of Palm Beach, and Jesse took a moment to savor it. The yacht continued north.

As he stepped into the room, he was immediately impressed not only with the décor, which included a large painting of New York City and the Statue of Liberty at early evening, but with the attractive, young brunette sitting behind a flat-screen computer. She looked up and turned his way as he entered and closed the door. He spoke as he strode to the long desk. "Good morning, ma'am, I'm Jesse Hawkins. I have an appointment with Mr. Rabia at ten-thirty." He held his briefcase with both hands in front of him.

"Good morning, Mr. Hawkins. Mr. Rabia has been delayed. He asked that I direct you to the conference room. The material you requested is there." She made another entry to the computer and stood. "Follow me, please. Would you like coffee?"

"That would be very nice. Thank you Miss . . . ." Jesse tagged along behind and was taken by the girl's shapely figure. She appeared to be about twenty-four or so.

She held the door to the conference room and entered behind him. She said, "Miss, Jernigan, uhh . . . Harriet. Please call me Harriet." She led the way to the long oak table in the center of the room where four small stacks of paper graced the far end. She indicated the chair and said, "And you? How do you prefer to be called?" She smiled and her white, even teeth glimmered.

Jesse looked at the scant paperwork and, controlling the wee angst trying to gain a foothold, turned toward her. "Please call me Jesse." He looked at his watch. "When do you expect Mr. Rabia?" He looked around the room at various paintings, mostly of the Florida wilderness.

"He should be here before noon." Harriet moved toward the door, and turned to face Jesse. "I'll bring you coffee. Do you take sugar and cream?"

"Black, please. Thank you." He turned back to the table.

Each small stack had a sticker denoting the year. He removed his jacket, draped it over the adjacent chair and stood over the stacks for a minute. While standing, he removed the clip from the 2002 stack, a mere three pages. The scarcity didn't surprise him – that was the first year – the year of receipts from Kahid Mosque. On the Balance Sheet he noted the real estate in Ft. Pierce at $235,000 and cash of $15,153.18 and the offsetting accounts, Contributed Capital in the amount of $250,000.00, $153.18 in Retained Earnings. The Cash Receipts Schedule reflected $250,000 from Kahid Mosque and interest income from Bank of America. The Income Statement, for the period September 26, through December 31, reflected only the bank interest. The accounts had been generated through use of a standard computer accounting program.

Angst continued to build and pushed against the remaining elation. The dingy vacant house in Ft. Pierce came to mind. *Is this why it's vacant? No funds?* He glanced through the window and out to the waterway – no boats were in motion. The American flag above the waterfront restaurant waved briskly in the breeze. He was reluctant to face what he halfway expected in the other stacks, and started to sit when Harriet came into the room. The tray she carried held a cup and a pot of coffee. Her smile quickly faded as she placed the tray on the table.

She asked, "Is there something wrong?"

Jesse immediately realized his face reflected his disturbed state, and quickly produced an acceptable smile. "No, nothing wrong. Just looking at that placid waterway and wishing it was the weekend so I could be out there enjoying it. You get out there much?"

She turned and looked out the window. "No. I only remember being out there one time." She turned back to him. "Sounds like you go out a lot. Maybe . . . ." The phone in the front office rang. "Got to run." She raced out of the room.

Her faint perfume caused a mysterious feeling deep within. Jesse stared after her for a few moments, then poured a cup of coffee and reached for the stack for the next year. He removed the title page, stared in awe at the Balance Sheet and compared it to the data for 2002. A sort of exhilaration began making its way through his body – something a bit strange here. Farouk Mosque was receiving and spending money apparently without a functioning mosque. He fought to control his building emotions, drank the coffee in one gulp and poured another cup full. *Okay, let's get down to business.*

The material indicated donations of just under $4,000,000 and a new account titled Building Reserve with a similar balance. Jesse could hardly contain the eagerness caroming inside his stomach as he flipped to the Cash Receipts section to determine the source, and was amazed to see that most individual donations were in excess of $300,000, the donors all with Mid-Eastern names. The donations were all even amounts and seemed to come in regularly each month in relatively similar amounts – only the donor name changed.

Jesse's heart fluttered. He was on to something big, and he fought against the idea of running straight to Feldman to tell him. No way would Danny not agree to turn this case over to the Criminal Investigation Division now. He leaned back in the chair, ran a hand through his hair and finally reached for the coffeepot and another cup of coffee. The coffee eased the growing eagerness somewhat, and a saner, more logical mind resumed control.

In 2002 the mosque received funds to help get it started in St. Lucie County, and was used to purchase land there. In 2003 the mosque received donations from wealthy donors, most likely for the same purpose – to build a mosque and to spread the word of Islam. Anxiety began to take hold again. He drank the rest of the coffee and refilled the cup. How much money did it take to get a new mosque off the ground and running smoothly? He was afraid to look at the next year. But yet, the mosque property remained vacant after more than three years! Jesse re-stacked the 2003 papers and pulled 2004 in front of him. He had to be a cold, no-frills accountant, sticking to the hard facts no matter how much he wanted them to be something else.

Jesse eased the top page off the stack and stared agape at the Balance Sheet. He had been expecting virtually no change from 2003. The Building Reserve had increased to almost eighteen million dollars! He rubbed his eyes, picked up the page and brought it closer to be sure he wasn't seeing things. He said aloud, "What the hell's going on here?"

Harriet Jernigan poked her head into the room. "Anything wrong, Jesse? You need more coffee?"

Jesse, momentarily startled by the voice, quickly collected himself and turned in the chair. "No, Harriet. Everything's fine, just talking to myself." He smiled to re-assure her. "I do that sometimes during an audit. Get so wrapped up in it, you know." He stood and moved toward the window, his eyes still on her. "Yes, I would like some more coffee . . . if it's not too much trouble."

Harriet moved to the table and collected the tray. Jesse stared out into the waterway. She glanced that way for a moment and said on her way out, "Maybe you can take me out there one of these days."

Jesse turned, her fragrance finally reaching him. "You mean it?"

Harriet's word reached him before she stepped through the doorway. "Yes."

Sunlight played out just below the window and Jesse looked at his watch – eleven-thirty. Should he call Amy for lunch and share what he'd found? A slight trace of Harriet's aroma lingered. Three small boats raced north, each seemingly trying to reach the inlet first. For a moment Jesse was down there with them. That moment of respite was quickly gone as the revenue agent part of him took hold again. He turned back to the table as Harriet re-entered with the coffee.

She placed the tray on the table and said, "Mr. Rabia has returned and will be available to meet with you for a few minutes before lunch." Her eyelids fluttered and she moved to the door. "Let me know when you're ready."

"Thank you, Harriet. Need about fifteen minutes. Ready then. By the way, can I use that phone over there for a local call?"

Harriet smiled. "Sure, go ahead." She closed the door behind her.

The calmness he had forced upon himself now departed as he made his way back to the table and the task at hand. He quickly flipped to the 2005 Balance Sheet and saw that the Building Reserve had now increased to over forty-three million dollars. The figure boggled his mind. Where was it all being held? Where is it all coming from? The Balance Sheet only reflected a cash balance of $4,217.66 – the same amount as 2003, plus accumulated interest income. He delved into the stack and retracted a bank statement for December 31 – balance, $4,217.66! The statement listed individual deposits and transfers of like amounts to another account number. The Cash Disbursement journal in the accounting records reflected the transfers going to the Building Reserve and corresponded with the bank statement.

Jesse tried to comprehend this large buildup of cash and its transfer to another account. Was this another bank account for the mosque, or another completely separate entity? He was still stewing with this question when the door opened and Syed Rabia entered the room.

"Mr. Hawkins." Syed strode toward Jesse, his right hand partially extended. "I trust you have found everything in order."

Jesse pushed the chair back from the table and stood to face Syed. Jesse was immediately impressed with the man's demeanor, his dress, and his looks. For some reason Jesse had been expecting a heavier and darker man, more Arab-looking. This man, with a light tan complexion, well-groomed brown hair and clean-shaven, could have been taken for many a European. The man strode purposefully and confidently. Jesse extended his hand and grasped Syed's, matched the firm grip and backed away to reveal the stacks of paper on the table as Syed moved closer.

"Yes, Mr. Rabia, everything seems to be in order. I do have a few questions, though, but first allow me to express my deep appreciation for your cooperation. Harriet is a jewel. You're fortunate to have someone like her on board." Jesse probed deep into Syed's light brown eyes and found support there that this was indeed a man to be respected – a man of honor and conviction. He felt a tinge of sadness that his chosen job was to impose grief on people – especially a person like this one seemed to be. He enjoyed the job when facing obvious tax cheats, but many were like this man – maybe time to opt for early retirement.

Jesse's mood quickly jumped back to the case at hand. This man was in control of this mosque and therefore deeply involved in what appeared to be a clear importation of money for some reason other than the mere institution of another mosque in the state. He was on the board of Allied Paint who clearly was hiding money in a foreign bank. There was definitely more to the man than met the eye. He might even be the one that had tried to have him killed. Feldman's words rang loud and clear, "Be on the alert, Jesse."

Syed moved closer to the table and touched the separated papers that Jesse had been working with. "Yes. Harriet is a wonderful person, and you are right, I am fortunate to have her working for me." He idly flipped through the papers. "You said you had questions."

"Yes." Jesse selected the Balance Sheet and pointed to the item Building Reserve. "If this is a bank account, do you have the statement?"

Syed took the statement from Jesse and seemed to study it for an extended time, which was only a moment. "This is not a bank account; it is an investment."

Jesse's eyebrow arched slightly and he said, "I note the mosque purchased land in Ft. Pierce, apparently for the purpose of constructing a building, and was titled Building Reserve in the books. The additional funds received over the years continued to be charged to that account." Jesse remembered researching court records and could not recall any other real estate purchases by Farouk Mosque. Jesse continued to search Syed's eyes for changes that would alter his first impression of the man. "Does this account reflect additional purchases of real estate?"

Syed didn't flinch. His facial expression and bodily demeanor remained unchanged. "The entire purpose of the funding was to initiate the Farouk Mosque in St. Lucie County. For various reasons, economics being a major one, it was decided to postpone construction until a more appropriate time. Donations continued to come in, and I proposed investing the money temporarily until the time was deemed right by the leaders of the mosque – excess funds could be used to fund other mosques around the state."

"Is the total amount invested in real estate?"

"A Limited Liability Company controls the funds. That is, as funds flow in to the mosque, they are transferred to the company, which invests primarily in Florida real estate."

"What is the name of the LLC and who controls it? Does it file an income tax return?" Jesse noted the slight flicker at Syed's brow and the sudden momentary eye diversion.

"Yes. Florida Land, LLC, files an income tax return on a fiscal year basis as a corporation."

Jesse fought hard to keep his growing excitement from showing. "Who controls that company?"

"I do."

There was a tap on the door and Harriet poked her head into the room. "Please excuse me, Mr. Rabia, but your luncheon appointment is in five minutes. You want me to call and delay?"

"Yes, Harriet. Tell him I will be ten minutes late. I am finishing here now." Harriet backed out of the room and Syed returned his attention to Jesse. "I must go now. Will you need more time?"

Small doubts began to creep in again. Feldman wouldn't extend the case with this explanation. Could this operation really be legitimate? Surely it didn't take this kind of money to start a new mosque. Who were the contributors? Was there a monetary connection to Allied? Maybe the records for 2006 would provide enlightenment. "I'll need a few more minutes before lunch. I'd appreciate it if you could provide me with the Mosque's accounting records for the current year, and, if possible, another meeting with you this afternoon. After my review, I will only need a few minutes. Do you think you can arrange it?"

Syed, with a glance at his wristwatch, began moving toward the door. "I will have Harriet provide you with those records now. I should be back in the office by two-thirty. I will make time for you." He went through the doorway.

CHAPTER 31

The pleasant aroma emanating from Maury's Café followed Jesse to Amy's car. Jesse placed both hands on the door and bent down to look into Amy's glimmering eyes. She had been overly excited with the information given to her during lunch, and felt certain the Farouk Mosque case would be received at CID with enthusiasm.

Jesse still had doubts and continued to try to calm her down. "Wipe that grin off your face, gal. I've still got a way to go before I'm ready to forward it. I'd rather you not say a thing to Gerald until I'm absolutely sure. You remember how he was when I tried to interest him before. Not sure I completely trust him anyway. I'll—"

A deep frown wiped the grin from Amy's face, and she blurted, "What do you mean you don't trust him? Not that Arab ancestry thing again, is it?"

Jesse, a bit shocked by the outburst, removed his hands and stepped back from the door. "Hold on, hold on. I just don't want to take any unnecessary chances until I have a better feel for what's going on. I'd rather that we keep this between us a while longer." He bent down, put his hands back on the door and peered into her eyes. "Okay?"

Amy's face eased. "I'm sorry, Jesse, for yelling. It's just that I've worked closely with Gerry for the last three years, and I could never get used to thinking about him in that way. He's a good man, Jesse – as good an American as you or me." Her face showed deep concern and she placed one hand on his. "Of course I'll keep our conversations strictly confidential. You know that."

Jesse placed his free hand over hers. "Don't fret none, gal. I know I can trust you, but . . . ." He rubbed her hand and she placed her other hand on top of his. "The past several weeks have been like no other in my life and . . . you've been the calming influence for the past two." He gazed into her eyes and saw small tears forming. He extracted his hands, gently patted hers and stood back from the door. "It's got to the point where I'm always on the defensive – ever expecting the grim reaper to appear out of nowhere."

"Count on me, Jesse." Amy grinned big again and inserted the key into the ignition. "I look forward to working this case with you, though – be like nothing I've ever experienced if it turns out like you say."

Jesse smiled, too. "Right now there's a few big ifs. Maybe I can get those out of the way this afternoon." Amy's car came to life as Jesse moved toward his own. "I'll call you tonight after I'm finished."

Amy blew him a kiss. "You be careful, Jesse."

CHAPTER **32**

Harriet's image lingered for a moment after she left the conference room, then Jesse turned to the task at hand. Throughout lunch with Amy the thought about donors and how they could affect the outcome of the examination continued to plague him and created the doubts lingering in his mind. During the earlier look at the records he had been so rapt with how the Building Reserve balance had grown from 2002 to 2005, and where that money was, that he had completely overlooked the Cash Receipts journal for 2004 and 2005.

Jesse's eyes were glued to the stack of papers marked 2006 as he removed his jacket and took the chair. He was eager to tackle that pile, but first he must satisfy his need to identify donors. Would they be the same as 2003? Who would be giving such large amounts for a project that had never gotten off the ground? He moved the 2004 stack in front of him, took a deep breath, and flipped the cover page off to reveal the Balance Sheet. He hesitated, then chose to review the Cash Receipts page. His total case revolved around this issue.

The first entries on the page indicated the same kind of activity as 2003 – large donations from individual donors. He felt a moment of dismay. He would have a hard time proving these weren't legitimate donations even though they were not being used to build a mosque. Then his eyes settled on several small donations interspersed between larger amounts near the end of the page. He looked for the source and immediately drew in a deep breath – "Various". He turned to the next page and saw the same type of entries. A lot of money was being lumped under the heading Various. He rubbed his chest, trying to lessen the tingle emanating therefrom. This was serious, and if his immediate solution to the question reverberating in his head was correct, this case was on its way to the criminal division.

Jesse quickly moved to the end of the stack and extracted the bank statements. After choosing a book entry for June, he compared it to the bank statement for the same period. One item on the bank statement in the amount of $9,200 was shown as a deposit to the bank, a clear indication that it wasn't several checks, and therefore had to be – cash! He drew in a deep breath to fight off the rising excitement – this was the case he had been seeking – the case of a lifetime. He pushed the chair back and stood.

Amy came to mind and he moved toward the telephone across the room. He hesitated. Hold on, boy. Get a grip on yourself. This case wasn't solid yet. Far out on Lake Worth a large yacht was making its way south, likely after a wonderful day on the ocean. His children came to mind again.

He moved back to the table and calmly shuffled through other bank statements, comparing them to the various accounts as he went. To him the amounts were definitely cash. Fighting the overwhelming urge to share his findings with others, he methodically opened the accounts for 2005 and, as expected, found the same type of transactions, except more cash. His expanding exhilaration took control, and he strode again to the window, looking out but really seeing nothing, his mind completely absorbed with what he had discovered. There seemed to be no other explanation but money laundering. But, for what purpose? That was the next object to tackle.

For a split second he was at the airport in Stuart, and the Arabic student pilot flashed across his eyes. Terrorists planning another World Trade Center! *I knew it.* His first impulse was to collect his things and get back to the office.

But wait a minute. His accounting mind, fighting for a position in his thoughts, took hold and brought him back to sorting facts.

Something was wrong – didn't tally. What was it? He moved back to the table and stared at the stacks of paper, his excitement still dominant, but . . . then it hit him square in the stomach. He gasped for air. Those single "cash" deposits could possibly be various checks listed on a deposit receipt and entered on the bank statement as a single deposit. His thought process blurred. He felt faint and took hold of the chair for support. In a sort of bewildered state, he ran a hand through his hair and looked blankly at the various pictures on the wall – everything seemed far off and indistinct.

Logic again took hold of his dazed mind. He needed more information. Harriet probably had made the deposits and would have copies of receipts. He moved to the door, his feelings now neither positive nor negative. Back to collecting facts.

Harriet, deeply engrossed in some project, had her back to him when he entered the lobby. She flinched and turned to him when he spoke.

"Harriet, need your help."

"Oh. Jesse, you startled me. Yes, what can I do for you?" She smiled. "I can't go out on the ocean with you until after five." Her smile turned impish. "Can you wait until then?"

The smile was tantalizing, but Jesse controlled himself and smiled, too. This was a girl that aroused his emotions, and if he didn't watch out he would have a conflict between her and Amy – something he didn't want. "No. Unfortunately, the ocean is out for today. Have to keep my mind on work – job to do." He moved closer to her desk and held out the bank statement for last December. "Just need to verify a deposit." He pointed to a particular deposit.

"There've been several of these small deposits, and I would like to know what they're made up of."

Harriet took the statement, studied it for a moment, retrieved several booklets from the bottom of a file cabinet and sorted through them. "Ah. Here's what we're looking for." She scanned the pages, and when she came to a number, said, "An exact match." She held the receipt book for Jesse to see. "Cash collections."

"Harumph!" Jesse coughed abruptly, and immediately covered his mouth with his fingers.

Harriet, with a slight frown, looked up at him. She paged through the book. "It seems that all of those small amounts are cash. I get cash to deposit on a daily basis." She handed the book to Jesse. "Is this what you're after? Do you need the other months?"

Jesse, now in complete control of his senses again said, "Yes. If it's not too much trouble, could I get the ones for 2004 and 2006 also. Just want to scan through to be sure they're all the same."

She took the book from him. "Sure, no problem. It'll take me a few minutes. I'll bring them in."

"Great. Thanks a lot, Harriet. You've made my job a hundred percent easier." Jesse moved toward the door to the conference room. "Maybe you could make a copy of one of the receipt books for my file." As he stepped through the doorway, he said over his shoulder, "This weekend may be a good time to go out on the ocean."

Back at the conference table, Jesse looked with dismay at the stacks of receipt books Harriet had brought in. Instead of the expected exhilaration, the accountant remained in control and juggled the facts to place them in reasonable order for logical thinking. The mosque was receiving substantial cash donations without a functioning mosque, but that didn't necessarily mean that cash was coming from overseas, or that the operation was illegal. The large donations from named donors seemed out of line and extravagant, but that, too, didn't prove illegality. And Syed – he seemed on the up and up, and had provided a reasonable explanation for the funds being transferred to another entity. But what about the LLC? Why would it be investing in Florida real estate when that market had been weakening for some months now? And, if this was a money-laundering scheme, why run it through the mosque in the first place?

Jesse, a bit perplexed with the facts and their possible connotation, ran a hand through his hair, took the chair, opened the 2004 accounting records and began to reconcile the entries to the bank statements and deposit receipts. He then moved on to 2005 and found that all of the small deposits were indeed cash. The big question now was how to show that the funds were not from normal operations and that they were being used for some other purpose. The idea of a terrorist plot would not go away.

Jesse stacked all the accounting records on the other side of the table and moved the 2006 records in front of him. He wasn't sure now why he had asked for this year. If the findings were similar to the other years, he would be no further ahead than he now was. Probably a waste of time. His eyebrow arched when he noted the increase in the Building Reserve account – now in excess of seventy-five million!

Exhilaration began to push on the accountant mentality, and he thumbed through the pages to Cash Receipts. Receipts were quite similar to the other years and his eagerness waned again. He flipped the page – the same. The next page – the same. Jesse was quickly becoming bored with this part of the examination. He routinely turned to the next page, and as his eyes settled on an unusual entry, there seemed to be a catch in his throat and the familiar tingle in his chest – a deposit of $1.5 million from Provident Paint. His right hand went, without conscious effort, to his throat and massaged it. *God Almighty.*

Jesse was too absorbed to hear the door open when Syed entered, and was a bit alarmed at the sound of his voice.

"Mr. Hawkins, did you find everything to your satisfaction?"

Although Jesse didn't recognize the voice, he assumed it was Syed and twisted in the chair to face him. *Control, boy. Facts, get the facts.* "Mr. Rabia. Yes, sir. Everything's proceeding nicely." Syed moved to the table and stood next to the chair. Jesse closed the journal for 2006, moved it away and brought the one for 2004 in front of him. "Have a few questions and I'll be finished with the mosque." Syed said nothing and waited patiently for Jesse to continue.

Jesse opened the journal to Cash Receipts and slipped the corresponding bank statement aside. "I've noted that the mosque, in addition to the continuing large check donations, has received numerous cash donations of varying amounts for both 2004 and 2005. The donor's names are not shown. The entries are listed as various." Jesse brought a journal page and the bank statement to the forefront for Syed's perusal. "What is the source of these cash donations? I question it because there is no active mosque."

Syed took the papers and studied them for a moment. "Yes, I can understand your concern." He placed the papers back on the table, stared at the paintings on the wall for an extended moment, then looked directly at Jesse. "The explanation is quite simple however. A portion is received through Kahid Mosque collections, and I, along with others concerned with the new mosque, petition mosques all over Florida and the Southeast for donations. Most have agreed to set aside a portion of their receipts for our purpose. Cash arrives and is deposited on a regular basis." Syed adjusted his tie. "That has no effect on our tax status, does it?"

Jesse's mind tumbled. His perspective of this man was changing rapidly. He still saw an intelligent businessman, but doubts were beginning to take hold about his honesty. The man was obviously thinking fast to provide satisfactory answers and it apparently made him nervous. Jesse was now certain he had a big case brewing. "No, that doesn't affect the tax status, but what could have an effect is the use of those collections. If that use is not solely for the purpose of the mosque, that is, its religious purpose, the mosque could lose its tax-exempt status, and therefore have to file tax returns and pay tax on the non-related income."

Syed's facial expression did not change and he said, "I explained that to you before. Money was collected to build a mosque to facilitate the growing Muslim population in St. Lucie County. Unfortunately, we have encountered numerous obstacles in our path, which our engineers and lawyers are attempting to resolve. Hopefully that will be done in the coming months and we will begin construction without further ado."

As Syed continued to rehash his old argument, Jesse's mind was trying to sort through the accounting records for expenses having to do with construction plans and expenses. That thought hit him like a thunderbolt – he couldn't remember any expenses. This man was lying through his teeth. How to go forward from here? Should he push with more questions? He thought again about the attempts on his life. This could be serious – he had to discuss it with others. But, he must ask at least one more question. "The mosque has collected over seventy-five million dollars. How can we hold that to be all for religious purposes?"

Again, Syed didn't blink. It was as if he had already contemplated that question. "I've posed the same question to

160

my superiors, and the answer is; we will use the amount necessary to build our mosque, then donate the balance to other mosques in the country for their religious purposes and for new mosques to handle the ever-growing Islamic population. In other words, we don't anticipate that funds will ever be used for non-religious purposes."

Jesse was thinking fast. This was the opportunity to press on with the examination and see if he could determine what was being done with the funds going into the LLC. Even if all the donations were legal, the money received from Provident Paint in 2006 indicated a tie to Allied, and therefore a tie to the senator, definitely solid justification for pulling his return. It also indicated that Allied's profits were being shifted to Provident, a foreign "bank account", for the sole purpose of avoiding taxes in this country – out and out fraud. But what about the attempts on his life – his children?

Maintaining his professional demeanor, Jesse said, "That explanation sounds reasonable, but the amount of money involved creates a wee bit of a problem. I'll need to run it by my boss before a final ruling is made." He stood and gathered his notes. "I'm sure you understand the need for that."

Syed smiled. "I have been my own boss for so long now it is not easy to think of reporting to one, but I think I understand your need." He extended his hand and Jesse took it. "Will you be needing anything else at this time?"

Jesse removed his hand and placed his notes inside the briefcase. He picked up on the fact that Syed operated his own business. Was that also connected to the operations? "No, not at the moment. If I do, I'll call. And, Mr. Rabia, I can't thank you enough for the splendid cooperation I've had while here. If I'm unable to speak with Harriet, would you please convey my thanks and appreciation for her help?" Jesse, for some strange reason, still held a deep respect for this man. He extended his hand again and said, "Thanks again. I'll be in touch if necessary."

CHAPTER **33**

At home in the den, Syed stared unseeing at the book-lined walls, his hand resting on a book he had chosen to read to extract from his mind the events of the afternoon. The book was not open. He knew his explanation had not held water with the revenue agent, and it was simply a matter of time before the agent would be back. What should he do? Had it been a mistake to run the check from Provident Paint through Farouk Mosque? The agent didn't mention the transaction, yet he had been looking at the records for 2006. Surely he hadn't missed it and was fully aware that Allied purchased its paint from Provident. *There is the tie to Allied, and, therefore to me.*

A tinge of fear struck as he recalled using the same words at a meeting with Abdullah. Would he be targeted like the others? Doubts clouded his mind. Abdullah was like his father – he had said so on numerous occasions. Surely he would not think of such a thing. But yet, there seemed to be something much more sinister going on than just shuffling money.

Syed struggled to stay with the problems at hand and to concoct a valid purpose for the Provident money going to the mosque. Past mistakes tried to take hold, but he wouldn't jump to conclusions, realizing that the exigencies of the moment often led to undue trouble.

Syed's sole reason for getting involved in the operation had been to facilitate his homeland's economic expansion. That was the purpose laid out by Abdullah, Imraaz, and his father. Since then it seemed to be one small deviation from morality after another. He still could not comprehend the need to launder money for the simple task of funding the purchase of a business. Initially he had arranged for overseas money to go directly into a special LLC controlled by Imraaz, from which funds were extracted to purchase business interests.

After the World Trade Center disaster, Abdullah and Imraaz had explained that it was important to not broadcast the fact that it was Mid-Easterners purchasing the interests. By then Syed had been sufficiently harassed by the U. S. Government that he completely understood their reasoning. They had suggested using Kahid Mosque for the first money-washing, but he had devised the scheme of creating another mosque for the sole purpose of masking the money. The plan was to have funds come in to Farouk Mosque as donations, then transferred to a new LLC, which in turn would purchase real estate, the sales of which would produce legitimate cash that could then be used without risk to purchase going businesses or start-ups.

Then came the momentous opportunity to acquire Brisbane Paint, LTD in England along with his supreme scheme to keep all profits from the sale of paint in an offshore entity. The beauty of that acquisition lay in the fact that it was the U. S. government that provided the funds and a senator responsible for the whole thing. This was sure to be an excellent source of funds for years to come. He had been elated with his coup and the word was out that he was soon to be honored by the top echelon.

Then the murders began. And he had, against his better judgment, been drawn into the action. Through Abdullah's insistence, Syed had been brought into direct contact with Hamza even though Abdullah gave the orders. Just why Mendez was killed, he would never know. Then the attempts on the revenue agents' lives. All for what purpose? Had none of that happened, Mendez's tax return would have been examined and that would have been the end of it. As it was, those events sent Jesse Hawkins searching ever deeper. Syed held a bit of respect for the agent and his zeal to uncover unpaid taxes. He admired a person who worked hard at their particular task. Would Abdullah send Hamza out again?

"I'm home."

Mary's voice shattered his thoughts and he turned to look toward the open door. Not seeing her, his troubled mind returned to the problems stored there. Syed opened the book in an effort to move on to other topics. He had barely started to read when Mary breezed jauntily through the doorway and made her way to the file cabinet at the far side of the room. "You seem unduly dour. Nothing wrong, I hope. We're still on for dinner and the theater, yes?" She opened the top file drawer and sorted among the files there.

Mary's fragrant aroma arrived at the desk and, as usual, her normal cheerfulness brought immediate relief. Before he could react further, she extracted a file, moved behind Syed, and still holding the file, encircled him with her arms. She whispered in his ear, "I love you sooo much," then tenderly kissed him on the cheek.

Syed, exhilaration surging through his body, removed the file from her hand, stood and turned to take her in his arms. He buried his face in the fragrant, dark brown hair hanging below her bare shoulders. She was the most beautiful and loving girl he had ever met in his life. The problems and thoughts of a moment before were non-existent. He murmured, "I dearly love you, Mary Rabia. You are the most fortunate event in my life." They continued to embrace and the events of that date four years ago flooded his memory.

The chance meeting had indeed been fortuitous. Mary had been only ten years old when she came to this country, with little exposure to Islam. Her mother, a Muslim of Arabian descent, had escaped to the United States after the brutal killing of her Jewish husband by the Iraqi regime in 1980. Neither of Mary's parents had been religiously oriented during her life and especially since coming to the United States. But in 2002 her mother, for some unknown reason, had regained her belief in the teachings of the Prophet Mohammad and had attended a special event hosted by the Kahid Mosque. Practicing Muslims had come from all over South Florida. Syed would never forget looking through that vast crowd and locking his eyes to those of the most beautiful woman in the world. She had seemingly made the first move, but it was he who had pushed the issue, and within three months they were married.

He unlocked his arms and moved back slightly, just enough to get a good look at her face. He wiped away a tear from her cheek with his thumb and kissed her on the mouth. They clasped each other again and he said, "I will forever love you."

Mary squeezed with her arms. "And I you. Life could not be any better."

They eased their hold, backed off a bit and gazed admiringly at each other.

Mary moved to the other side of the desk, picked up the file and opened it. She smiled at the slight frown on Syed's face and said, "Now, back to work before we leave for a pleasant evening."

"Do we have to work now? What work could be so important at this time?"

Mary extracted a sheet from the file and slid it across the desk in front of him. "As I've been telling you, lot sales have been dropping off for the past few months but, this month they've dropped dramatically." She waited for his reaction to the sales data on the sheet. He merely looked up at her.

"I need to determine if you wish to continue making transactions even though, in most cases, Florida Land will realize losses. Or if it's necessary to continue realizing cash flow. I know that was important to you before." Her facial

166

expression did not convey inquisitiveness beyond the questions asked.

Soon after devising the plan to mask the money sources through the purchase and sale of real estate, Syed, managing a fledgling financial management company and tending to money acquisitions for Farouk Mosque, had found his time to be severely limited. His solution had been to have Mary take over the duties of Florida Land. Her job was solely to purchase and sell lots throughout Florida, which she did almost exclusively using the Internet. Although she had questioned the purpose of the business, she had backed off after his explanation that the business belonged to the mosque and that funds were being amassed for its needs.

His mind turned again to the problems he was wrestling with, and the additional one that had bothered him ever since he determined that mosque business was not completely on the up and up. He regretted dearly that he'd kept small secrets from her. If this caused him to lose her, he would kill himself. There was absolutely nothing in this world more important than Mary. "Yes. Sales do not look promising, but you continue with the transactions. I will consult with Abdullah soon." Syed looked at the desk clock and stood. "I guess we better ready ourselves if we are to enjoy our night."

Mary smiled, stood, replaced the file in the cabinet and moved hurriedly to the door. Over her shoulder she said, "I'm first in the shower," and disappeared.

Syed's thoughts turned again to the problems ahead.

Would Hamza be called in again?

In Miami, Hamza Nazim watched the man casually stroll along the sidewalk, then signaled to his cohorts at each end of the block to close in. The man seemed unconcerned until he spotted Hamza crossing the street and moving toward him. He rushed forward before seeing a man walking hurriedly toward him, then turned to go back, then saw the other man closing in. Looking in desperation at Hamza, he turned and ran into the alley.

Hamza pulled the man off the high fence at the end of the alley as the other two men gathered close. The man's eyes darted in every direction, unable to settle on any one object. Hamza, with his left arm against the man's chest forcing him against the fence, placed a large knife at the man's neck and slowly moved it sideways. Blood oozed from the slight incision. The man's eyes bulged with fear but didn't move.

Hamza's voice matched the effect of the menacing knife. "You promised to repay the loan three days ago. You have done this before. You need a lesson." He moved the knife across the neck and more blood seeped out.

The man struggled. His eyes darted about wildly. "I had the money to repay you. Somebody stole it from me . . . . Please . . . ."

Hamza stepped back as he put pressure on the knife and moved it across the neck. Blood spurted as the man slumped to the ground.

Hamza's cell phone chimed.

CHAPTER **34**

"Mr. Hawkins?" The question reached Jesse as he closed the door to Jacob Kirschner's reception room. He looked up to see a pleasantly beaming face through the opening into the clerk's office. The young woman rose and walked to the opening as Jesse crossed the room.

"Yes, I'm Jesse Hawkins. Good morning."

"Good morning, sir." Still smiling, the young woman removed a wisp of blond hair from her eyelid as she arrived at the counter. "Mr. Kirschner is expecting you. Please follow me." She moved away, opened the door and led him down the hall to the conference room. She flipped the light switch. "Please have a seat. Mr. Kirschner will be right with you."

A slight hint of flower blossoms lingered as the receptionist retreated. Jesse surveyed the room of Senator Walker's CPA and placed his briefcase on the long table. Rays of sunlight streamed in from the large window that made up most of the wall. The view was of a tall building across the street. Another wall was covered with books and the other was almost covered with a large scene of the Everglades. A white egret stood on one leg, peering out across the placid, glimmering water.

"Mr. Hawkins." A tall, slender man about forty years old entered the room and reached to take Jesse's hand. He carried a single file and a yellow legal pad. "Tell me what you need, and I'll try to get it for you."

Jesse, a bit startled, took the hand. "I don't need much, and I don't imagine this will take but a few minutes." Jesse, without sitting, opened his briefcase, extracted the file and opened it. "It seems that Senator Walker received a check in the amount of $150,000 from Allied Paint Corporation in

2005, and I can't find where he reported it on his return. I only see his Senate wages, some interest and dividends and a few capital transactions. Also I—"

"$150,000 from Allied Paint?" Jacob opened his file and flipped through the pages and his own notes. Without looking at Jesse, he seemed baffled and said, "I don't recall such an amount, and I don't see any mention of it in my notes." He looked up at Jesse. "Are you sure it was received in 2005?"

Jesse removed a sheet of paper from the file and held it up for Kirschner's review. "The check, clearly written in December 2005, was endorsed by Senator Walker." Jesse experienced a pang of doubt as Kirschner took the paper and examined it. *My God, could this check have been received and endorsed in 2006?*

Kirschner, looking more puzzled, kept his eyes glued to the paper. "Well, as you say, the check was written in '05 and Senator Walker clearly endorsed it, but . . . ." He wiped his glasses with a handkerchief and held the paper for closer inspection. "I can't make out exactly when the check cleared the bank." The puzzled look left his face, as if he had arrived at an answer, and he looked at Jesse. "Since it wasn't written until late in December, perhaps the senator didn't receive it until January. That could explain why it wasn't reported in '05." He handed the paper back to Jesse.

Jesse, fighting to keep his face from showing dismay at his failure to clearly determine the date it had cleared, took the paper and scanned it, hoping to come up with an answer before he had to respond. But wait a minute. It didn't really matter when it cleared, what mattered is when the senator received it. That's when it should have been reported. Jesse looked again at the date on the check: December 14, 2005. It wouldn't have taken more than a week for the check to get to the senator. He started to feel in control again. To lock it up, he would have to go back to Allied and obtain a copy of the correspondence accompanying the check. He almost smiled when another thought hit him. What if Allied won't share the correspondence? What if they've destroyed it? "The question is," Jesse said, "when did the senator receive the check? If it was in 2005, then it is reportable in 2005. I think that's easily answerable with a phone call to the senator." Jesse looked directly at Kirschner with his most positive demeanor.

"Well, I agree. If it's not reportable in '05, I guess it would surely be reportable in '06." He glanced at Jesse, his brow a bit squinched. "Assuming, of course, it is in fact income anyway. So it behooves me to determine when he received it. I'll call him now." Kirschner moved to the end of the table toward the telephone.

"Before you do that, I have one more question."

Kirschner's hand paused over the phone. "Shoot."

"The senator sold his house in 2005 and I don't see any mention on the return. "Did his gain not exceed $500,000?"

Kirschner again looked a little puzzled and moved back to his file. "Wait a minute. I seem to remember something strange about that transaction." He started to go into the 2005 file, then said, "Okay, now I remember, that was a screwed up deal. Hold on, let me get the 2006 file." He left the room and was soon back with another file.

"Now, let's see." He removed a sheet of handwritten notes and studied them for a moment. "Okay, here's what happened. The transaction was supposed to have closed on December 27, but because of some entanglement it didn't actually close until January 9. Something to do with when the money actually changed hands, as I recall. But, according to my preliminary calculations, it will not be reportable."

"I don't understand. The court records I saw indicated a closed sale in December. I have a copy of the court documents." Jesse rifled through his file.

"Yes. I know. Like I say, there was some big bugaboo and it didn't get closed. The courthouse recorded the sale for '05 and it took the attorney on into January to get the filing corrected." Kirschner moved to the computer nestled among the books. "Here, let's see if the records have been updated." He began to enter data into the computer.

Jesse moved around the table and stood behind him to see how he did it. This was an area in which Jesse was definitely lacking and he berated himself for not learning how to research on-line. Most of the agents were doing it and he had promised himself that he would soon learn, but it always seemed to be put off for another day.

A document appeared on screen. Kirschner said, "Ah, here it is. This is the original, recorded in December – the one you have. Notice it's marked void." He shifted to the next screen. "Okay, here's what we're looking for." He turned and indicated for Jesse to come closer to see.

Sure enough, the document was official. Jesse thought back on his audit of Allied and the fact that he had been unable to find the purchase recorded on the books for 2005. This result caused him no grief; he hadn't really expected an adjustment because of the special rules for the sale of a residence. But did it bode for something other than tax? Why had Allied sold the property at such a large loss only months after its purchase? Was it a payment of some kind to the senator? Jesse asked, "Can you make a copy of that for me? Make one of the original also to show that it has been voided." The document he saw in April had not been marked void – he was sure of that. When was it marked? Jesse moved back to his side of the table. "Well, I guess that takes care of that issue. Will you call Senator Walker about the check?" He made notes to his files.

"Yes. Hold on a minute. I'll go to the printer." Kirschner returned, handed the copies to Jesse and moved to the telephone. "Hello. This is Jacob Kirschner, Senator Walker's CPA. Could I speak with his assistant?" He placed his hand over the mouthpiece and gave a thumbs up to Jesse.

"Mr. Benson, I'm here with the revenue agent and he has a question. There was a check in the amount of $150,000 written to the senator by Allied Paint Corporation in 2005. The agent is questioning why that amount was not reported on the senator's tax return for 2005. Can you help?" Again Kirschner placed a hand over the mouthpiece and spoke to Jesse. "He remembers the transaction but wants to review his records to be sure. Be just a minute."

Jesse's angst continued to build. Was it possible the check had not reached the senator until January? What else could go wrong on this case? Maybe he was being too overzealous as Danny always said.

"Yes, I'm here." Kirschner spoke into the phone, then listened. His look conveyed perplexity. "Yes, I understand. The check was deposited in December to the senator's campaign fund." He frowned at Jesse. "Can you tell me why that was? The check was made payable to the senator." He paused again, apparently listening to dialogue from the other end. "Okay, I understand. Will you send copies of records to verify what you say?" Kirschner again raised his thumb in Jesse's direction, and returned the phone to its cradle.

"Mr. Benson said the check represented contributions to the senator's campaign fund by Allied employees. Each year the corporation seeks contributions from its employees and then remits one check payable to the campaign committee. For some unknown reason, in '05 the check was made payable to Senator Walker, who simply endorsed it and turned it over to the committee." Kirschner grinned and moved back to the side of the table. "Does that answer satisfy you?"

CHAPTER **35**

Does that answer satisfy you? Does that *answer satisfy you?*
The words echoed in Jesse's head as he walked to his car.
His case against the senator seemed to be fading fast. If the
$150,000 payment was really a campaign contribution, there
would be no fraud and not even an adjustment. There would
be additional taxes imposed on Allied because Allied had
listed the payment as outside services and deducted it from
income. What was the real nature of the payment and why
had it been made? If it was an expense, what service had the
senator performed for Allied? Did Allied's employees really
make individual contributions, or was this really a
contribution from Allied itself? If it was a corporate
campaign contribution, for what purpose was Allied making
it? And then there was the purchase of the senator's house by
Allied at a price higher than the obvious value. Just what
connection might there be between the two?

Jesse reached to open the door to his car and stopped
short as the revelation struck a cord. The fact was, the
$150,000 had been paid to the senator and entered on
Allied's books and tax return as Outside Services. Not a
campaign contribution. What the senator had done with the
money was irrelevant to that particular misfiling. Jesse's
spirits soared again. Until he could determine the true nature
of the expenditure, his criminal case against the senator was
not over yet. His meeting with Feldman was in one hour. He
opened the car door.

"Mr. Hawkins."

Jesse turned to see a young man in a sports jacket walking
fast toward him. He did not recognize the man.

The man handed Jesse a card and said, "I'm Arthur Reid,
with the *Washington Post*. I heard you were auditing Senator

Martin Walker, and wondered if I could ask you a few questions."

Jesse's face reflected his bewilderment. He had never before been approached by a member of the press. He was at a loss to respond. "I . . . I—"

"Please forgive me, Mr. Hawkins, but I would be most appreciative if you could spare me a few moments. The *Post* is doing a story on the senator. Could we go somewhere and have a coffee or something?"

"I'm sorry, Mr. Reid, but I'm not allowed to discuss the senator's case with anyone outside the Internal Revenue Service."

"I understand, but maybe I could help you with questions you might have."

Jesse wondered how a reporter could possibly answer any of his questions. Nobody that he knew of was eager to help a revenue agent. "Why would you want to help me?"

Reid appeared overconfident. "Like I said, the *Post* is doing a story on the senator and it's my job to tie up the loose ends. We suspect the senator is into something illegal and we'd like to know what it is . . . for the good of the country." Reid peered deep into Jesse's eyes as if to underline his last utterance. "By the way, how did you get started on the senator's tax return? Through Allied Paint?"

Jesse struggled to control the look of astonishment he knew must be spreading across his face. How could Reid possibly know that? Reporters seemed to have a way of getting information that was normally unavailable to the likes of people like Jesse. What did he mean by something illegal? *Maybe I ought to play along with this guy. Who knows?*

Reid continued, "Did you know that Allied is really owned by Brisbane Paint Company Ltd., in England?" To Jesse, Reid seemed a bit too smug.

175

Jesse retaliated, "Did you know—?" The thunderbolt struck. The corrected court records stood out in his mind as if he was looking at them again on the computer screen. The reason he had not detected the purchase and sale of the senator's house on Allied's books was plainly revealed. It had been purchased by the LLC managed by Syed. In his mind he zeroed in on the image and, sure enough, there was Syed's signature.

Jesse got into the car. "I'm sorry, but I really must run to make my other appointment." He closed the car door, entered the key in the ignition switch and looked at Reid. "Arthur, you might want to check the public records." He turned the key and the engine purred.

Reid looked at the business card Jesse placed in his hand, grinned and backed away as the car moved backwards. "Thanks, Jesse. Let's have lunch. I'll call."

CHAPTER **36**

Michael Gibson looked up and grinned as Jesse approached his desk. Jesse couldn't hide his elation at the recent turn of events in a case that initially seemed doomed to mediocrity. He was onto something bigger than he had ever expected. He tried to mask his feelings and laid his briefcase on the desk. "How's it going, Mike? Any juicy cases?"

"Not much on this end. Anything new with you? Any more attacks on your life? How's the case going?"

Jesse felt the need to rub it in a little – to tweak the appetite of the mad scientist and watch him drool. "This thing has expanded beyond my wildest dreams. Every time I examine one case, another one of more interest pops up. Think I've got a criminal case and . . . ." He looked at Michael and saw the intense interest gathering there. "Could go a lot further, maybe . . . like 9/11." He watched disbelief replace the interest, and inserted other files into his briefcase.

"Come on, Jesse. What've you got?"

The reporter's smug statement about Allied flashed in Jesse's mind. Jesse's response had been automatic and he had almost revealed the identity of Provident Paint. He would have to be a lot more careful if he was to overcome his eagerness to let others know of his coups. "I'll let you in on it later. Right now I've got to meet with Danny and Gerald." He took delight in letting Mike know that he was meeting with the head of Criminal Intelligence.

As he walked away another thought popped up. The paint was manufactured in England, sold at a low price to Provident, and then sold at a high price to Allied. An agent waved to him and he automatically waved back, but his mind wouldn't let go of the information. How was the senator connected to that operation? Aha! In 2006, money had been transferred from Provident to Farouk Mosque and, he suspected had been transferred to the LLC, and the loss on the home sale he'd attributed to Allied was likely taken by the LLC to offset other gains. He decided he would definitely audit the LLC. Should he make the appointment now? A look at his watch showed him he was out of time.

Feldman looked up from his work when Jesse entered the office and motioned for him to take a chair. Jesse laid the briefcase on the desk and sat. In the seconds he had left, he reviewed in his mind the case he would need to submit to get accepted by CID. All the facts seemed a jumble. *Damn it, why didn't I take more time to get this perfect?* He extracted papers from his briefcase.

Feldman finally cleared the papers from his desk and said, "Gerald will be a few minutes late." Feldman, as usual, seemed unduly impatient. It was nearing time to quit for the day and head for home. "Jesse, I sure hope you've got something worthwhile. We've all got a lot of work to do, with deadlines looming every instant. Gerald had to go to great lengths to make time for this meeting, and he didn't hesitate to let me know it." The door opened. "I sure hope you've got something this time."

Gerald Singleton entered, shook hands all around and took the chair next to Jesse. He glanced at his watch. "What've we got?"

The doubt Jesse had about Singleton's heritage flashed in his brain and was quickly gone. Amy and Danny trusted him, so would he. "At our last meeting, I explained the need to audit Allied Paint Corporation and Senator Martin Walker. You both agreed that we would go ahead with those." Jesse glanced at Feldman and back to Singleton. "There was a small glitch, but we overcame it and moved ahead with both audits."

Singleton asked, "What's the small glitch?"

A frown appeared on Feldman's face as he spoke, "A little pressure from Atlanta, but we worked it out. It's okay."

"About the senator's return, I imagine." Singleton seemed to understand the problem and the possible consequences if anything went wrong. "Go ahead, Jesse, bring me up to date."

Jesse, still grappling with the proper presentation, moved his chair so that he would be able to give both men equal attention and said, "Let's start with Allied. I examined them initially because of a small payment by them to the deceased taxpayer, Mendez. That led to the payment of $150,000 to the senator for Outside Services. I had also determined, through a review of court records, that Allied had purchased the senator's house in 2005, and within a few months, sold it at a loss. That transaction was not reflected on the books of Allied." Jesse noted the blank faces on both men.

"During the audit, I managed to learn that Allied was sold early this year. Three of the board members have Arab names, one of whom lives in this community. Mr. Syed Rabia was the referral for Mendez, who was a recent convert to Islam and a member of the local mosque." Singleton seemed bored and looked at his watch.

Jesse continued, "Allied didn't make a profit in 2005 as well as in the two preceding years." Still no interest in either man. "The gross profit percentage seemed too small to ever result in a profit, and a look at purchases led to a company in Nassau. That concerned me, so I flew over there and determined there was no such company on the island." The eyelashes of both men flicked up. Jesse felt better.

Before Jesse could continue, Singleton said, "I understand you have a small plane. Did you fly that over there?"

"Yes." Jesse grinned. "That was the first time I'd ever crossed the ocean outside sight of land. A little tense, but

exhilarating, too." Jesse could continue talking about flying, but thought better of it.

Feldman asked, "So what did that tell you, Jesse?"

"At that moment it told me that Provident Paint, the company in Nassau, was a mere bank account." Outright interest was now beginning to show on the men's faces and Jesse's confidence grew. "I have subsequently determined that a company in England is the manufacturer of the paint."

"How the hell did you determine that?" Feldman's face reflected his usual incredulity.

"If you will, let me hold back that source until you decide where we're going with this." Jesse didn't want to let them know that he didn't rely on the source one hundred percent. When Feldman relented, Jesse continued, "The information did allow me to come up with a possible transaction sequence. Brisbane Paint in England sells the paint to Provident in Nassau for a paltry sum, realizing little or no profit. Provident sells the paint to Allied at a high price, effectively keeping the untaxed profits offshore. You will recall that Allied does not make a profit."

Singleton, with awe written all over his face, looked first at Feldman then back at Jesse. "Jesse, I'm damned impressed with your deductive ability. That is some mighty fine sleuthing, but . . . how're you going to prove it? Even assuming the English company is as you say, where do we go from here? Did you determine a further connection to the senator?"

"I audited the local mosque because of a connection to Mendez. He was the trustee of a real estate trust, and I," Jesse glanced at Feldman, "kind of felt there might be some sinister meaning hidden there." Feldman grimaced and started to speak, but Jesse overrode him. "When I later determined that the replacement of Mendez as trustee was Syed Rabia, the Arab I mentioned earlier as a board member of Allied, I . . . " he again looked at Feldman . . . "with Danny's approval, examined the mosque. They had not filed a return and I didn't find any adjustments that would've required them to." Singleton seemed ready to interject but held it.

"But that audit led to the audit of the Farouk Mosque, headed up by none other than . . . Syed Rabia." Jesse paused long enough for the significance of that knowledge to sink in. "Kahid Mosque, in 2002, funded the Farouk Mosque with $250,000 which was used to purchase property in St. Lucie County."

Singleton looked at his watch for the third time and said, "I'm afraid I don't understand what the audit of a mosque has to do with my question about the senator." He tapped his watch. "There may be some possibilities with Allied, but I'm running out of time, Jesse. We may have to arrange another day."

Jesse could not understand how these investigative people passed right over the Arab connection. Maybe too long in the administrative role. "That St. Lucie property was never converted into a mosque." No reaction on the faces. "The Farouk Mosque, over the next four and a half years took in donations, mostly from Arab names, amounting to seventy-five million dollars – none of which was used for the mosque." He now noted huge expressions of awe.

Singleton said, "My God. What—?"

"To your question about the senator, this year the Farouk Mosque received $1.5 million from Provident Paint, the offshore bank account. That money was transferred to an LLC as were all the other receipts by the mosque." Jesse drew in a deep breath, realizing that he had not actually tracked the $1.5 million into the LLC. He decided to not correct himself. "I have subsequently learned that the sale of the senator's house actually closed this year, which answers my question as to why the sale didn't show up on Allied's books."

Feldman leaned across the desk, his interest now plainly exhibited. "But I thought you said that court records indicated the house was sold in 2005."

"That gets a little complicated, but it was all explained when I met with the senator's accountant this morning. The court records have been corrected to show the purchase by Florida Land, LLC in 2006."

"Florida—" Singleton was cut off by Jesse.

"The same LLC that received all the money from the mosque." Jesse felt more sure of himself after this successful recap of events, even though he hadn't gone into the larger possibilities.

Feldman looked at Singleton. "What do you think, Gerry? See anything there?"

Singleton said, "This is a very interesting but complicated case. Right now I'm not sure just what it holds. There definitely are some strange things going on, but are they criminal? That's the question I have to wrestle with. I ask that Jesse make a formal report so I can study it in detail." He looked at his watch and stood. "I've got to be on the move, guys." He reached for Jesse's hand and Jesse stood, too. "Jesse, I don't know just where all this will lead, but I want you to know that I think you've done one hell of a job here and you're to be congratulated." He squeezed Jesse's hand. "One thing further before I go. How did the senator's exam go? Did he report the $150,000?"

"No." Jesse noted the extreme interest on Feldman's face. "But, his aide says the money was a political contribution from Allied's employees. Says Allied made a mistake when they made the check payable to the senator. I've got to follow up on that."

"God. I'll be late. Jesse, keep me up to date. Danny, let's go over this again after we've had time to study Jesse's report." Singleton headed for the door.

Feldman stood and began to stuff material into his briefcase. "Jesse, I agree with Gerry. You've been very thorough . . . as usual, and even though I give you hell about your inquisitive nose, it definitely is an asset to the Service." He moved around the desk and took Jesse's hand as they headed toward the door. "I take it you're going to examine the LLC."

"Yes, I am, and I hope I can learn what all that money's being used for. Something strange going on. Terrorists maybe." Jesse looked at Feldman and grinned. Feldman frowned.

CHAPTER 37

"Hi, Jesse. Ready to go out in the boat?" Harriet's voice reached Jesse as he closed the door behind him. The question and the import caused a bit of a stir in him, but the other problems remained in the forefront.

Jesse had arranged for another look at the Farouk Mosque books for 2006. Syed had seemed a little upset when Jesse had called him after the meeting with Feldman. Syed's recollection of his last meeting with Jesse was that the mosque audit was complete and the explanation of the use of mosque funds satisfactory. Of course, that was the impression Jesse had conveyed, all the time knowing there was definitely something sinister going on with all that money. While here before, he had neglected to determine as a fact the disposition of the Provident deposit. Hopefully he could derive that information without stirring up too much anxiety in Syed.

He walked to her desk. "How goes it, Harriet? Yeah, I'm ready. You?"

Harriet stood. "Let's go." The grin spread across her face and her eyes twinkled.

"Yeah, sure." Jesse propped his briefcase on the desk and grinned just as big. "One of these days, huh?"

A small pout formed. "Well, it's Thursday. Only two more days until the big weekend. Maybe . . . ." She retook her seat behind the computer. "The information you requested is in the conference room." A small smile re-formed. "You need anything else, let me know. Want coffee?"

"Thanks a lot, Harriet. No, think I've had enough coffee already." He moved toward the conference room door. "I really appreciate your cooperation, Harriet. I may need more of it."

A quick scan of the material on the table revealed that $1,500,000 had been received and transferred to Florida Land, LLC on January 6, 2006. Jesse's heart raced and he sought out the bank statement. He knew it would confirm the transfer, and sure enough, it did. Everything fit now to tie the senator to Allied and therefore Jesse's justification for pulling the return. He now had to prove the $150,000 payment was taxable to the senator and try to figure out the purpose of shifting the purchase of the house from Allied to the LLC. How were they able to do that? It had to be linked to further money washing.

He tried to recall images of the first court recordings. The original court recordings showed the purchase of the property by Allied in late December 2005 and the subsequent sale in February at a lesser value. Later, the first recording was voided and redone to reflect Florida Land, LLC as the purchaser. He had neglected to follow up on the recordings of the subsequent sale to verify that it, too, had been voided. He now wished that he had a laptop and the expertise to search court records to prove his theory that it was, in fact, the LLC that had sold the property.

The big question was, how were they able to shift the purchase to the LLC, and why would they want to? Jesse suspected a payment to the senator for something. The words of the reporter rang in his ears, "We suspect the senator is into something illegal . . . ." Was the re-recording a result of political pressure? What effect did all this have on his case?

Jesse extracted the tax return for Florida Land for 2005, which he had received by fax Wednesday afternoon. A quick scan of the return revealed nothing unusual.

Jesse was almost at Harriet's desk before she responded to his approach with an involuntary jump. "Oh, Jesse. You scared me. Don't sneak up on me that way."

Jesse grinned. "Didn't sneak. You were so wrapped up in your work, you didn't pay any attention to me." Harriet didn't grin back. "Hey, I'm sorry. Didn't mean to alarm you. Forgive me?"

She turned away from the computer, faced Jesse and smiled. "Yeah, guess I was caught up in my task. What do you need?"

"I would like to see the books of Florida Land, LLC, for the last three years plus the 2006 year-to-date. Can do?"

A small frown crept up on Harriet's face. "I guess it's okay, but I'll have to check with Mr. Rabia first. He's in with a client now." She looked at the clock on the far wall. "Probably another half hour or so. Is that a problem?"

"That's okay. I'll kill a little time." He decided to dig a little. "Maybe go across the street and watch the boats go by." Jesse headed toward the exit.

Harriet's frown widened. "Ooooh, you would."

Jesse paid for the coffee, and on the way out to the large porch overlooking the waterway, he noticed a magazine with blaring headlines: "Al Qaeda Has Nukes". He moved to the magazine rack, flipped to the cover story, and a quick scan indicated that bin Laden had, over the years, acquired nuclear weapons and materials from several sources, including the Soviet Union, and had enlisted knowledgeable scientists to perfect the weapons.

Jesse placed the magazine on the rack and walked out on the wood-planked porch. The boats moored to the adjacent docks were almost a blur. Jesse's mind was caught up with the idea of nuclear weapons and the Arabs he was dealing with. A speedboat raced by, sending water tumbling toward the parked boats.

What was all that money being accumulated for? He knew for certain it was not all for a mosque, if for one at all. He knew, too, at least in his overactive mind, that a group of radical Muslims were out to destroy the United States. He remembered another story he had read not long ago where bin Laden had warned the American people of another imminent strike, one much worse than the World Trade Center, which had only been a token of what was to come. Are we asleep at the wheel again? Could it possibly be that he was in the vanguard with his idea, and no one else would listen? He had to get other, more experienced minds involved. How much did he have to unearth before they would take him seriously?

He drank the rest of the coffee and looked at his watch. Thirty-five minutes had gone by since he left Rabia's office. He turned and headed in that direction, more determined than ever to find the hidden link.

CHAPTER **38**

Syed Rabia, standing facing Harriet's desk, turned as Jesse opened the door. "Ah. Mr. Hawkins. Come, let us talk in the conference room." He moved to the door and held it as Jesse entered the room.

"Harriet tells me you wish to review Florida Land's books. May I ask why? I understood that your examination was completed when you were last here."

"As I told you then, I was concerned if mosque donations were being used solely for tax-exempt purposes and also that I would have to consult with my supervisor."

"I thought I had explained that sufficiently. Those funds were to be used for the construction of a mosque and that any excess would be distributed to other Islamic functions around the country."

"Yes, sir. You did, and I apologize for any inconvenience I've caused." Jesse looked into Syed's eyes and thought he saw a flicker of understanding there. "The mosque has collected a lot of money which doesn't seem to be used for anything. So right now the question remains. Is the mosque exempt from tax? That's why I asked to see the records of the LLC."

"Again, I am unsure exactly what you are looking for and wonder if I should consult with my tax man first. Please understand that we have nothing to hide. It is . . . ." Syed seemed to be trying to decide how to proceed.

Jesse took advantage of the pause. "I know that funds received by the mosque are immediately transferred to Florida Land and are recorded as Building Reserves on the mosque's books. That entry indicates to me that Florida Land is owned by the mosque. My job is to determine what those funds are being used for. Like I said, I'm not trying to make things hard for you, but I have to do my job."

Syed ran his hand through his hair. His face seemed to connote understanding of Jesse's plight and that the examination would be conducted with or without his consent. "I know you have your job to do, and I understand your position: it is just that this is all so new to me. I have never been examined before and it is not one of my best experiences." A small smile appeared. "I guess it is all right. I will have Harriet bring the materials to you."

Jesse extended his hand, which was grasped by Syed. "Thanks a lot, Mr. Rabia. I really appreciate your cooperation. I'll take as little time as necessary." Jesse's stomach growled with anticipation as Syed departed the room.

Jesse first compared numbers on the 2005 balance sheet to the tax return and was not surprised the two documents were in agreement. It also didn't really surprise him that the cash balance was nominal. The plan, according to Rabia, was to keep the funds invested in Florida real estate to take advantage of the boom. What did surprise him, though, was the relatively small amount of real estate on the books. It should be more in line with the seventy-five million transferred from the mosque. His anticipation quickened. He looked again at the tax return balance sheet and took special note of five million dollars in real estate, a receivable of seventy million dollars and a thousand dollars in cash. Money was going into something other than real estate. Where?

A closer look at the general ledger caused Jesse's pulse to quicken. The account titled Loans Receivable, Hemisphere Equities, LLC, revealed numerous entries, large and small. He quickly compared those entries to the sales journal and noted similar entries. It appeared that as land was sold, the proceeds were transferred to Hemisphere. *My God, what have I got here?* He leaned back in the chair and stared unfocused at the pictures on the wall. The money was being invested in real estate as Rabia had stated, but sales proceeds were going into some other investment. There were pages and pages of entries.

A thought occurred to him and he flipped the pages to the sales journal. He counted the thirty pages and was astounded at the number of sales. He looked again at page one of the tax return and was astonished that the numbers hadn't affected him prior. Cost-of-Sales was greater than Sales. They were selling the lots at less than they paid for them, and selling them rapidly. Were they simply trying to outfox the probable real estate recession?

He pushed the 2005 books out of the way and went back a couple of years, a boom year for Florida real estate. Everyone seemed to be in the game, all making quick money. Sales outstripped costs by a small margin. Again they seemed to be buying and selling rapidly. The next year reflected a small loss. Their purpose definitely was not to make money in the real estate market. What was the other investment that had prompted them to overlook solid land profits?

Jesse strode over to the large picture window and its view of the waterway, his mind ablaze. Who was the owner of Hemisphere? The mosque? Who ran that show? Syed? Would this trail never end? Where did it lead? Could he find the answers? There definitely was something hidden here and he had to find it. Could he convince the powers-that-be?

All boats were moored at the restaurant pier. Seemed to him that somebody should be out there enjoying the wonderful weather and placid water. The next thought occurred suddenly. What about the receipt of funds from

Provident? Did that go into Florida Land as he suspected? He almost ran back to the table and picked up the stack of papers. The $1.5 million had been received in January and paid out the same month. His heart racing again, he quickly turned to the real estate page and noted the entry that corresponded with the purchase of the senator's house. A few entries down showed the reduction of real estate by a similar amount. The property had been sold. Had they realized a loss? He turned to the Sales page and saw an entry in the amount of $1.1 million. In just a little over a month the LLC had taken a loss of $400,000. This was after an appraisal by Mendez! There was no question in Jesse's mind that the transaction was a payoff to the senator. For what, he didn't know, but he did know he would find out.

The red light flashed on the cell phone. "Jesse – Arthur Reid. Have you seen the headlines in the *Palm Beach Post*? Call me."

CHAPTER **39**

The secretary, startled at the sound of the door slamming, looked up as Senator Walker strode purposefully across the room. She thought better of saying anything that might further agitate the senator's current mood. She had seen the morning *Post*.

The senator breezed right by her desk, not even stopping to peer into the out-basket, as was his norm. "Sylvia, hold my calls until I tell you." At the door to his office, he turned and said, "Tom is due in one hour. Send him right in."

"Yes, sir." She wondered if her words reached him through the noise of the door slamming behind him.

Sylvia retrieved the newspaper from a desk drawer and reread the headlines. "Senator Martin Walker accused of taking bribes." She shuddered, replaced the newspaper in the drawer and resumed her normal duties.

Martin glared at the newspaper on his desk and, in a moment of uncontrollable rage, swept it onto the floor and stared at the wall without seeing. Where had the reporter gotten his information? Of course it was public information, but what would have prompted him to go there? The earlier report about his relationship with Allied Paint had already caused rancor within his party, and now this. He had to put this behind him for the moment while he took care of the immediate problems.

He stared at his briefcase and forced himself to remove the files that contained notes from the immigration meeting this morning. If he was to assure passage of key elements of the bill, it would be necessary to spend the rest of the afternoon on the phone, calling in favors. For his part, the meeting had been almost a waste of time after Senator

Gordon McCormick shoved the morning *Post* in his face before the meeting began.

The meeting had resolved none of the issues facing the unrestricted border crossings. Martin felt sure terrorists were infiltrating the country along with innocent workers seeking jobs to help their families in Latin American countries. He knew in his heart that one day soon, if the Senate and House failed to resolve their differences, the country would pay dearly. In his mind he could see terrorists mixed in with laborers making their way across the desert waste, while others routinely entered in the normal manner with passports and visas from friendly countries.

Martin caught himself staring at the papers while he recalled his meeting this morning with Senator McCormick.

Gordon said, "You're smiling so I take it you haven't seen the paper this morning." He handed the paper to Martin.

Martin's smile vanished immediately as the headlines virtually leaped out at him. "No, I haven't seen it. Same reporter as before? What's he up to this time?"

"Don't really understand the whole story. Haven't taken the time to read much more than the headlines, but it has something to do with the sale of your house in Florida. Yes, the same reporter who started this thing with the Navy paint contract a few months ago. As I remember, he was claiming bribery then, too." Gordon held the door for Martin. "Looks like the competition is really out to do you in this time. Anything to it?"

"I'll have to read it myself, but at first glance it looks like he's taken a giant leap, as is usual with most reporters when they feel they're on to a big story." Martin handed the paper back to Gordon and stepped through the door to the Senate hearing room. "I sold my house this year but it had nothing to do with the paint company. It was purchased by a company that to my knowledge has no connection to Allied Paint Corporation. I have no idea how the reporter came up with that connection." He looked at Gordon as he moved away to his assigned seat. "I'll look deeper into it after the meeting."

Martin was brought back to the present as the door opened slightly and Thomas Benson's head peeked around. "Are you ready for me, Senator?"

"Yes. Come on in, Tom. Hope you've got some good news for a change." Martin motioned for Benson to take the chair in front of the desk. "What's this business in the paper this morning?" He looked at the pages scattered on the floor.

Benson collected and folded the paper, and, while still holding it, sat in the chair. "We're facing some tough issues, Senator. Not only this one but the IRS examinations aren't going away. Now—"

"What do you mean? I thought the agent accepted that I deposited the check from Allied into the campaign fund. That's changed?"

"Your accountant in Palm Beach called and said the agent was maintaining that you had received payment for some service rendered to Allied and that you had failed to report it. A . . . ." Benson hesitated and looked solemnly into Martin's eyes. "A criminal offense."

Martin gasped and placed his hand on his throat. "A criminal offense? I explained that the company's employees had always made donations to the campaign. How could it be a criminal offense?" Martin leaned out across the desk and stared at Benson. "What the hell's going on here, Tom? That some rookie agent?"

"I understand he's been with the agency for fifteen years or so. Definitely not a novice. My sources at IRS say the agent is not only examining you and Allied but has branched out to include two mosques in the area and a company associated with them."

"What the hell do two mosques have to do with me?"

"I'm not sure, but one of the companies he's auditing, Florida Land, LLC, is the recorded purchaser of your house." A stunned look appeared on Martin's face. Benson continued, "I thought it was Allied that had purchased your house. That's what the reporter said in his earlier article."

Martin breathed deeply and leaned back in his chair. He knew all about that switch in courthouse records. He'd paid dearly, in money and political capital, to affect that alteration. He knew, too, that it was the offshore company that had provided the money for the purchase, wiping it completely off Allied's books. "It was Allied who was originally listed as the purchaser. I'm not sure just what happened there, but I do remember there was some paper shuffling . . . ." Martin tried to collect his thoughts. How deep to go? "But that's not really relevant. What prompted the reporter to search the courthouse records and determine the difference in selling and purchasing prices, which he alleges is a monetary benefit to me? As I understand it, Allied had an appraisal done and everything was legit." He sat up straight in his chair again. "How did you find out about Florida Land?"

Benson seemed to be studying a picture on the wall. "I had a contact down there search the records and, because of the other audit, I called Buchanan at IRS and he told me about the Florida Land audit. Regarding the reporter, I only know that he was in Palm Beach and that he got his information from the court records. He also knows, he spells it out in his article, that Allied is owned by a British company who sells paint to a Bahamian company who sells to Allied, and alludes to an offshore bank account used for laundering money." He looked straight into Martin's eyes.

Martin blinked, stood, walked to the large window and stared out into the afternoon. His political life flashed before him. His career had been fashioned around an ardent desire to be a statesman – to do right for every citizen. Had that overriding hunger led him to this? Such pettiness in all humans. He continued staring into the sunlight, lost in thought.

Finally he turned back to face Benson. "Tom, I'm facing some rough times. This may be it for us." He walked back to the desk, but stood behind the chair. "I can understand if you decide to leave me, but I need to tell you the whole truth. You—"

"Don't worry about me leaving you, sir. We've been together too long to even consider such a thing. I have a hunch I already know what you're about to tell me anyway."

"You do? How could you?"

"You've got to understand that if you rub elbows with smart people, some of those smarts rub off. I've been associated with a smart man for many years." Benson stood and smiled.

Martin smiled, too. "You're a good man, Tom. What will you do if I don't get re-elected?"

"Maybe I'll run for your seat."

"By God, maybe we could pull it off." Martin sat in the chair. "So you knew all along that I made sure Allied got the Navy contract in exchange for sizable political contributions year after year?"

"It took me awhile, but it finally dawned." Benson reached across the desk and grasped Martin's hand. They both squeezed extra hard and placed the other hand on top.

"How do we handle the political thing, Tom? What do we do about the revenue agent and the criminal charge?" Martin's major concern was the bribery charge. If that was provable, he could end up in jail – his entire career a shambles. He couldn't live with that.

CHAPTER **40**

Syed, standing next to his beloved books while looking out the window, dialed the number and waited. The revenue agent had just left and Syed was in a deep stew wondering where all this auditing would lead. Would the agent audit Hemisphere? Had it been a mistake to allow the audit of Florida Land? The phone rang five times before the line opened.

"Yes, Syed. You have news?" Abdullah seemed pleased at the call.

"Abdullah, a pleasure to hear your voice. Are you at a time and place for a short conversation?"

"I am in the middle of a meeting, but I can speak with you for a moment."

"You are at the university?"

"I am in New York on urgent business."

Syed drew in a deep breath. "In New York? Please forgive me, Abdullah. I would not have called if I had known. I am—"

"Do not be disturbed, Syed. It is always a pleasure to hear your voice. I have traversed the country since our last meeting. I should be in Florida on Saturday. We can speak more then if necessary. But continue. You had a matter of importance?"

Syed started to apologize more but thought he had better get on with his message and not tie up Abdullah any longer. "It is about the revenue agent. You will remember that after he audited the Farouk Mosque, and because of my explanation, pursuant to your advice, that all mosque funds would eventually be used for religious purposes, he seemed satisfied, and I assumed the audit was over.

"This morning he came back for another look. That didn't seem like too much of a problem, but then he wanted to see the books for Florida Land. I was really at a loss as to what to do. I had fears that he would question why proceeds from real estate sales were transferred to Hemisphere. I thought of calling you then for advice but went ahead and made the decision to let him see the books. I now wonder if that was the right move. He did not let on, but I suspect he will follow up with an audit of Hemisphere, which will negate our explanation of using the funds for tax-exempt purposes. I do not know where it will lead, but I thought it wise to alert you." Abdullah didn't respond for what seemed like several minutes and Syed became alarmed. "Abdullah, are you there?"

"Yes, I am here. I was trying to collect my thoughts." Abdullah hesitated again. "I, too, am unable to ascertain the possible outcome of such an audit. Would it merely affect the taxability of the mosque or would it have a ripple affect on other long-term and short-term objectives?" Abdullah paused. "Hold on one moment. I will walk outside."

Syed knew the long-term objectives included the acquisition of United States corporations in particular areas of business and manufacture. He had no tangible knowledge that Hemisphere was involved in any of the other activities vaguely alluded to by Abdullah on various occasions. The periodic conversations with Imraaz had never divulged any other use of funds going into Hemisphere. Syed remembered Abdullah, in that moment of agitation at the mosque, where he had ranted on about the killing of millions of Americans. He remembered, too, the last meeting when Abdullah had pleaded with him to stay with the operation for a short while longer. Why was Abdullah in New York? Was this the short-term objective? Did this have to do with the millions? Abdullah's voice interrupted his thoughts.

"Syed. I think the strategy should be to delay the agent. If we can delay him for two weeks, the outcome will not matter. I am surprised that he did not question you about Hemisphere when he was with you. That can only mean he suspects something and will follow through with full force. There is nothing further for you to do in that regard. Continue transferring funds as before. I will call Imraaz when I disconnect with you."

Syed was unable to control himself. "Does your trip to New York have anything to do with an attack on the United States and its people? Is that going to occur in two weeks?"

"I cannot talk with you now. I will tell you about the plan when we meet for the trip to Miami next week. I can only say there will be a momentous and historic event soon."

Syed fought to control the rising internal panic and the building terror he felt. "Will there be another try on the agent's life? Will you contact Hamza?"

"No. Rest assured of that. I will contact Hamza when we visit Miami, but for another assignment that has no relevance to the audit you speak of. I must go now. I will see you next week."

The chatter among the five men ceased as Abdullah re-entered the building. He walked to the front of the room and turned to face them as they gathered around. "Please forgive me. Before I was unfortunately interrupted, we were discussing the project and your individual needs." All the men were dressed in business suits befitting their societal position. "All of you have been chosen by the leader of the *mujahadeen* for this most important project, and I have been chosen to provide you with funds necessary to accomplish your role in this mission."

Abdullah turned to the desk and withdrew five files from his briefcase. "You each were recently visited by the al

Qaeda representative, as was I, at which time you verified your cell and specified your individual needs." He opened the first file, noted the dollar amount, opened the suitcase, removed a titled packet and passed it to one of the men. He continued until all the men had their individual packets. "I assume this cash will be sufficient. Any questions?"

A young man placed his packet into a briefcase and said, "When I met with the representative, she merely said the attack would take place within the month. Have you been given the precise date when we are to activate our people?"

"I am like you. I do not know the exact date and time, but I will know precisely when I receive a coded message. When I relay that to you by telephone with the code 9999, the time will be soon after that." Abdullah knew the date would be within two weeks after the shipment arrival at Allied in Miami, which was scheduled for Monday. He did not doubt that it would easily pass through the port's detection system. "The fact that you are receiving the extra funds at this time is assurance the time is near." One of the men started to speak but Abdullah continued. "While I cannot be sure now, I am expecting D-Day to be two weeks from Monday. I should be in touch with you in one week, which will provide you with sufficient time to remove your families from the city. When I contact you, within two days of the 9999 call, you will have one hour to activate your plan."

Another of the men spoke, "Will you have a role in the disaster that is to befall New York City?"

"I can only say that I will be involved to a greater extent than any of you, with Allah's blessing. His rule is imminent. Allah be praised."

The men all responded as one. "Allah be praised."

CHAPTER 41

The soft, musical tone of the cell phone caused Imraaz Amed to glance briefly at his coat draped over the empty chair next to him. He looked apologetically at the eight board members, four on each side of the long conference table, and said, "Forgive me, gentlemen. This must be an emergency. Excuse me for a second."

Imraaz turned back to the coat, extracted the small, silver phone, opened it, unsurprised by the identity of the caller. He spoke to the men, "Just as I expected." He stood. "Please forgive me, gentlemen. Take a moment and have refreshments. This will not take long." Phone in hand, he exited the conference room and stepped into the hall.

With a slight tingle of anxiety, Imraaz gazed into the handset. Telephone calls from this man were most unusual, and this call could only mean one thing – the time was near. On the one hand, he was glad for the awaited apocalypse and what it bode for the people of the world, but on the other, he had, through his business dealings and personal connections developed over the past several years, taken a certain liking to his life in the United States. Generally he felt sure that would not change for the worse, but from somewhere deep in his being doubts arose from time to time. His strong Islamic upbringing forced out such negative thoughts.

"Abdullah, nothing amiss, I trust."

"Imraaz, good to hear your voice. Are you available to talk freely?"

The apprehension returned. A female staff member stepped into the hall from an adjoining office and strode toward him. He smiled and nodded greetings to her. She did likewise and moved on down the hall. "Yes, I am in the hallway at the offices of Universal Chemicals."

"In Iowa? Good. Everything okay there?"

"Yes, everything is fine. We are moving along in accordance with the plan. I was in the middle of a board meeting when you called, but I am free to talk with you. Is this what I think it is?"

"Yes and no. The time is at hand, but your operation has been put on hold for the present. The purpose for my call is the revenue agent. Have you been in touch with your office?"

My operation on hold? What does that mean? "No. I will call when I am finished here. What is this about a revenue agent?"

"The agent examining Allied Paint has extended his reach to Syed's operation and now it seems it may extend to yours. We must do all possible to thwart such an event."

"What has the agent found with Syed's operation that would send him to me? That tax situation does not affect Hemisphere and what we do. There are no tax issues with my operation that I know of. I am afraid I do not understand." Imraaz created a mental picture of his operation, seeking anything out of the ordinary that would trigger a tax examination. Hemisphere simply received capital from Florida Land, LLC, invested it in U.S. corporations and businesses conducive to the necessities of the owners, and dutifully reported interest and dividends on timely, professionally prepared income tax returns. He was unable to fathom why a revenue agent would be auditing Hemisphere.

Abdullah said, "I agree with you but this agent is aggressive. He may be onto more than mere taxes. An examination of the books of Hemisphere would not only reflect the legitimate acquisitions of American businesses but . . . ." There was a pause on the other end and Imraaz knew immediately what was to follow but was still unable to fully comprehend Abdullah's cautionary actions. Abdullah continued, "An examination would lead the agent to me and that could possibly affect the timing of the operation. You will remember what they did to me after the World Trade Center coup. We must delay the agent at all costs."

Imraaz's mind ran at full speed. His forte was business – the reason others chose him for this position. He had never had any encounters with the likes of revenue agents or other government officials on such mundane matters. His job had been to acquire companies in the chemical, energy, nuclear, and transportation fields and organize them with sufficient staff that would allow their use and deployment to further the goals of Islam – and Allah. Although he knew full well of the ultimate goal, and he supported that wholeheartedly, he had never been involved in the details of that part of the operation. "You say this agent is aggressive. How will I deter him if he persists?"

"Imraaz, I need two weeks without the interference of this man. I will do what is necessary to have that time. I feel certain that you can find a way to put him off without my having to resort to other methods." Abdullah's mood changed for a moment and he chuckled. "Use that creative mind of yours."

The chuckle disarmed Imraaz for one second, but the thought of the two killings and the attempts on the current agent's life took top position. He had never understood the reason for those killings and attempts. The Mendez affair had remained an enigma to him. What did a simple real estate agent have to do with anything? "I will do what I can. Trust me."

"I do trust you, Imraaz. I rely on you. I will speak further with you when I return next week." The phone went dead.

Imraaz, somewhat puzzled with this turn of events, went back into the conference room to the awaiting board members. The talking quickly subsided when he entered and took his seat.

"Now. Where were we?" Imraaz sorted through the papers on the table.

Imraaz shook hands with the last of the board members, gathered the papers and placed them in his briefcase. Overall it had been a productive meeting. He was within reach of full control, and therefore would have the ability to alter company policy when the time came to distribute chemicals for the ultimate goal. He retrieved his cell phone and entered the number of his home office in Florida. Before he could speak, the pleasant voice of his secretary altered his mood.

"Yes, Mr. Amed. I trust your meeting went well. Will you be coming home tomorrow?"

"Yes, Virginia, I will fly out this afternoon and will be in Florida in the early evening. I have a few other matters to see to so I may not be in the office until Monday morning. Is anything of importance pending?" Imraaz could hear papers being shifted around.

"Nothing that can't wait. You should take advantage of the weekend and relax after your long trip."

"Yes, I may do just that. There was nothing else?"

After a long pause she said, "Oh. Yes. A gentleman from the Internal Revenue Service called, wanting to speak with you."

"Did he ask for me by name?"

"No, sir. He asked to speak with the president of the company. I gave him your name and told him you were out of town. He said he'd call back."

"You didn't tell him when I would return?"

"No, sir."

"Good. Several of my projects are expected to consume a considerable amount of time during the next two weeks. I need to postpone meeting with him until after that. Can you handle that for me?"

Another pause "Yes, sir. I'll take care of it."

"Thank you, Virginia." Imraaz pocketed the phone and smiled with self satisfaction.

CHAPTER 42

Jesse stood as Amy approached the table, accepted her peck on his cheek, and sat as she rounded the table and took her chair. He gave the waitress the high sign and looked at Amy. "I've already ordered for both of us. Should be out in a minute or two. Figured you'd be on time."

Amy smiled. "You're getting to know me quite well, aren't you?" The waitress brought another cup of coffee to the table. Amy looked up at her and they exchanged smiles. "Guess Mildred is too, huh?"

Jesse smiled and felt good inside. One day he'd have to get real serious with Amy – maybe even ask for her hand. "Yeah, the way it is when you get to be regulars – and tip well."

Amy sipped the hot coffee. "Anything new?" She took another sip. "I take it you saw the *Post* yesterday."

"Actually I didn't see the paper until late. Received a telephone message from the reporter after I left the audit."

"You received a message from the reporter? How would he know to get in touch with you? Why would he?" The frown on her face deepened and she looked intensely at Jesse. "I don't—"

"You've been gone all week and I haven't had time to bring you up to date on the latest happenings. I guess Singleton told you of his interest in my examinations."

"No. He wasn't in when I got back yesterday and, of course, I haven't been in yet today. What gives?"

The waitress came with their food. The tempting aroma wafting up from the plate stirred the building hunger in Jesse. He started to take a bite but hesitated. "I met with the senator's accountant on Tuesday and learned that the sale of the senator's house didn't close until this year, coinciding with money received by the Farouk Mosque from Provident Paint in Nassau."

Amy's eyes widened and she laid her fork on the plate without taking a bite.

Jesse continued, "From a look at the senator's 2005 return, I knew he hadn't reported the $150,000, but they're claiming the money was a campaign contribution from Allied's employees." Jesse noted the grimace on Amy's face. He salted the eggs and forked a bite into his mouth. "I don't know if that's the case or not, but I'm not buying it. I think it's fraud, and Singleton may think so, too." He forked more food into his mouth and washed it down with coffee. "Anyway, as I was about to get into my car, the reporter came up and introduced himself. Hinted that maybe we could be of use to each other."

"Is that how he got his information he reported in the paper? You gave it to him?"

"No. He didn't get it from me, but after he gave me a bit of information, I did suggest that he ought to search the public records." Jesse thought back to the moment with the reporter. "I explained to him that all my data was confidential but then, in a snooty kind of way, he told me that Allied and Provident were both owned by a company in England. In a rash, to show him that I knew as much as he, I almost told him that Provident was only a bank account. I caught myself in time, but I realized that he just may be able to give me some useful information. That's when I suggested the public records."

Amy took the last bite of food and placed her knife and fork on the plate. "What do you make of his charge that the senator is taking bribes from Allied?"

"I agree with him. You'll remember it was Allied that was initially listed as the purchaser of his house and it was only through some strange machinations that the purchase was re-

recorded as a 2006 transaction and the purchaser changed to Florida Land. That's an LLC I haven't yet told you about. Anyway, the house was sold after only a month at a substantial loss. I've always questioned why any sane person would do such a thing – always figured it was some kind of payoff to the senator." Jesse finished his breakfast and wiped his mouth with the napkin. "Not sure if the apparent overpayment is taxable or how the IRS would be involved in payoffs – bribes." Jesse drank the rest of his coffee and signaled for the waitress to bring more. "By the way, the reporter apparently didn't discover the public record changes. His story said Allied bought the house. I made the same mistake."

"Where do you go from here?"

"I talked with Danny Thursday afternoon and he tentatively agreed the return should go to CID, at least for discussion – he's still a little worried about the political fallout." The waitress came and filled their cups. "But the big thing that's got my imagination on fire is the other LLC." Amy's eyebrow arched. "I mentioned Florida Land, the LLC that purchased the senator's house. The new one is Hemisphere Equities, LLC, and it gets its money from Florida Land after the real estate is sold. It looks to me like the whole procedure is a big money-washing scheme – not sure just why. Right now I'm unable to determine where Hemisphere invests the money."

"Have you examined Hemisphere yet?"

"Not yet, but Danny okayed pulling their returns for all open years, and I had them faxed to me Thursday afternoon. There's no specific details, but the balance sheet shows an account titled Other Investments. All three returns show the account, and it gets larger over the years. So whatever they're investing in, they're not selling."

"Have you made arrangements to audit them?"

"I tried yesterday afternoon, but the secretary said the president was unavailable at the time – said I should call back. I plan to do just that right after we leave here. Amy, I think I'm on to something much bigger than even I could imagine."

Amy's brow arched again. "Nothing's bigger than you could imagine, Jesse." The brow dropped and she grinned showing her white, even teeth. "I'm not sure I understand. There're too many examinations going on. I can't seem to keep up with them and what they mean. Help me."

Jesse's phone toned and he looked at the screen – Arthur Reid. Jesse looked at Amy and said, "The reporter." He pressed the talk button and said, "Hello."

"Jesse, Arthur Reid. You have a minute? Did you get my message?"

"Hey, Arthur. Yeah, I got your message. Sorry I haven't had time to answer, and sorry that I don't have time to talk with you right now. I'm at breakfast with a colleague. We'll be leaving soon. Can I call you back? Is there anything urgent?"

"I have some information you might find interesting. Can we meet in the IRS parking lot when you get back from the restaurant?"

"Okay, I'll meet you there." Jesse looked at his watch and at Amy. "About thirty minutes?"

"See you then." The phone went dead.

Jesse closed the phone and laid it on the table. "The reporter wants to meet with me in the parking lot when we get to the office. I said about a half hour. That okay with you?"

"Sure, that's fine. What do you think he wants?"

"Don't know. I imagine he's still trying to pick my brain. You know reporters." The waitress came and placed the bill on the table. "But Amy, if CID accepts any part of this case,

I want them to assign you to work with me. Do you have time?"

"I'm up to my neck right now, but I don't know who else would be in a better position to work with you. I would sure like to work with you on it, but I guess we'll have to wait and see. You were going to summarize for me."

"Well I sure hope you can. Can't think of anyone else in that department I'd like better." He reached across the table and took her hand in his, patted it, then sat back in his chair. "Okay, let me recap for you and see if you agree with my conclusions. You understand how the senator is connected to Allied, I believe." When Amy didn't respond right away, Jesse asked, "Don't you?"

"I understand that Allied paid him money which they classified as an expense and he's now claiming it is a campaign contribution. I think that issue may be worthy of a criminal investigation." Amy paused and Jesse felt a sense of satisfaction that somebody finally agreed with him on something. He was eager to respond but held it. Amy continued, "I'm not sure what to make of Allied's purchase of his property and the subsequent sale at a loss. Too many *ifs* there at the moment, but it sure looks like some kind of a payoff. But is that tax fraud? There certainly is some reason for Allied's interest in the senator, but does it fall within our duties? What is he doing for them, and is it illegal?" Amy waved at the waitress and indicated a coffee refill.

Jesse said, "I agree with everything you said, and, like you, I don't know the reason for it all. The reporter called it a bribe. For what, he didn't say. Maybe I can get that from him when we meet in a few minutes. Another thing, too, how and why did they manage to have the court records changed from 2005 to 2006? These are definitely questions that have to be answered." Jesse looked at his watch as the waitress refilled their cups.

"Well, if I can get the senator transferred to CID on the omission issue, others can take it from there. The important thing is that he is connected to Allied and Allied is owned by Arabs. And, outside of some tax issues, I think there's something very sinister going on. Follow me.

"Allied is owned by a British company, which I suspect is also owned by Arabs, and they are definitely keeping profits in an offshore bank account – Provident Paint. In my mind this is fraud, and I imagine the British tax service would be interested in the information as well. Provident Paint is the source of funds used to purchase the senator's house.

"Now, the Farouk Mosque, headed by one Syed Rabia, who is also on the board of Allied, receives large donations from Arabs, and a lot of cash supposedly from various mosques around the country. According to Mr. Rabia, all of these funds have been collected to build a mosque in St. Lucie County." Jesse took a sip of coffee and looked over the cup rim to see the effect all this was having on Amy. Her face remained devoid of expression. "This fund-raising began in 2002 and has collected over seventy-five million dollars through 2006. To date—"

"Seventy-five million?" Amy gasped audibly and placed a hand over her mouth. "My God, are you sure about that amount?"

"I'm sure, and not only that, none of it has been spent to build the new mosque – as of today."

"Where is the money going? Held in bank accounts?"

"They're investing it in Florida real estate through Florida Land. According to Mr. Rabia they're trying to keep the funds invested while waiting for approval from the government to go ahead with their construction plans. The problem with all this explanation is I find no construction expenses on the books, and they're flipping the land so quickly, they're not showing any profit." Jesse noted the change on Amy's face. "It seems to me the whole thing is a big farce. For some reason they're washing the money to keep it from being seen by the government, and that leads me to a conspiracy theory."

Amy said, "Something sure seems to be out of the ordinary. What in the world could it be? How to convince the higher ups? That part of it is out of our expertise."

"That's not all of it, Amy. You remember I told you about pulling the return for a Hemisphere Equities?" Amy nodded and Jesse continued. "Well, the reason I pulled it is because all of the sales proceeds in Florida Land go directly into Hemisphere. The money's not being used at all for mosque purposes – at least at this time."

"How are the transfers shown on Florida Land's books?"

Jesse fought to keep the satisfied smirk off his face. "Loan Receivable, Hemisphere." The smirk almost emerged.

Amy leaned forward – growing interest spreading across her face. "This is almost incomprehensible. What in the world is going on? What is Hemisphere doing with the funds?"

"That's what I hope to find out. I've got to get a look at those books. I'll call again this morning." Jesse looked at his watch and was amazed to see that he needed to leave now if he was to meet with the reporter. "You think I've got something here?" He glanced at the check, made a quick calculation of the tip, and placed the necessary money on top of it.

"Sounds like the case of a lifetime. Hope you can get it transferred." Jesse's eyebrow raised and Amy continued. "I'm sorry, Jesse, but now I'm having a bit of a problem with that. I can see the possible tax effect in the offshore activities but, with the scant information available to me, I've been unable to find the tax issue with the mosque, Florida Land or with Hemisphere. Have you found a tax problem with any of them?"

Jesse's gut wrenched, but he managed to keep a straight face. She had hit upon his known weak point, but what had changed her mind? Before, she had seemed certain the case was transferable to CID. He forced himself to say, "No, nothing material, except maybe loss of exempt status if the mosque isn't using the funds for religious purposes. The two LLCs haven't been examined completely yet." As an afterthought he said, "Maybe the funds received are income—"

"I think that might be hard to prove. I also know that without a provable criminal offense, CID won't take it." Jesse was having a tough time maintaining a straight face. Amy continued, "I definitely think you've got a chance with the senator's case, and a possibility with Allied and the offshore issue. That one could really be a coup for the department." Amy stood. "I have to admit I'm excited about the possibilities with those LLCs, but . . . I think you'll have to convince others about that, don't you?"

Jesse fought to control his plummeting enthusiasm. He knew she was right, but he also felt certain that something out of the ordinary was going on between Farouk Mosque and those LLCs, and he associated it with the sinister. How much time did he have to prove his case? "Yeah, you're probably right . . . and that could prove mighty hard to do without an intro from CID."

They walked out of the diner. Jesse smiled and said, "Tomorrow's Saturday. Want to go out on the lake?" Each placed an arm around the other.

CHAPTER 43

As he turned into the parking lot at the Internal Revenue Service, Jesse's mind continued to sift through a mix of possible results of a Hemisphere audit and a pleasant weekend on the water with Amy. Money from Florida Land was invested in a loan to Hemisphere, yet there was no interest income from that source reflected on the books or the bank statements. Obviously the money was being used for something other than investments or religious purposes – the building of a mosque in St. Lucie County was a farce. He had to audit Hemisphere. He had to convince others to get involved. This was more than a tax examination. Surely Syed was on to his probing and aware of his findings. The man wasn't dumb. Was it Syed that had first sent the killers? Would he turn them loose again? *It's getting scary again.* He scanned every car in the lot. The waving arm of Arthur Reid brought Jesse back to reality.

The reporter stood at the rear end of a parked car and waved Jesse toward the vacant spot next to it. Jesse pulled into the space and turned the ignition off. Before he could get the door fully open, Reid was there. Jesse pressed the door against Reid's stomach and emerged from the car. "You're right on time, Arthur. How's it going?"

"Going great for me, how about you? Who's the pretty girl?"

Jesse looked a little stupefied. "How'd you know I was with Amy? Spying on me?"

Reid grinned, "My job. No, really, I'm not spying, just trying to meet with you. I just missed you when you drove off to breakfast. I followed and was about ready to join you at the table when the young lady showed up. Decided to call instead of intrude."

Jesse grinned, too, but reflected that a reporter's job was a lot like his own – always intruding on somebody. "Amy's a colleague. We're good friends."

"A colleague? You mean she's a revenue agent, too?"

"Oh yeah. One of the best in the criminal division."

"I didn't realize there was a separate department for that. Guess it makes sense though. Are you in that department?"

"No. All agents start out in the field and may eventually move into CID if they're good enough and have the desire."

"Will the senator's case be transferred there? Is that what you were discussing at breakfast?"

Jesse leaned his back against the car and studied the man. Jesse was impressed. Reid appeared to be about thirty, and his mind seemed to jump far ahead of the obvious. Hemisphere came to mind and Jesse wondered if Reid would be a benefit to him in that area if there were no tax issues involved. "You know I can't discuss the senator's return with you." Jesse's mind ran back to Thursday when he wandered out to the restaurant on Lake Worth and saw the magazine headline, "Al Qaeda Has Nukes".

He said, "What makes you think it should be transferred to CID anyway?"

"I only know that Allied pays the senator money each year and that they show losses on their tax returns. Something fishy there." Reid paused and looked away as if in thought. "Did he report that on his tax return?"

Jesse took a deep breath to control his astonishment at the man's persistence and depth of curiosity and moved away from the car. "Come on. Let's go inside out of this sun. We can talk in the conference room maybe."

Reid seemed to finally recognize the heat and looked up at the blazing sun. "Great idea." He trailed a little behind Jesse but soon caught up. "By the way, I never did thank you for the tip."

Jesse held the door open and they both moved inside. "The tip?"

Reid seemed a little bewildered at Jesse's question. "You know, about the public records."

Jesse closed the door to the conference room and they took chairs on opposite sides of the long table. "Oh, yeah. I remember. That where the headline came from? How'd you determine there was a bribe?" Jesse smiled. "Stretching it?"

Reid's smile was bigger than Jesse's. "Yes. I guess I did stretch a little. I saw where Allied later sold the property for quite a bit less than they paid for it and immediately figured it was a payoff. My sources had already told me the senator was receiving money in exchange for the Navy contract, but I didn't know exactly how it was happening. I—"

"The Navy contract?" Jesse blurted that out and instantly rebuked himself for revealing his knowledge.

"Come on, Jesse. You audited Allied. Surely you know they sold to the Navy."

Jesse knew more than that. He knew the Navy was Allied's main customer. "Sorry I reacted that way. You were saying about your research of public records."

"What I was trying to tell you was that I went back to the courthouse yesterday and found that the records had been altered to show the senator's house was sold and purchased, not by Allied, but by a company named Florida Land." Reid looked smugly at Jesse, and when Jesse didn't respond or alter his composure, continued. "I did a little more research of State and Federal records and determined that a naturalized citizen of Arab descent controls the corporation."

Jesse fought to control his expression. "His name?"

"Syed Rabia." Reid looked intently at Jesse. "Jesse, I suspect this may go a lot further than my original suspicions of bribery by the senator. My nose tells me something corrupt is cooking."

Jesse had a warm feeling inside. Finally here was someone on the same trail. His respect for Reid deepened, and he realized that Reid might be of considerable help in fleshing all this out. But how was he to team up with him? He must be careful to not reveal confidential tax information. He stood. "Let me just say this, Arthur. My nose is taking me in the same direction as yours is taking you. I'm trying to work out in my mind how we can help each other." Jesse started toward the door and Reid followed. Jesse shook Reid's hand. "Let me think on it."

CHAPTER **44**

Jesse pulled out the file marked Hemisphere from his desk, flipped to his notes on top of the tax return, reached for the telephone and punched in the number. The phone on the other end rang five times before the message came on in a pleasant voice. "You have reached Hemisphere Equities. I am away from my desk or otherwise unable to answer the telephone. Please leave a message at the sound of the tone. Thank you for your patience."

Jesse grimaced and stared at the telephone receiver. This was his third try within the hour since his meeting with Arthur Reid. He knew it was Friday but at three o'clock someone should still be in the office. His gut told him he was being stalled, and that stirred him up more.

Jesse thought of Reid and how the reporter's astute abilities and forwardness could be of benefit. What kind of information would have to be given up to get that sharp nose to join in the hunt? Other than the senator and Allied, tax issues were scant, but the flow of money most certainly was leading to something out of the ordinary. He knew the money to buy the senator's house came directly from overseas and suspected that the other payments did, too. There was no question that Syed Rabia controlled the initial flow of money, and that he was lying about building a mosque. Money flowed into Farouk mosque, then into Florida Land where it was washed, then into Hemisphere and thereafter invested in something. The ultimate question is what is the purpose for this elaborate charade? Why would legitimate businessmen go to such lengths? Perhaps Reid had connections in high levels of government that could get someone interested and launch a full-scale investigation.

He looked at the telephone receiver, trying to decide whether to try again or simply mop up loose ends and get ready for a pleasant weekend on the water. That thought warmed him for only a minute and was soon gone when he viewed the open cases in the desk drawer. In addition to four normal cases that he hadn't even set appointments for, the major ones, the mosques, Allied, and Florida Land, all needed immediate action – adjustments or no-change. He looked for a moment at the file for Hemisphere lying on the desk. *Telephone identification.*

Jesse removed the phone from his pocket and, as he flipped it open, it chimed. He gazed at the dial, a bit annoyed at the intrusion into his insight. The call was from his ex-wife. She was calling from her cell phone. Was she not at home? He let it chime itself out and dialed Hemisphere using his cell phone where his name was blocked. He had used this ploy several times when making appointments with taxpayers he suspected of being a little shady. *Why haven't I thought of this before?*

"Hello. This is Hemisphere Equities. How may I direct your call?"

Elation spread through his body at the sound of the pleasant voice. "Hello. This is Jesse Hawkins with the Internal Revenue Service." He detected an audible intake of breath. "I would like to speak with Mr. Imraaz Amed. You said earlier that he would return this afternoon. Is he in?"

There was a long pause and Jesse suspected the receptionist was going to hang up. "Miss—"

"Mr. Amed has not returned and . . . when I spoke with him yesterday, he said, because of unforeseen business complications, there was a possibility that he would not return until a week from Monday. Can you wait to speak with him until then?"

"It's important that I speak with him as soon as possible but, if he's not expected back right away, I guess I'll just have to wait. Will you please give my call priority when Mr. Amed returns?"

"Yes, certainly, Mr. Hawkins. I'll see that he gets your message as soon as he returns. Thank you for your patience and understanding."

The phone went dead and Jesse thought the receptionist's voice sounded relieved. This was a put-off if he'd ever heard one. For some reason they didn't want him to see the books. What could he do about it?" Jesse looked up and saw Michael Gibson coming across the room. He wasn't in the mood to listen to his chatter and questioning. He tucked the Hemisphere file in his briefcase and met Gibson mid-way across the room. "How goes it, Mike? Got any good cases?"

Gibson jerked his head toward Jesse as if seeing him for the first time. "Huh? Huh? Oh. Hi, Jesse. Yeah. Yeah. Sure. You're the only one with any cases. How goes it with the senator? CID status yet?"

Jesse didn't want to tell Mike just yet that the returns for both Allied and Senator Walker had been transferred to CID on Thursday. "Got to run. Talk to you later." Jesse breezed past Mike and went directly to his car without talking with anyone else. It was time to play reporter.

Jesse browsed the magazine rack at the kiosk just down the street from the office building that housed Hemisphere. The attendant, a skinny old man, busy with something at the other end, paid little attention to Jesse who was keeping an eye on the entryway to the building.

In his heart, Jesse knew the receptionist at Hemisphere was covering for her boss who apparently had called her for no other reason than to stall Jesse. Why? What had he to hide? Jesse knew also that he had to find some way to examine Hemisphere's books. The idea to stake out the office came to him when he had seen Mike coming across the room back at the office, and the timing had been perfect.

It was now only an hour and a half before quitting time and if Mr. Amed was going to return today, he should be doing it any time now. Jesse scanned across the line of magazines at the various topics: the war in Iraq, business mergers, top members of the billionaire club, a seductive actress with nine-tenths of her breasts revealed, more political scandals, the president's lies. Far at the end, the headlines he'd seen before, "Al Qaeda Has Nukes" blared out at him.

Out of the corner of his eye, he detected movement and saw a dark-skinned man in a blue business suit get out of a taxi at the curb. The man paid the driver and entered the building. Jesse ran and got inside as the door to the elevator began to close.

He waved at the man in the elevator and yelled. "Hold that door, please." Arthur Reid would have been proud of him – might even offer him a job as a reporter for the *Post*. The man placed his hand on the door and Jesse entered. "Thank you, sir. That was close."

The man merely grunted, nodding at Jesse but remained engrossed in his own thinking on the ride to the fifth floor. Without acknowledging Jesse, he left the elevator, turned to the right and walked determinedly down the hall. Jesse bent down to tie his shoe, then followed and watched him enter through a doorway midway down the hall. Jesse's heart quickened as he measured his pace. He walked past and read the sign on the door; Hemisphere Equities, LLC, 501.

Jesse's mind raced as he continued down the hall. Should he go back and confront Amed right now or wait until Monday. He felt quite certain that Amed would be in the office next week. He stopped at the end of the hall, trying to come up with the right decision. Finally he took the stairs to the first floor lobby and went to his car. He opened the door, remembered his ex-wife's call, and dialed her number.

No answer.

CHAPTER **45**

The red light on the intercom flashed and Senator Walker pressed the button. Sylvia's voice evinced concern. "Senator, Mr. Edward Buchanan is on the line. I'm sorry, sir. I know you said you didn't want to be disturbed. Shall I—?"

"Thank you, Sylvia. I'll take the call." His mind still tangled with the mishmash of congressional issues intertwined with personal problems, he activated the line, "Ed. How're things? Trust you got that examination squelched. Elections are just around the corner, you know."

"Good to hear your voice, Senator. Why aren't you on the course? On Fridays we're supposed to be at the club with the boys."

"I'm sure you didn't call me to remind me of that. Good news?"

"In a way I was hoping you would be on the course. The news I have is not good, and I want to apologize for allowing it to get this far." Buchanan paused, and Martin, normally stoic when faced with everyday issues, felt a moment of panic.

Buchanan continued, "Even though I applied heavy pressure all the way from the top man in Jacksonville to the supervisor in Palm Beach, your tax return was transferred to . . ." an inordinately long pause . . . "the Criminal Investigation Division."

Martin gasped. "What does that mean? Criminal investigation? For what? Criminal? For Christ's sake, Ed, I'm no criminal. I can't imagine—"

"They said something about omitted income. Money received from Allied Paint Corporation."

Martin recalled the conversation with Benson. "We explained that to them. That was a campaign contribution from Allied's employees. None of that was used for personal purposes. Is that all they have?"

"A campaign contribution? I don't understand. What would make the agent call that an omission of income?"

Martin thought of the reporter and wondered if there was a connection. "It makes no sense to me. Political witch-hunting?"

"I doubt that – at least not by the revenue agent. I'll have to find out the details."

"I'll talk to my aide. He handles things like that. I know he talked with the accountant that prepares my tax returns. He said it was all taken care of. I can't imagine . . . ."

"One more thing, Martin." Buchanan paused and Martin grimaced. "They also turned Allied over to CID. I'm still not sure of your connection to them – why they make political contributions to you. I never did understand that *Post* article. Not sure I can help in that arena, but if you think I can, fill me in."

A pained expression formed on Martin's face and he stared at the painting of his boyhood farm – the old barn with the door open and chickens pecking at the ground. His mind tried to take him back there – to those joyous and peaceful times. He could almost detect the smells emanating from the barn.

"Martin?"

"I've been their staunch supporter for the Navy contract for many years. They provide a good product at a competitive price and they reciprocate by helping to keep me in the Senate. That's really all there is. Happens all the time. My opponents are simply trying to make a political issue of it and that's the whole reason for all the hullabaloo by the press." Martin thought of calling his aide who was much better at handling these details. "On what grounds was Allied turned over?"

"The agent suspects tax evasion. They say—"

"Tax evasion? What the hell would send them in that direction? To my knowledge, Allied sells paint to the Navy, and that's their sole business." Martin, unaware of specifics, had purposely stayed away from the issue because of mild suspicions that Allied had an offshore connection, which was the source of the larger contributions to various campaign funds around the state, as well as funds to purchase his house. "Do you know the details?"

Buchanan hesitated. "I'm sorry, Senator but they say that Allied, a subsidiary of an English company, is sheltering its profits in a Bahamian bank account and . . . ." Buchanan's pause was longer than usual.

"Yes, Ed. Go on. What else?"

"That Bahamian bank account provided the funds to purchase your house in Florida and the public records were changed to remove Allied's name."

Martin felt like he had slipped off a scaffold, hanging on with one hand, momentarily expecting to plummet to the ground five stories below. Dread gripped like a vise. Again he thought of his rise from a poor farm youth to his present position and his early zeal and passion to side with the people of the country. "These are details I leave to my assistant, Ed. Let me get him in here to explain. I'll get back to you when I obtain more facts. Anything else?"

"Martin, let me again express my sorrow that I was unable to thwart the examination and prevent the apprehension I know it must be causing you. I just wish there was more I could do."

"Don't fret about it, Ed. I know you did your best, and I'll remember it. Thank you for your efforts."

"Is there anything else I can do for you at this time?"

"No. Thanks again. I'll be in touch if necessary. You can count on my support, Ed. Bye, for now." Martin, deeply depressed that all of that information was in the top echelon of IRS and with all the events of recent weeks, punched off the intercom system, took a deep breath, leaned back in the chair, closed his eyes and allowed his mind to carry him where it would.

The ancient smells returned and for a moment he was a thirteen-year-old milking the cow in the dilapidated barn. The sound of a wagon approaching on the old rut-filled dirt road caused him to look around the cow and see his father jump off, wave to the other miners, and walk toward the house. He itched to run to him and give him a big hug but knew better. After a long night in the mine, his father would not be in the mood for hugs. The harsh smell of coal dust drifted in as his father, face and overalls coated in black, walked by the barn door. The old, young man forced a smile and waved at Martin as he passed. He was a loving parent, as was his mother. They spent their time encouraging Martin to do better than they had, planning to some day break the ties with West Virginia and move to Florida. His grandparents had already moved there some time ago.

Martin's mind jumped ahead three years. He saw himself fighting to contain the tears as he threw a handful of dirt into the deep hole that held his father's coffin. Soon thereafter he and his mother joined his grandparents.

His mind propelled him ahead. Within two years, with the benefit of an academic scholarship, he was at the University of Florida competing in student government affairs, and three years later he was president of the student council. Government and serving the people were his ardent passions. Before graduating, he ran for the Florida House of Representatives and, because his sole opponent was killed in an auto accident, was elected and served nine years, before moving to the Florida Senate. Within eight years he was elected to the U. S. House of Representatives and within another six moved to the U. S. Senate in 1976.

A muted tapping brought him back to the present. Martin looked at his watch and nodded at the face peeking around the door. Thomas Benson, with one sheet of paper in his hand, strode to the desk and, at an additional nod from the senator, took the chair.

"Are you ready to discuss these, sir?" Benson laid the paper on the desk.

All of the other thoughts that had been both tormenting and placating were forced to the background. He sighed. "Good a time as any. Where are we in the polls?"

"We're still behind, but not far. You're favored by forty-six percent and we can bring that up by election time with the right planning."

"You're talking about the Navy contract. We'll see about that. What about the issues?"

"Yes, sir. The Navy contract issue won't go away. As a matter of fact it's getting worse."

"On with the other issues, Tom."

Thomas looked at the paper. "Yes, sir. On immigration, most polls are in favor by a large margin for your position of tighter controls at the borders and establishing English as the official language, but they're negative on the president's call for providing legal status to those in the country illegally, and an automatic chance at citizenship. They're definitely negative for the House's position of charging all illegals with a felony. We may have to move away from the president to some degree while still protecting your lead in the polls."

Martin ran his hand through his hair, leaned way back in the chair and stared at the ceiling. He said, "We're spending too much now shoring up the Mexican border while most of the known terrorists come in from Canada." He leaned forward and hovered over the desk. "I suspect those who are going to hit us again are already in the country, perhaps home-grown – biding their time. You know, with an E-2 visa, immigrants are allowed in if they're buying businesses that create jobs. I wonder how many of those are avowed terrorists? We definitely have to be strong in this area, regardless of politics – if we're to survive as a nation." His voice quivered for a second. "Anyway, go on. What else?"

"Another big issue where the people are divided 60/40 is racial profiling. Folks have a tendency to get rabid when this topic is mentioned in conversation – on both sides. Right now we're on the right side, but you know what happens in the course of a campaign."

"I know very well, but again, I have to come down on the side of what's best for most of the people. We must remember that it was persons of Arab descent who struck on 9/11, and it's those of the same ilk who vow to do it again – only this time much worse." Martin paused and his resolve stiffened to normal and he looked directly into Thomas's eyes. "This time it could very well be with a nuclear bomb." The eyes widened – questioning. "I've heard rumors of al Qaeda's use of the term 'Hiroshima' when promising future attacks."

"Do you really think they'd go that far?"

"I don't think it, I know it. And that's the reason we must have the grit, and the laws to back us, to find those who vow to destroy this country and our way of life. We don't want to go to the lengths we did during World War II with the Japanese, but we must be able to identify those who are most likely, and unfortunately, most are of Arab descent." Martin forced his zeal to calm. "We have to ensure that our campaign material spells out our position clearly without purporting to abridge a citizen's rights."

"We're already on track and we'll work to increase our position in the polls."

"Okay, what else?"

"Well, there are several, but an important one is in your state—"

"Oil?"

"Right. As you know, this one is a tightrope walk. Either way could be disastrous."

"Yes, and nothing will change that except higher oil prices. Big problem. Remove limits on production and endanger the beaches, or compromise. Well, my position is clear . . . ."

The intercom light flashed again and Martin pushed the button.

"Senator forgive me for interfering, but Mr. Bruce McDonald said he needed to speak with you. Shall I . . .?"

Martin's insides tightened – his divorce lawyer. "Ask him to hold one minute, Mrs. Bauer." Martin pushed the off button and his emotions, conflicting violently, betrayed his remorse at having to postpone further discussion with Thomas. He thoroughly enjoyed topics to do with bettering the lives of citizens – his whole life. "Tom, we can continue later this afternoon. Are you free?"

"Yes, sir. I'll make time." Thomas stood and picked the paper from the desk.

"Before you go. Earlier you said something about conditions at Allied getting worse. What did you mean by that?" Martin's mind was trying to shift back to the nagging problems of his life.

Thomas averted his eyes for a second, then looked straight at Martin. "That is the one issue that could take us down, Senator. The press is building its story which can only strengthen the opposition." Thomas paused and drew in a deep breath. "And now, my source tells me that not only is

Allied evading taxes and laundering money through its
associate companies, but . . . it's now owned by Arabs."

CHAPTER **46**

Jesse, briefcase in one hand, subpoena in the other, hesitated at the door to Hemisphere Equities, his mind in turmoil. He had been in that fix since Sunday when he'd gone to see the children and no one had been home, a large For Sale sign dominating the front yard. His phone calls over the weekend to his ex-wife had gone unanswered, and he'd continuously berated himself for not taking her call Friday. Why had he not asked the children to go out with him on the boat Saturday? Even though this audit had been hard won, and that side of him demanded a fight, the image of his children and their fate refused to diminish. *Where's Thelma gone with my children?* He had to find the answer to that question, but he had to get into the audit, too.

Jesse steeled himself, knowing that the subpoena would be served today, either to Mr. Amed or to his secretary, and the audit would begin. He reached for the doorknob, paused, and removed the cell phone from his belt, intent on calling his ex-wife. But after dialing the first three numbers, he remembered the secretary telling him earlier that after today, Amed would be gone for a week. Replacing his phone, he turned the doorknob and entered the office.

Virginia Moorehead, a middle-aged brunette with hair neatly knotted in a bun, turned her head away from the computer screen and faced Jesse. Her facial expression, while pleasant, seemed to question his reason for being.

Before she could offer a question, Jesse said, "Good morning. My name is Jesse Hawkins. I'm with the Internal Revenue Service." Her expression changed to one of disbelief. Jesse continued, "You may recall that I spoke with you on Friday about meeting with Mr. Amed. Is he in?" Jesse stood in front of the desk, noticing a very slight hint of perfume in the still air. From the changing face, Jesse could detect uncertainty. He was amused, but his outward appearance did not confirm that. Would she lie?

Virginia turned toward Jesse and smoothed her dress to cover her knees. "Mr. Amed is not— " The door to the inner office opened and Amed stepped through the doorway.

"Virginia . . . ." Amed stopped short when he realized someone else was in the room. He nodded at Jesse and directed his attention to the secretary. He looked again at Jesse, this time with a hint of recognition, then away. "Virginia—"

"Mr. Amed, this is Mr. Jesse Hawkins with the Internal Revenue Service."

Amed, in utter disbelief, jerked around to stare into Jesse's eyes. "Uh. Uh." He collected himself. "Yes. Mr. Hawkins is it? What can we do for you, sir?"

Jesse maintained his strictest professional demeanor. "Pardon me for interrupting, sir, but the 2005 tax return for Hemisphere Equities has been selected for audit. I would like to review the books and records for that year and the two preceding years. I thank you in advance for your cooperation."

Amed had recovered completely and now appeared as the professional manager he was. He turned to the secretary. "Virginia, do we have the books here, or are they with the accountant?" Before she could answer, he turned to face Jesse. "We may have to get the records from the accountant. Can you wait? I will call him." Amed moved toward his office.

"Mr. Amed, I have a subpoena for the records." Jesse handed the subpoena to Amed who did not take it. "I would like to look at the records that are here. Is that possible?"

Amed ignored the question. "A subpoena? Is that normal?" Although Amed was now facing Jesse, he didn't move to take the service.

"No, sir. It isn't normal, and I apologize, but I'm facing a deadline placed on me by my superiors, and when I was unable to arrange an appointment with you, they instituted this procedure." Jesse's cell phone chimed softly. "I'm sorry." He turned the phone off. "I have no recourse but to pursue the audit. Please understand, sir."

Amed took the subpoena and read through it. "Is there something wrong that would lead them to go to this extent? Were tax returns incorrectly filed?" He turned to the secretary, obviously stalling for time. "Do you know anything about this, Virginia?"

"No, sir. The accountant usually comes in about the middle of the month. I don't believe he's been in this month yet." The telephone rang and Virginia, with a positive nod from Amed, answered it and, after the pleasantries, said, "Yes, sir, I'll see if he is available to take your call." She cupped the mouthpiece. "It's Mr. Barton. He said you were expecting his call."

"Yes. I'll take it in my office." Amed turned to Jesse. "Can you wait a few minutes, Mr. Hawkins?"

"Yes, sir."

Virginia said, "Mr. Hawkins, you can wait over there on the couch if you prefer. Would you like coffee or a soft drink?"

"No thanks, ma'am. I'll just sit over there." Jesse moved to the couch, his mind afire with the possibility that he would get to audit this morning. As he looked at the two paintings on the walls – one, some kind of manufacturing plant with smoke billowing out of a tall stack, the other, a mosque overlooking a broad, placid river – the thought of his children re-emerged.

Amed put the call from Barton on hold and switched to another phone. He spoke with his accountant for a few minutes, then placed another call. Before he could speak into the phone, Abdullah's voice on the other end said, "Yes, Imraaz, you have important news? I am driving with Syed to Miami for a visit to the Port."

"Please forgive me for interfering, but I thought I should talk with you first before making a decision."

"A decision on what?"

"The revenue agent you mentioned in our previous conversation. He—"

"Revenue agent? Has he called?"

"He is here now." Imraaz waited for a response and when none came, said, "He wants to audit the books of Hemisphere now."

"Can you not delay him?"

"He has presented me with a subpoena that states I am to make records available to him now."

"A subpoena?"

"Yes. I talked with my accountant and he said if I didn't comply, the agent would return with law enforcement officers and compel compliance. What do you advise?"

After a long pause, "I need time, Imraaz." He seemed to be weighing his limited options. Imraaz bided his time and, Abdullah continued, "I suppose you must comply with the agent's demands, but I ask that you delay as long as possible. I guess it could be worse if we push the agent to enforcement." Another pause. "Keep me informed." The phone went dead.

Jesse remembered the phone call he'd had earlier and reached for his cell phone. Amed entered the room, and Jesse stood as Amed walked towards him.

Amed said, "Mr. Hawkins, I must leave for a few hours. I have called my accountant, and he will be here in due time to provide you with the books and records you require. I think he can answer most of your questions. I should return in the early afternoon for a few minutes, then I must leave again – be away for the balance of the week." Amed looked at Virginia, but spoke to Jesse. "Will this arrangement suffice?"

"Yes, sir. Thank you very much for your cooperation. I will complete my job in the shortest possible time. When do you expect the accountant?"

Amed looked at his watch. "He should be here within the hour. Would you care for refreshments?" He looked again at Virginia.

"No, sir. I'll take a short walk and return in a half-hour. Again, thank you for your understanding." Jesse, with briefcase in hand, nodded at Virginia and left the room. This was turning out better than expected. Within an hour he would have answers to the many swirling questions.

By the time Jesse reached the end of the hall and the door leading to the stairs, he remembered the phone call again and removed the phone from his belt. He almost dropped it when he saw the name on the display screen; Thelma Hawkins. *Damn it. Damn it.* He'd been trying to reach her all weekend and now she'd called. He had a great desire to punch something but instead pressed his balled fist against the wall until it hurt.

Calmed, he returned the call. It rang four times and he was beginning to boil when the line finally opened. "Thelma—"

"Where have you been, Jesse? I've been trying to reach you since Friday. Don't you even care about your children? Don't you—"

"What do you mean, 'care about my children'? They're okay, aren't they?"

"Yes. They're okay, but they wanted to say goodbye to their father before they left. I tried—"

"Thelma, what the hell are you talking about? Where are they? Where are you?" Jesse recalled the For Sale sign in the front yard. "Are you selling the house? You were supposed—"

"If you would answer my calls sometime, our conversations wouldn't have to be like this. But no, you're always tied up with your job or with . . . Amy."

"For crying out loud, Thelma, I called all weekend and *you* didn't answer. Where the hell are you? What've you done? Where've you gone with my children? You're not supposed to take them out of the city without my okay."

"I tried to get your permission, but you wouldn't answer the phone. I'm getting married next week. I told you that was coming."

It felt like his mind was being raked over red-hot coals – everything in a turmoil. His children were being taken from him and now they would be calling someone Uncle Charlie, or some such. He wanted to reach inside the phone and grab Thelma by the neck. "Where the hell are you, Thelma? Where are my kids?"

"The children are happy. We're in New York City."

CHAPTER 47

The accountant left the room and Jesse turned to the four neat piles on the large conference table. He had only requested the three open years. What was the fourth pile? He directed his attention to it and was surprised to see the numbers 2006. Interesting, but he would start with 2003 and compare the data to the tax return.

Jesse removed his jacket, draped it on the chair to his left and loosened his tie. Thelma's voice from an hour ago continued to reverberate across his brain and he had to struggle to remove it for the moment. In New York? What to do about that? Would he ever see his children again?

Still standing, Jesse removed the top page to reveal the balance sheet for 2003, noted the word *Investments*, and reconciled the number to the tax return. He flipped through to find the general ledger page for that category and the length of the list was not unexpected. He had halfway expected to see investments in real estate, but instead found the names of corporate businesses. Names like United Chemicals, Nuclear Power Products, Superior Energy, and Eastern Laboratories sent his mind racing towards an image of the World Trade Center. Why would these people go to such great lengths to cover up the money trail if these were simply legitimate business acquisitions? He ran his hand through his hair. *What am I on to?* All of a sudden fear grabbed him. He quickly scanned the room, his eyes wide and alert, halfway expecting to see the Arab barge through the door. *Calm down, Jesse. Get a hold of yourself.*

The 2004 records showed a doubling of the investment account and the 2005 a quadrupling of that. The amount through 2005, forty-five million dollars, almost equaled the total amount collected by the Farouk mosque – the money supposedly destined for another mosque compound. A look at the 2006 balance sheet as of April caused him to take a deep breath. Something wasn't right. He looked to the door again.

With the balance sheet in hand, he sat in the chair and stared at a new asset account – Operation Inner City. What in the hell was that? Jesse's heart raced and he felt like getting up and running to share this information with Feldman. He started to go looking for the source of that amount. *Hold up, Jesse. Get a grip.* He forced himself to shed the conspiracy theory and return to the auditor mode. Operation Inner City could very well be within the religious context. Some kind of program to help the needy. Was he chasing demons again? *Get on with the audit.*

Jesse reviewed and compared the records for all years and found nothing out of the ordinary. Some of the expenses could certainly be challenged, but probably not worth the effort. From a tax point of view, this audit was producing results similar to the other mosque-related audits. With the exception of the tax exemption issue, there wasn't much, but he knew in his soul there was more to it than that. The mosque was connected to Allied Paint, now in the hands of CID, and had received funds from the offshore bank account, which were used to purchase the senator's house. How were all these activities connected to a central plot? The feeling in his gut would not go away. How would he ever be able to convince others? The reporter? Jesse reviewed the chain of events and transactions.

Farouk mosque received money from overseas sources. That money was transferred to Florida Land, which invested in real estate, and in turn shifted the funds to Hemisphere Equities, which invested in particular entities. The investments centered on a few companies in chemical and energy-related businesses. It was as if they were trying to gain control of the various companies. He wondered about the size of the companies and the degree of control they had managed to get. Why had they gone to such great lengths?

Operation Inner City returned abruptly to his mind and he retrieved the ledger account to determine the payees. Were the payments for various religious projects? But regardless, if these payments were for religious or community projects, wouldn't the mosque have made them? Why run them through Hemisphere? Questions, questions.

There were several entries on the page, but all to one person.

"Mr. Hawkins, I trust you found everything satisfactory." Jesse flinched and swiveled in the chair at the sound of the voice.

Amed stepped through the doorway and strode across the room. "I see you were provided with all the data you requested." Amed indicated the piles with a sweep of his arm.

"Yes, sir. I found everything in order. I was just preparing to conclude for the day." Jesse stood to show respect. "At the moment I don't foresee any adjustments. I won't make a final judgment on that until I have the opportunity to review my notes."

Amed smiled. "Good. Good. Your results are not surprising. Mr. Stevens is a fine accountant. I rely on him one hundred percent. When will I hear from you with the final judgment?"

"Probably by the end of the week." Jesse began to place papers into his briefcase. " I do have one question before I go though, if you will—"

"Yes. Sure. What is it?"

"The payments to Mr. A . . . ah." Jesse glanced at a single paper. "Abdullah Zacaari." Amed's jaw slackened but quickly recovered. Jesse continued, "What were they for?"

Amed looked again at the papers stacked on the table, then back at Jesse. "I think those payments were made in this year. Did you have those records?" He moved closer to the table and looked intently at each stack. He picked up the smaller stack. "This is 2006. I thought you were only interested in the prior years."

"Those records were here when I arrived. I always audit—"

"The subpoena was for the other years." Amed's face began to contort and redden. "Do you have the authority to go beyond the subpoena?" He gripped the records with slightly trembling hands. "I don't believe you had the right."

Jesse's gut tightened and began doing somersaults. He knew without doubt that this examination, which started with a little nobody, Mendez, had a lot more meaning than he could comprehend, other than the terrorists he had imagined in the beginning. "I'm sorry, Mr. Amed but, yes, I am allowed to examine all records provided to me. My job is to determine the correct tax for the open years using whatever information is available. I don't see—"

"I will have to consult my attorney about this. I tried to cooperate with you and provide all you asked for." Amed slammed the records onto the table. "I do not think you had the right to look at those records." He faced Jesse defiantly. "Will that be all, Mr. Hawkins?" Without waiting for an answer, Amed said, "I think you should leave now."

CHAPTER **48**

Abdullah glanced at Syed in the passenger seat and spoke into the cell phone. "Yes, Imraaz. I am still in the car. You have information?"

Abdullah's right hand gripped the steering wheel tighter than usual and pain ran through his fingers. His eyebrow arched, and he looked mournfully at Syed. He had anticipated a peaceful trip with Syed to Miami – a time spent explaining the reason for the coming action. It was important to him that Syed, his informally adopted son, understand the necessity for *jihad* and the impact on the future of Islam and the people of the Mid-East if it was left undone.

Abdullah closed the phone. He didn't speak, but his frown remained.

Syed asked, "Anything I can help with?"

Abdullah released his tight grip on the wheel and forced a smile. No need to get Syed embroiled in this problem, too. "No, I don't think so. Let us enjoy our trip. Perhaps we shouldn't accept additional calls." His smile broadened and Syed returned one as big.

A slight smile remained and Abdullah stared straight ahead, contemplating what he considered to be a rigorous drive once he left the turnpike and entered Miami proper. He hoped he would not miss the turn toward the port as he usually did. He glanced at Syed out of the corner of his eye and noted a serious demeanor. "We should be there in thirty minutes. Will your board meeting take more than an hour? Perhaps we can have lunch at the seafood restaurant overlooking the bay. What is the name?"

"I can never remember the name, but I agree we should go there." Syed seemed to loosen up. "The board meeting should not last more than one hour. To my knowledge there are no major topics on the agenda – quite normal, I think." He turned to look at Abdullah. "Will you join us?"

Abdullah was a little amazed at the offer. Although he was not on the board, and had refused the invitation to join, he knew everything of importance that transpired at each meeting. The call from Imraaz came to mind, and Abdullah thought of the revenue agent and his examination of Allied. What had become of that? He thought of Hamza and his failed attempt on the agent's life. How would things be now if his attempt had been successful, or if he'd been allowed to follow through? "No, I guess not. You will recall I have to see Hamza while here. I will do that during the board meeting." He pictured large crates being lifted from ships onto waiting trucks and sought to detect the crate containing his anticipated shipment. Time was limited. He had to act without delay.

Abdullah paid the toll and eyed the tangle of highways ahead. "Steer me in the right direction, Syed. I always get lost on this leg of the trip."

Syed smiled and said, "Just follow this road; it will take you to I-95. I will show you where to exit."

Abdullah absorbed the sight of the mosque from the parking lot across the street. He was a bit early for his meeting with Hamza, but half expected to see him emerge from the mosque at any moment. Hamza had taken to heart the news that he had been recommended for a glorious event and had called several times seeking details and confirmation.

As Hamza exited the mosque, Abdullah left the car and moved to a bench nestled within a small alcove of oaks and colorful hibiscus plants. Hamza, dressed in slacks and tee shirt, an unusual beaming smile gracing his dark, wide face, joined him.

"Hamza, it is so nice to see you. Come, sit here." Abdullah patted the bench next to him. "When I come here, I think many years back when you were a mere lad. Now look at you, a grown man – a man among men. You have been well since we last spoke?"

"Oh, yes, sir." Hamza adjusted himself on the bench and gazed at Abdullah. "You have determined that it is I that have been chosen?"

"This is a very important opportunity and only a select few qualify. The decision has come from the *mujahadeen.*" Abdullah noted the questioning, negative look. "You have been chosen, by the will of Allah. It is you who will live on with the gratitude of all those who remain. Allah be praised."

"Allah be praised." Hamza could not control the exhilaration exhibited on his face. "I have always known that I was put here by Allah for a purpose. What am I to do?"

Abdullah remained serious and looked through Hamza's elation. "I knew you would be overeager. You are to give the ultimate, and the time is near. Are you ready?"

"I am ready. Allah be praised."

"Your name will be revered forever in the annals of Islam. Yours will be a life of wonderment in the after world." Abdullah paused to see the effect of those words, and seeing nothing but reverent awe, continued. "You will carry a suitcase to Times Square in New York City where you will realize your purpose as set forth by Allah. The resulting aftermath will leave millions of the infidel dead and suffering, as dictated by the *jihad.* This will be like nothing you have ever accomplished." He paused again, happy for his choice of Hamza and the eagerness reflected on his face. The choice was the right one. "Are you ready, Hamza?"

Hamza, no longer able to contain his emotions, leaped up from the bench and walked in circles, stopping finally to face Abdullah. "I am ready. I cannot wait. Allah be praised.

When do I leave? How will I go? When do I get the suitcase?"

CHAPTER **49**

A family of seagulls swooped low to the pier, then, squawking at a high pitch, soared into the breezy, salt-laden air as the crane lifted a container from the ship and swung it onto the waiting truck. Abdullah watched as the truck, with its cargo of paint destined ultimately for a Navy port in the northeast, moved away toward the train yard and another took its place.

Abdullah kept his eye on the truck as it slowed to go through the newly installed detector, the first of its kind in the port area. The screeching seagulls brought his attention back to another container being swung to a waiting truck. It, too, departed to the waiting train for its unknown destination.

Abdullah flinched when Syed, who had returned to the Allied office after their relaxing lunch overlooking Biscayne Bay, asked, "Will we be heading back soon? I have a few items to take care of before tomorrow."

Abdullah turned and faced Syed, then back toward another container being hefted by the huge crane. "Yes, just a moment or two more." He looked back at Syed. "Isn't it amazing? The power of those huge cranes? The skill of the workmen? I take it you have watched the unloading of supplies before."

"Oh, yes. It is interesting to watch."

Abdullah stared at the crane as it deposited its load on the truck and swung back for another. Two more containers were swung and deposited. Abdullah, a slight frown on his face, wondered if this part of his trip was in vain. Would the expected shipment arrive? He looked at Syed, then at his watch.

When the next container was halfway to the truck Abdullah saw the message he'd been waiting for, and the frown was replaced with a slight smile. "There it is . . . ." He caught himself and forced the smile away.

Syed shaded his eyes with his hand and peered at the container, then turned with a questioning look at Abdullah. "What is it? Is that a special container?"

"See the numbers 9999?" Abdullah pointed to the top left of the container. "That is significant." He took Syed by the arm and followed the truck as it moved out. "Come, let us see if it gets through the detector." He noted the question on Syed's face. "I will explain, but first we must go to the train yard where the material will be stored separately." Abdullah smiled as the truck passed through the detector – the advanced packing material worked as planned.

"The material? There is material other than paint on the truck? Why wasn't I informed?"

Abdullah moved toward his car. "Come, we will ride to the train and watch the unloading. It is important that I take the package as soon as it is deposited at the warehouse."

"It is your package?" Syed raced to keep up and entered the car as Abdullah started the motor and shifted into reverse. "Is this connected with your trip to New York? You were to explain that to me."

"I will explain all to you, but first let us get the package. I had not expected to have to rush and be so anxious, but the audit of Hemisphere has brought a change in plans." Abdullah thought of his parting words to Hamza. *You will travel by car, first to my university in Orlando where you will receive instructions in the use of the suitcase, and then to New York. I will see you at the campus on Wednesday at one o'clock.*

Crates of paint were being removed from the marked container and transferred to the waiting railroad car when Abdullah pulled up next to the small Allied warehouse. He watched in anticipation as crate after crate was removed from the container. The small package, specially wrapped, was likely situated in the center of the paint to further deter detection.

His elation grew when the workman removed a suitcase-sized object from the truck and handed it to a warehouseman, who dutifully signed a receipt and moved toward the warehouse. Abdullah drove to the door and confronted the man as he was about to enter the warehouse. "I am Abdullah Zacaari. The package you carry is for me." He handed the man his driver's license, signed the necessary paperwork, accepted the package, and returned to the car.

Syed, standing by the passenger door, asked, "What is that and why was it shipped with the paint?" He looked at the item wrapped in a sort of foil unknown to him.

Abdullah placed the package onto the back seat and shut the door. "Get in, Syed. It is time to go." Abdullah, unable to control his happiness that all had turned out so well, grinned as he got into the car, "Everything will work as planned – except sooner."

CHAPTER 50

Abdullah took the ticket from the tollbooth operator, laid it in the small receptacle and turned north onto the turnpike. He flipped open the cell phone to make the necessary calls, glanced at Syed's agitated look and knew he would have to inform him of the upcoming events before calling the cells in New York.

"This is an exciting time, Syed. One we will likely never again experience during our life on this earth. It has sometimes been trying for me, and I know it has been trying and distressful for you." Abdullah looked sympathetically at Syed, who frowned but seemed eager to learn the facts.

"After the *fatwa* issued by the Imam of Manhattan in 1999, it has been the position of the *mujuhadeen* to wage an open *jihad* against the Satan of the world, the United States of America, the occupier of our beloved country and perpetrator of the Israeli occupation, and . . . disenfranchisement of the Palestinian people for all these years." Abdullah realized his voice was rising with his building passion, and he fought to subdue it. Syed seemed to be listening intently.

Abdullah continued, "I know you abhor violence and I respect that in you. I, too, abhor it." He looked quickly at Syed with understanding, then back to the road. "I know, too, that you are a devout Muslim and will go to the extremes necessary to protect the faith and its followers. This Satan has vowed to alter our country and its traditional beliefs. It is the will of Allah that they be prevented from further aggression." His voice quivered and he gripped the steering wheel with both hands. "We must do all within our power to assist in Satan's destruction." He stared straight ahead and tried to ease the building emotions.

Syed's voice reflected his growing concern. "Does the planned action involve the killing of millions of which you previously spoke?"

Abdullah remembered the outburst at the mosque several weeks ago and silently berated himself for his inability to control his emotions when considering the aspects of the *jihad* against the Great Satan. "You understand it is not our overall mission to kill, but it is necessary to defend ourselves. Our people are under siege, with many killings and atrocities being perpetrated on a daily basis. We are at war. We—"

"I understand that we must stand up for our rights and beliefs, but killing millions of innocent people? Is that within the teaching of the Prophet Muhammad? The wish of Allah?"

"It is unfortunate, I know, but the people of America freely elect their representatives and are, therefore, actively involved in the war." Abdullah glanced at Syed and saw a glimmer of understanding. "If we are to be successful and rid the world of infidels, we must be resolved and steadfast. It is the duty of all Islamists to spread the word of Allah and the great prophet. And no, neither Allah nor Muhammad condone killing, but we must protect ourselves, and therefore it has been declared that killing is justified in such a war."

"How will millions be killed? How will killing millions solve our problem? The Great Satan is too big and strong to capitulate because of an isolated incident." Syed appeared to be taking the information without qualms.

"We are only the beginning. Similar projects are set to occur in major cities throughout the country soon after. The plan is to destroy the infrastructure and the economy in one fell swoop. Unfortunately, millions will likely be killed during the attack." Abdullah's voice began to rise again. "Millions will lose their jobs and the economy will spin into the greatest depression ever known." He looked too long at Syed and began to veer off the road, but quickly recovered. "It is then that the Islamic faithful will step in under the guidance of Allah."

Abdullah looked at the cell phone screen, punched the button and the soft chiming stopped. "Yes, Imraaz. We are just now exiting the turnpike. What do you have? Did all go well with the revenue agent?"

"Abdullah, it has not gone well. I acted too hastily and have jeopardized your project."

Abdullah's throat constricted for a moment, but he immediately calmed himself, knowing that his decision to hasten the operation had been a good one. No matter what happened now, the project would proceed – and be successful. "Calm yourself, Imraaz, everything will be all right. How did you act too hastily?" Abdullah winked at Syed in an attempt to ease the concern seen there.

"The agent looked at the records for this year and asked about the payments to you. I am afraid he will go looking for you. I ran him off."

"You what? You ran him off? What did he say?"

"I told him I had to talk with my attorney, and he simply said okay. He packed up his things and left without a further word. I think he was quite taken aback at my tirade. Again Abdullah, I want to apologize for losing my composure."

Abdullah's mind catapulted forward to the steps and timeline to D-Day. This turn of events could seriously affect the project if the agent was able to activate other government agencies. But why would he? He was looking for taxes. "Do not worry, Imraaz. Continue with your operation. I will be in touch in a few days. Goodbye for now."

Abdullah saw the concern on Syed's face. "The agent has extended his examination to me."

Back on the turnpike after leaving Syed at his office in West Palm Beach, Abdullah settled in for the two-and-a-half-hour drive, his mind ablaze with the coming activity and timing. He had been given a range of two weeks, and now, because of the revenue agent, he had to tighten it by more than a week. Hamza was expected in Orlando on Wednesday and could make it to New York in one full day. Abdullah decided it was best to delay as long as possible so as to provide cell members ample time to remove their families from the city.

Abdullah thought of Syed and his apprehension about the upcoming violence. Syed, a devout Muslim, would hold fast to his faith, and his support was assured. *But what about my daughter?*

He dialed each of the cell members and gave the same message. "9999. D-Day is Friday afternoon. You will receive a final call one hour before." He breathed a deep sigh of relief. The decision was final.

The next order of business; He had to convince his daughter to leave New York without delay. He dialed her number.

CHAPTER 51

Syed, hardly able to control his boiling emotions, said goodbye to Abdullah and got out of the car at his office building. In a car across the lot, Syed noticed a young man looking his way. At first glance, Syed wondered why the man, who turned his head away, was interested in him, but the recent moments with Abdullah and the revelations during the trip back from Miami quickly forced out any other thoughts trying to gain a foothold. He waved at Abdullah's departing car, noted the sun peeking around the high-rise buildings in the area and hurried in the opposite direction toward the entrance to the office building – the man in the car completely forgotten.

Syed reached for the doorknob to his office when the slamming of a door caused him to look down the hall. The man from the parking lot waved and hurried away from the stairwell door.

"Mr. Rabia. Can I have a word with you, sir?" Arthur Reid, panting, walked at almost a run. "Forgive me, sir. I ran up the stairs, hoping I could speak with you for a minute before . . . ." His breath became more measured as he reached Syed. "May I?" He produced his press badge. "I'm a reporter with the *Washington Post* and have a few questions. Only take a minute."

Syed's thoughts of Abdullah and his plans for the immediate future quickly became entangled with the image of the recent newspaper headlines – "Senator Martin Walker Accused of Taking Bribes from Allied Paint Corporation." The article alleged that Allied had not only made cash payments to the senator but also had purchased his house and immediately sold it at a loss. At that time Syed had felt certain the near future would bring a confrontation such as this one now. He had broached the subject with Abdullah but no concrete reaction had been forthcoming.

Syed deliberately looked at his watch. "I am sorry, Mr. Reid. My time today is severely limited, perhaps another day?" He placed his hand on the knob and twisted. The door opened, he stepped partially inside and turned to face Reid. "How can I possibly be of interest to the *Washington Post?*"

"Again, let me apologize for any inconvenience, Mr. Rabia. I'm doing a story on Senator Martin Walker and his connection to Allied Paint Corporation." Reid moved near to the door as if he planned to enter with Syed. "The public records regarding the sale of the senator's house were altered. Allied is not now shown as the purchaser. The new purchaser and subsequent seller is Florida Land – a Limited Liability Company managed by you. Can you tell me—?"

"I am sorry, Mr. Reid, but I really do not have the time today." Syed tried to close the door, but Reid applied pressure and eased his way into the room. Syed's secretary looked startled as the two men entered and stood at the door.

Reid said, "I need to know the connection between the two companies and why the transaction was altered in the public records. Can you shed any light there? What is your connection to Allied? Are you aware of the cash payments to the senator?"

Syed, now alarmed by all the attention and questions, nodded at Harriet and moved toward his office – his mind spinning almost out of control. "The closing agent made a mistake and it wasn't determined until later. It was finally rectified and that is the cause for the alterations. The county accepted the lawyer's explanation." Syed opened the door to his office and stepped through. "I really must go, Mr. Reid." He closed the door behind him.

Syed had just sat at his desk, his mind afire, when he heard a light tap at the door.

Harriet peeked around the door. "He's gone. Are you all right, Mr. Rabia? Is there anything you need before I leave?"

Syed looked up, his face still reflecting concern, "No, Harriet. You go on home." He forced a slight grin. "I am fine. A lot on my mind right now." He glanced at the files on his desk and placed his hand on them. "You go ahead now. I will see you in the morning. Lock up when you leave." Harriet nodded, and closed the door behind her.

His life was on the cusp, never to return to any degree of normalcy. He had strived so hard to be successful in this great country; but now his growing business, soon to be thrown into an abyss with the coming collapse of the economy; the possible loss of his wife because of his complicity in the upcoming disaster; his citizenship meaningless; his internal conflict with his religion and the interpretation of it as determined by some; his whole life ruined because of his decision and his love for Abdullah. What was he to do?

The ringing of the telephone interrupted his thoughts. He looked at it with a blank stare, then noted the caller – his wife. Should he take it in his present state of mind? Should he dare to tell her of what was about to happen? Could she ever possibly understand his reason for participating? Sharing the information with his wife was the only way he could continue living. He pressed the button and opened the line.

CHAPTER **52**

Jesse, gasping for breath from his dash down the stairs, stood with his hand on the car door and stared at the upper floors of the building. With his mind ablaze with runaway plots and subplots, he could readily imagine the buzz of activity going on behind those windows. Imraaz pacing wildly in his office, yelling at the secretary, cursing the accountant for providing the information for 2006, trying to reach others by telephone. Jesse grinned and entered the car. What concoctions of witch's brew had he uncorked? His skin tingled as an eerie feeling raced through his body. Would they call the killer in again? He looked all around.

He pulled into the Revenue Service parking lot, cut the engine, and took deep breaths in an attempt to calm himself. He had to be controlled and logical in his presentation to Feldman, and that would be quite difficult because he couldn't comprehend exactly what he faced. This case had developed into something way beyond the norm. He leaned back against the seat and allowed his body to go limp. Thoughts, facts, and fantasies with real-life, dark-skinned gremlins ran rampant and left him unable to organize a viable presentation. The cell phone rang. His mind cleared for a second and he reached for the device, starting to accept the reporter's call, but thought better of it. He would return the call after his meeting.

The disruptive event that had so effectively been placed to the rear of everything else suddenly loomed in the foreground. All other matters were of secondary importance to the loss of his children. Conflicting images fought for control: happy faces as they dodged incoming waves at the beach; fear as they huddled against the side of the boat; Thelma's tirade and her threat to keep them from him; the

For Sale sign on the front lawn. He beat his palms against the steering wheel and yelled to the wind, "Damn you. Damn you!" He regained control and looked around, pleased that no one was in earshot. It was four-thirty, he'd better hurry.

Feldman was obviously annoyed by Jesse's late entry, but he waited patiently for Jesse to begin his presentation.

Jesse asked, "You don't think we ought to get Mr. Singleton in here to hear this? We'll need him if it goes where I think it should." He had lost his fear of Singleton since the two cases had been accepted in the Criminal Division.

"Get on with it, Jesse. We'll call him if it warrants." The familiar frown spread on Feldman's face as he looked at his watch.

"First off, I'd like your permission to pull a few returns. Maybe we could have Mrs. Morrison do that while I'm here. I can review them this afternoon."

"This have to do with your reason for being here?"

"Yes." Jesse unfolded a paper and handed it to Feldman. "I'd like to pull Abdullah Zacaari, Syed Rabia and Imraaz Amed."

Feldman handed the paper to his secretary when she entered and said to Jesse. "Do not begin active examination of these people until I give the go ahead."

Jesse nodded his agreement. "Okay. I think what we have here goes beyond mere tax examinations. I've followed every lead and, with the exceptions of Allied Paint and the senator, have not found any significant adjustments." He noted the dismal look. "But, I think what I *have* found warrants the expertise of other areas of government."

"Jesse, am I hearing you right? You have collared me here this afternoon to talk about issues other than tax? I've gone along with you so far, and you have proven yourself with the other taxpayers, but now you're saying flat out that there are no tax issues. What the hell is it? We *are* in the tax business you know."

"Yes, I know. I know that, Danny, but what I've come across will even make your mind imagine weird things. I tell you, there's something mighty damn strange going on." Jesse noted the slight smirk and the impatient look but stood his ground. "Let me recap quickly what I've discovered; then you decide."

Jesse extracted a file from his briefcase and laid it on the desk. "The audit of the mosques began because of the ties to Syed Rabia, who is the trustee of a mosque's land-trust and a board member of Allied Paint Corporation. Allied is owned by a British company which is owned by Arabs." Feldman shifted in his chair. "The company has developed a scheme to divert income to an offshore bank account, known as Provident Paint. Allied has close ties to Senator Walker who has been accused of taking bribes in exchange for securing the Navy contract for them. As you know, the cases for Allied and the senator have been transferred to CID." The impatient look deepened and Feldman squirmed.

"Farouk Mosque, initially funded by Kahid Mosque, has received millions of dollars from overseas sources and has attempted to wash that money through the purchase and sale of real estate via an LLC called Florida Land, which is managed by Syed Rabia. A review of those records definitely reveals that there is no valid religious or business purpose for that operation. Washing money seems to be the main goal.

"Now, Florida Land transfers that cash to another LLC called Hemisphere Equities, which is managed by Imraaz Amed. That company uses the money to purchase interests in various businesses around the country." The frown from

Feldman melted somewhat, as if he was beginning to see some part of what Jesse saw.

"Virtually all the companies purchased by Hemisphere are involved in the production of chemicals, nuclear materials, drugs, etc., which indicates to me they have a plan to eventually use those materials for no good in this country." Feldman's brow arched and Jesse had a good feeling. Things were looking up.

"Mr. Amed kicked me out of his office when I asked about the payments to Abdullah Zacaari – payments to an account titled, Operation Inner City."

"He kicked you out? What happened?"

"These payments occurred in 2006, and my subpoena didn't go beyond 2005. The accountant inadvertently brought the records for 2006 along with the others, and I took the liberty of browsing through them. When I asked the nature of the expenditures, Amed blew his stack – said I didn't have the authority to look at material for that year. I told him I had the right to look at everything available, but he didn't buy it. I packed my things and left and came straight to talk to you."

Feldman leaned back in his chair, stared for a minute at the ceiling, then back at Jesse. "All very interesting – and, as you say, very, very strange. You have any idea where all this might be leading?"

"In my heart, I know without doubt that it's heading toward disaster for this country, and I think it will be a hell of a lot worse than 9/11. But to be perfectly honest with you I don't have facts to back me. I would very much like to have others with more expertise in this area – somebody that may have knowledge of these people, prior experience. Maybe the information we have would be enough to send them on the hunt." Jesse stood and walked around the back of the chair. "Big question for me is, who do we contact to push the information in the right direction." He leaned on the chair with both arms. "What do you think?"

Feldman reached for the phone. "Let's go see Gary."

CHAPTER 53

Gary Singleton listened intently to Jesse's recap of the latest events and coupled it to the other information that had convinced him to add Allied and the senator to his caseload. He expected big repercussions from those cases, and this latest bit of data could either add or subtract from his status with the Service.

On the one hand, he agreed with Jesse. The facts and circumstances were indeed very unnatural – like nothing he'd ever experienced. On the other hand, it was impossible for him to reach the same conclusion Jesse had. Nothing in the facts presented made a verifiable case for some major plot against the United States. But yet, what if Jesse was right that Hemisphere's specialty acquisitions led in that direction? What if the money paid to Zacaari was in fact being used to fund terrorist cells throughout the country? That was a distinct possibility, and he shuddered at the name of the account title – Operation Inner City. What else could that mean but disaster?

Singleton picked up the phone and said to Jesse, "I have a personal friend in the local FBI office. I'll call him." He noted Jesse's grin as he waited for someone to answer the phone. "Jesse, I'm not sure I understand all you've told me, but I think you've done one hell of a job of tracking this thing, and, as I hear . . . sometimes at the risk of your life." He glanced at Feldman and said to Jesse, "I'm going to recommend that you be transferred to CID." Jesse's grin broadened into a large smile. He, too, glanced at Feldman who also sported a smile.

Singleton spoke into the phone. "Hello. This is Gary Singleton with the Internal Revenue Service. Can I speak with Special Agent Monroe?" He listened for a moment then said, "Tell him I have information, which may be useful to him."

When Monroe came to the phone, Singleton spoke for several minutes, relating the shortened history of the Mendez case and the action taken by CID. He then went into more detail about the latest discoveries that were more relevant to the FBI. He listened for an extended period of time and said into the phone, "Yes. I understand, Billy." He looked at Jesse. "The revenue agent and I are at your disposal. Call me as soon as you have some news. Thanks for your time. I appreciate it. I owe you." He listened for another second and hung up the phone.

Singleton spoke to both Feldman and Jesse. "The agent said that Abdullah Zacaari was a person of interest until just recently. The agency had tried to prosecute him after 9/11 and even had him imprisoned for awhile. They eventually had to let him go for lack of evidence, and although they continued to tail him, were prevented by the court from bugging his phones. After several years without finding anything of interest, they were called off." He noted Jesse's saddened face and the concern showing on Feldman's.

"He said the information had merit and that he would forward it up the line. He was hopeful it would receive positive attention."

Jesse, over-exuberant, bounced along as he made his way across the room. Things were going his way for a change. It was twenty past five and only a few agents were still at their desks. The neatly stacked tax returns on his desk were first to catch his attention, and he was eager to review them. A glimmer of his children flickered across his mind and he decided to give his lawyer a call in the hopes he may still be in.

". . . at the sound of the tone, please leave a message." Jesse frowned but accepted the response as normal for this time of day. He thought of calling Thelma again, looked at the returns and thought better of it – wouldn't do any good anyway. Tomorrow he'd see what his legal options were. He sat at his desk, sorted the pile into three stacks, and picked the first at random – Syed Rabia.

The front page of the return revealed Wages, Interest, Dividends and Partnership Income for a total of $135, 472. Page two showed nothing out of the ordinary. Interest and dividends on Schedule B were typical from banks and brokerage houses. Jesse was interested in what entity Syed used for his business and skipped to Schedule E. The income shown for Financial Management, LLC corresponded with the amount shown on page one. He would have to pull that return to verify that Syed was the owner.

Where did the wages come from? A schedule at the end of the stack showed Mary Rabia as the wage earner – the source – Financial Management, LLC. What did she do for the firm? He hadn't seen her at the office while he was auditing the mosque and Florida Land. Why didn't Syed take wages if he was running the firm? To escape the payment of payroll taxes?

Jesse pushed the stack aside. May be worth a further look. Good way to apply pressure, too. Syed, who seemed to Jesse to be an honest man, appeared to be caught up in something that caused him to lie. Did Syed know what the plot was?

He shifted the next return in front of him – Abdullah Zacaari.

CHAPTER **54**

Sunlight filtered around the buildings across the street as Jesse locked the door to his small apartment and walked down to the curb. He picked up the newspaper, started to remove the plastic wrapping, then thought better of it and tossed it onto the passenger seat of his car. He was in a hurry to make sure he caught Feldman early enough to get his approval to audit the returns he'd received yesterday.

Although he was most interested in Zacaari's return because of the payments to him from Hemisphere, he would have to put that off because of the necessary trip to Orlando. He knew, too, that he'd have trouble with Amed, especially since the last meeting. Maybe he'd try to pop in on Rabia, even though there didn't appear to be much in the way of adjustments.

A sleek, yellow BMW turned in front of him at the light. Jesse tensed and tingles ran along his skin. He thought of Singleton's comments yesterday. None of them believed the "attacks" on him were deliberate or had anything to do with a conspiracy. To them, both of the occurrences were unfortunate accidents. In a way, he could understand their thinking. Mishaps do occur, and usually when least expected. But Jesse knew without any doubt that the "accidents" were blatant attempts on his life. That dark, square face at both occurrences could not be considered a chance appearance.

The image of his two children pressed against the side of the boat resurfaced. He cringed and tightened his grip on the steering wheel. The For Sale sign replaced the image and he made a mental note to call his lawyer today. He forced himself to loosen the grip and said out loud, "By God, if I knew where they were living, I'd go there today. Seems to me her boyfriend was from New York. Oh yes, she said she was in New York. Maybe I . . . ."

He pulled into the parking lot and found several spaces for his choosing. As he turned the ignition off, he noticed the newspaper headlines vaguely through the cellophane wrapper. Something about it was familiar. He stripped the wrapper off and unfolded the paper, and his astonishment overran every other thought or feeling in his body.

PUBLIC RECORDS ALTERED TO CONCEAL A REAL ESTATE TRANSACTION BETWEEN SENATOR MARTIN WALKER AND ALLIED PAINT CORPORATION.

Jesse could hardly control himself. No wonder the reporter had tried to reach him yesterday. He looked around, and seeing no one else in the lot, began reading the article.

'In December 2005 Allied Paint Corporation, according to the original records, purchased the senator's house for $1,500,000 and sold it two months later for $1,000,000. Later, in 2006, the records were changed to reflect Florida Land, LLC as the purchaser and subsequent seller. The transaction points to a payoff to the senator by Allied in exchange for securing the Navy paint contract, and the alteration of the records was to obscure the connection between Allied and the senator, which is the subject being taken up by a special Senate committee.

Senator Walker has managed to override all suggestions and demands that the Navy contract be awarded using a competitive bidding system. For the past ten years Allied has gained the contract without any other manufacturers having the opportunity to bid, and there are many who would do so if given the chance.

It has been determined that Allied Paint Corporation is owned 100% by Brisbane Paint, Ltd, a British company that manufactures the paint in England and sells it to Provident Paint Corporation in Nassau, who in turn sells it to Allied. All profits are realized by the Nassau company, leaving no profits for Allied or Brisbane, and therefore no tax revenues for either the American or the British governments.

A review of the senator's campaign records for the past ten years reveals sizable direct political contributions from Allied. . . .

Jesse whistled and quickly scanned the balance of the article, which reiterated pieces from the previous article and expected repercussions from candidates on both sides of the aisle. This reporter really had a nose, and knew how to stretch the truth – he couldn't possibly know the details between the three paint companies regarding selling prices, etc. He obviously didn't know that Allied expensed the payments on its income tax return, nor could he know that Provident is merely a bank account. But in effect he'd guessed at what Jesse knew as facts – the companies were keeping profits overseas. He also, at this moment, couldn't possibly know that Provident had provided the funds for the purchase of the senator's house.

Jesse laid the paper on the seat and got out of the car. The reporter had the means and the gall to question many knowledgeable people. *Can I work with him without revealing confidential information?* He entered the reporter's number.

CHAPTER 55

Jesse turned into the parking lot across the street from Syed's office building to review his thoughts before trying to meet with Syed. Unable to reach the reporter, Jesse had decided, on the spur of the moment, to see if he could extract any information from Syed that might be relevant to Jesse's al Qaeda plot theory. He knew he would not be able to confront Amed about Hemisphere again without a new subpoena, and the trip to Orlando was out of the question – at least today. His chances for an interview were slim without benefit of an appointment. He positioned his car so he could see cars entering the parking lot across the street as well as view the boats out for a pleasant day on the water.

Two small boats far out on the waterway raced by. Jesse recalled the disastrous day with his children and their near death. What were they doing in New York? Did they miss their Daddy? How was he to get them back? The magazine article headline flashed across his mind, *Al Qaeda Has Nukes*.

Jesse was about to go into the restaurant and get a cup of coffee when he saw Syed's car turn into the office building parking lot. He strained to identify the driver but was unable, and by the time he walked across the street, the person had vanished.

Harriet was not at her desk when Jesse eased the door open. He turned his attention to the magnificent painting of the Statue of Liberty over the sofa. The painting caused his heart to beat a little faster even though he knew that it meant much more to many of those coming from other countries.

Harriet closed the door to Syed's office behind her. "Jesse, what are you doing here? You don't have an appointment, do you?" She moved behind her desk and laid a sheaf of papers there.

Jesse jerked at the sound of the voice and turned to face her. "No, I don't have an appointment. Just wanted to smell that sweet perfume again." He stood in front of Harriet's desk as a large smile spread across her face. "I took a chance that I could speak with Mr. Rabia for a minute. I apologize for popping in this way. Think he'll see me?"

"I'll see." She moved to the door, but before entering asked, "Been out in the boat since you were last here?"

Before he could answer she entered Syed's office and soon emerged. "Mr. Rabia will see you." She held the door open. "But, just for a minute, Jesse. He's very busy at the moment."

For just a second, Jesse's nerves tried to wrest control. Had he acted irrationally coming over to force this meeting? There was nothing materially wrong with Rabia's personal tax return. He wished now he had ordered Rabia's business return before rushing over here. That entity, Financial Management, LLC, was the source of the wages to Mary Rabia, and he knew that Rabia was part of whatever was going on with the perceived plot, which was of major importance now, so he felt a sense of urgency. Jesse steeled himself and stepped through the doorway.

Syed Rabia sat behind a large desk with a questioning look. The wall to the left was covered with shelves lined with books. Jesse moved to the desk. "Please forgive me, Mr. Rabia for intruding this way. I felt a great need to speak with you right away and worried that I might not be able to secure an appointment. Can you grant me a moment of your time?"

"This is a very trying time for me, Mr. Hawkins, but have a seat." He glanced at the clock on the wall and moved papers to the side. "I only have a few minutes. Is this about Florida Land?"

"There are a couple of things I'd like to talk with you about." Jesse laid his briefcase on the desk and withdrew a file. "Because of all these related entities, I pulled your personal return and—"

"My personal return? Whatever for? Is there something wrong? I don't see—"

"It's just routine, sir. I have not noted anything out of the ordinary, but I do have one question." Jesse opened the file and removed the tax return. "I see here that your wife receives a salary from the company. I didn't realize she was an employee of yours." Jesse knew this was a lame question but he had to get started some way. "What position does she hold with the company?"

Syed seemed a little peeved with the question but stated without equivocation, "Mary performs small jobs for me from time to time and this is my way of letting her know that I appreciate her service. Is there a problem with the payment? Are there other issues?"

"No, there are no other issues, and the payments are not a problem. Just curious that's all." Jesse reinserted the file into the briefcase and looked directly at Syed. "The main reason I came was to inform you about the audit of Allied Paint."

Syed's brow raised. "Allied Paint? I know you are presently auditing the company. Do you have questions for me? Allied's president would be in a better position for questions of day-to-day business."

"Mr. Rabia, I have developed a deep respect for you from our brief meetings and wanted to be right up front with you." Jesse noted a slight alteration in Syed's demeanor. "And because you are on Allied's board, I'm able to discuss matters with you." Syed's brow remained raised.

Jesse continued, "Because of Allied's financial relationship to Senator Martin Walker and its connection to Provident Paint in Nassau, the audit has been transferred to the Revenue Service's Criminal Investigation Department."

Syed's brow lowered and he leaned forward to the edge of his desk. "Just what does that mean?"

"That means the Service suspects criminal fraud and specialists will prosecute the case. It also means that certain individuals, such as yourself could be in jeopardy." Jesse felt a touch of remorse for causing this man pain, but Syed was deeply involved in the scheme to bring money into this country, and Jesse had to uncover the reason.

Syed, with definite concern now reflected on his face, said, "I am not aware of these connections you speak of, Mr. Hawkins."

Jesse knew Syed was lying and fought his instinct to retaliate against an opponent. He composed himself and stood, knowing that he was again placing his life in grave danger by what he was about to say. "Mr. Rabia, please allow me to help you. It will only do you harm to oppose me. I know, and you know, that Provident deposited $1.5 million into the account of Florida Land. The money was used to purchase the house of Senator Walker. You know that all the money collected from so-called mosque donors was never intended to start a new mosque, but rather to fund some scheme by transferring all the money to a company for the purpose of buying going businesses in this country. Businesses that manufacture products that can be used to cause destruction to America and its people."

Syed seemed perplexed and in deep thought with all this information but said nothing.

"Something sinister is imminent, Mr. Rabia, and I aim to find out what it is before it's too late. I feel that you can help me. We can help each other. If you will work with me, I will do all I can to protect you from criminal charges and see that your otherwise good name is not smeared."

Syed continued to offer nothing.

Jesse continued, "You probably saw the newspaper this morning. That reporter is investigating Senator Walker for taking bribes from Allied. Reporters are probably the most persistent people on earth. He knows about you, and he knows about Abdullah Zacaari and Imraaz Amed. You can bet he will track you all down in his quest for a story. He will spread your name all over the nation. It won't be a fun time." Jesse zipped up his briefcase. "Work with me, Mr. Rabia, and save yourself . . . and this great country."

Syed, looking painfully sorry and anticipatory, finally spoke. "I need to speak with the president of Allied. Give me a little time, Mr. Hawkins."

CHAPTER **56**

Syed walked to the bookcase and unconsciously withdrew a volume, flipping through pages he really wasn't looking at – his life virtually over. Should he call Abdullah and bring him up to date. Surely the newspaper in Orlando would cover the story of a prominent U. S. Senator taking bribes and manipulating court records. He replaced the book and walked back to the desk. The suitcase being placed in the trunk of Abdullah's car in Miami flashed across his mind and prompted him to recoil. He shuddered as he recalled his telephone conversation with Abdullah prior to the Miami meeting. In that suitcase was a device set to go off in New York soon. Abdullah, on at least two occasions, had predicted that millions would perish – a nuclear bomb! Was Hamza, a natural killer, part of the plan? Abdullah had met with him while in Miami.

What was he to do? Syed ran a hand through his hair, sat and stared at the ceiling. Mary, ever logical and thorough in her thinking, was where he should take these problems. After the trip to Miami, he had told her of his part in bringing money into the country for the purchase of businesses, of fraudulent use of the mosque and the LLC to disguise the sources. She had been aghast, since she was a participant, but seemed to understand how he could have gotten involved because of his father and Abdullah. The big question was how to remove themselves from further participation. She still didn't know of the money going directly to Abdullah in 2006 or of his plans for New York. How could he tell her that? But, even though he could only conjecture as to the total plan, he must open up to get her advice, and to keep her.

He picked up the phone, gazed at it for a long moment, started to hang up, then decided he must call her. He pressed the numbers.

Abdullah walked across the campus quad toward the lecture hall almost unaware of students and other professors, some rushing and others strolling leisurely toward their individual destinations. He rubbed his eye as a glint of sunlight flashed from atop a building on the easterly edge of the campus, his mind absorbed with the headlines in the morning paper.

Hamza was due tomorrow afternoon, and the plan, once activated would be unstoppable. The press had tied the senator to Allied and Provident and it would only be a matter of time before it led to the other organizations and the plan itself. The time was now. But what about his daughter? He had been unable to entice her to visit Florida at once, and in New York she could possibly be near enough to ground zero to be seriously affected. Yet if he didn't go through with it, then what?

He removed his cell phone and flipped it open. He would try to reach her again. She had not been answering her phone since their argument Monday. He started to press the numbers when the soft chime interrupted. The number on the screen belonged to Syed. A frown appeared. He's calling about the headlines. Abdullah was in no mood to talk with him and thought seriously about not taking the call, as the thought of his daughter's refusal to answer once more came to the forefront. "Yes, Syed. You are well? I am on my way to give a lecture."

"Yes. I am well. Please forgive me for interrupting you, but I thought I should tell you that the revenue agent paid me a visit the first thing this morning to tell me the tax examination of Allied has become a criminal case. He is threatening to charge me. I—"

"A criminal case?" Abdullah breathed deeply, his mind afire. "On what grounds?"

"He knows about the transfer of funds from Provident for the purchase of the senator's house. He knows that Provident is a sham and that paint revenues are being shifted overseas. He knows that Imraaz is using the money to purchase American businesses, and he suspects the products are to be used against the country. Abdullah, I don't—"

"Try not to fret about these things, Syed." Abdullah could see the wheels turning in Syed's head. One day he would snap and reveal everything. "Our holy mission is to proceed with the plan, and then all will be well again." He could hear heavy breathing at the other end of the line. "Stay calm, Syed. We must remain strong. A few more days."

"I am trying. Believe me, Abdullah. I am trying. The reporter came to see me on Monday, asking questions about the senator. He knows about you and it is likely that he will be in your area soon. You will prepare yourself?"

"I will take care of it. Do not worry." Abdullah walked up the steps to the conference building. "I must go now. Syed, stay with me and all will be well."

"I will stay the course. I will not betray you." There was a pause on the line; then Syed continued. "Is your daughter still in New York?"

Abdullah stared at the phone for a long moment, then said, "Yes."

Hamza, on his knees with arms spread out in front, palms flat against the floor, spoke to the altar at the far side of the mosque. "Allah be praised. Allah be praised. I know I have been chosen from the many who are qualified for this mission, and I am ready and eager to do your will. Friday I will be in your company." He placed his forehead on the floor and thought of his mother. She, as a good Muslim, would be proud that he had accomplished a worthy deed. He prayed silently.

CHAPTER 57

Senator Martin Walker, numbed and depressed beyond belief, placed the newspaper on the desk and removed the moisture gathering at the edge of his eyes with the tips of his fingers. Was this the end? The end of his political life? The end of his life?

He tried to focus on his many worthy accomplishments for the good of the people of the country, the main purpose of his political career, but the headlines kept the memories blurred. He laid his forehead on the desk, choked back a sob, and asked God for forgiveness. He immediately jerked his head up and sat back in his chair. *What the hell am I doing?* He'd never asked forgiveness for anything, had always faced his enemies. *I'll survive this crisis or . . . .* He opened the bottom drawer of the desk and placed his hand on the revolver.

A slight tapping at the door caused him to look up as Benson slowly stepped into the room. Looking a little agitated at the intrusion, Martin said, "Yes, Tom. I guess you've seen the paper? Another step backward, huh?"

"Yes, sir. I've seen it, and I'm getting barraged by the press and your colleagues." Benson moved to the desk. "Forgive me, sir for entering this way, but I thought I should confer with you before I give any formal interviews." At the senator's head gesture, Benson sat in the chair in front of the desk. "What am I to tell them, sir? Are the allegations true?"

Martin stood up, walked to the window and stared out into the light blue, cloudless sky. Gazing toward the White House, the thought of its historical splendor, breathtaking. He lifted the windowpane, leaned down on the sill and drew in a deep breath of the crisp, clear air. In his mind he was standing next to the podium ready to place his hand on the

Bible and take the oath of office to become the thirty-eighth President of the United States. His party had wanted him to run on two different occasions, but he had refused on the grounds that he could accomplish more for the people by staying a senator. Sometimes he wished he had made the run, often wondering where history would have placed him.

"Sir . . . ."

Martin turned to face Benson who was now standing and moving toward the window. "Yes, Tom." He began walking back to the desk. "Just thinking of past thoughts." He took his chair and Benson took his. "I know we've got to talk about this thing, but first I want you to know of my deep regret for not being more honest with you over the years. Frankly, I didn't think it important enough to have it interfere with all the other things on your mind." He ran his hand through his hair trying to sort out the facts and history and how it all had gotten to this point. What the hell; it didn't make a lot of difference now anyway.

"Look, like so many other things in the political world, this situation started out as a simple back-scratching tradeoff. Way back before you came on board, a representative from Allied Paint made a substantial contribution to a campaign committee that backed me and, through one of the personnel there, made known their desire to be considered for the Navy contract. That led to greater and greater campaign contributions and my going all out to support them." He looked into Benson's eyes and saw compassion and understanding. "But, I guarantee you, Tom, not one penny of the money ever went into my pocket."

"But, sir, the newspaper story alleges that Allied paid you more for your house than it was worth on the open market. I don't recall—"

"You're right. That was a payment I didn't forward to the fund. I was in a terrible bind from the divorce proceedings and searching for a way to keep from losing everything I had managed to accumulate over the years." The sadness that had been ruling was flicked aside and he again assumed the role of leader of the Senate fighting off the persistent demand for local grants. "In past years, Allied and its employees contributed to campaign committees that were committed to my re-election. This year, because of a weak moment, I requested a different mode of payment."

"But what about the allegation that you manipulated court records? What was the purpose of that?"

"What had started out as generally nothing unusual had blossomed by that time through the efforts of my opponents and their reporter friend into a national story splashed in all the major newspapers. You will remember all this started with the reporter questioning my backing of the Navy contract – strictly a political ploy. Again in a moment of weakness, I thought, erroneously in afterthought, that by changing the name of the purchaser I could remove the connection to Allied. As it turns out, it only poured more fuel on the fire." Martin stood and walked again to the window.

Without looking at Benson, he said, "This looks like the end, Tom." He stared out the window for an extended period and then turned to face Benson. "I will resign officially tomorrow."

CHAPTER 58

Jesse, walking towards his desk, his mind wrapped up in the tangle of options available, hadn't seen Feldman and jerked involuntarily at the sound of the voice. He stopped and faced him.

"Yeah, Danny. You've got good news?" Jesse saw no pleasing face and he fought to ward off negative thoughts.

Feldman waved for Jesse to enter his office and stepped back as Jesse entered behind him, moving toward his desk. "Come on in for a moment. Gary heard from the FBI." Feldman took his seat behind the desk.

Jesse remained standing. "I take it from the look on your face, they didn't take the case."

"I'm sorry, Jesse, but no, they didn't. Said there wasn't enough to overcome the problems they have with trying to re-elevate him to a person of interest. Said if you can come up with something they can work with, they'd be happy to try for a court order to overturn the restrictions placed by the prior court." Feldman stared at Jesse's sad face. "Hey, don't take it so hard. You did get the others transferred, and Gary wants you to go to work with him." Feldman grinned. "Don't know if I want to lose you. We see eye-to-eye on many issues. But, can't stand in the way of progress, and I know how much it means to you. You okay?"

Jesse gave a weak grin. The result was pretty much as expected. Nobody seemed to be capable of seeing what he saw. He knew the FBI's hands were tied to some extent because of their inability to prosecute Abdullah after 9/11, but Jesse suspected also that it took influence to overcome their built-in stubbornness to the facts presented by outsiders. Maybe the reporter could help in that regard. "Yeah, I'm all right. Well if CID does take me, I'll be just across the hall."

His grin broadened. "I'll still be able to pop in once in awhile." Feldman grimaced. "Thanks for your help, Danny. I better get to work."

On the walk to his desk, Jesse put a call in to the reporter.

CHAPTER **59**

Jesse leaned against his car door and said, "That was some story in the *Post*. You do get around." Arthur Reid grinned. "Arthur, I've only got a few minutes, but we've talked some about sharing information, and I want to talk with you about that now. Even though I won't share tax information with you, I want you to promise that everything I say to you today is strictly off the record. My name will never be mentioned."

Arthur's grin grew larger. "Jesse, I guarantee that's one thing you'll not have to worry about. I will go to jail before I reveal my sources, if that is their wish. I've never done it and never will. Trust me."

"The last time we met, you mentioned that you suspected there may be things going on beyond the bribery of the senator. I told you then that I had a like mind, but now I really believe that these people are getting ready to cause major disaster to this country."

Reid's grin vanished and his face reflected awe. "My God, Jesse. This is serious. You know something positive? What—?"

"Hold on. Hold on." Jesse stood away from the car and put his hand up. "I have some facts and I think they point in that direction, but there's nothing concrete. You understand?"

"Yes, very well. The way I operate most of the time. Go on, tell me what you can." Reid removed the pen from his shirt pocket and made an entry on his notepad.

"Okay. You know about the connections between Allied, Provident, and Brisbane, but did you know that the ownership of Allied changed this year and that there are several Arabs on the board?"

Reid whistled and restrained from talking at the hand gesture from Jesse.

Jesse continued, "Let me summarize as quickly as I can, so you can get the picture of these Arabs working together. Syed Rabia, who you know about, has devised a scheme to bring money in from overseas in the guise of donations to a mosque. That money is immediately transferred to Florida Land, who buys and sells land to further wash the money. It then transfers the money to a company known as Hemisphere Equities, managed by a man named Imraaz Amed." Reid whistled slightly again and wrote feverishly on the notepad.

"That company invests in American businesses that produce chemicals, drugs, nuclear materials, etcetera, and this year it transferred substantial funds to Abdullah Zacaari, a professor at the University of Central Florida in Orlando."

Reid stopped writing, looked questioningly at Jesse and acted as if he was going to speak.

Jesse continued, "The account those expenditures went into was titled Operation Inner City."

"What do you think that means? What's your take on all this, Jesse?"

"I think their original long-term operation was to acquire businesses that produced materials that could be used for widespread destruction and killings. Then something changed those plans and the money was diverted to cover other near-term operations. That term 'Operation Inner City' seems to mean something big is going to happen soon in a major city – maybe like New York." Jesse's heart felt like it was about to leap out of its mooring. He gasped audibly and slapped his head with the palm of his hand.

"What is it, Jesse?"

"I just thought of my kids in New York. I've got to—"

"Your kids are in New York? I don't understand."

"Last week my ex-wife took off with my children and the last I heard, that's where they are. I've got to call my lawyer to get them back here." Jesse fought to calm himself. It wasn't like him to lay out his personal problems to strangers. He had to finish here and get his lawyer on the line. "Let's continue with this, Reid. Like I said, there's nothing concrete but can you see what I see?" Jesse again had good control of his senses.

"I'm not a hundred percent with you, but I do get the drift of your thinking and think it's worth pursuing. Did you have something particular you wanted me to follow up on?"

"I would like you to first put pressure on Mr. Rabia. I think he is basically a good, decent man who may have gotten involved in this stuff innocently. I think with pressure and to protect his name, he may help us."

"I've already talked with him trying to get information about the connection to the senator. He refused to talk, but I think I can—"

"I don't remember seeing his name in your latest article. I think you should threaten to spread his name all over the country. You may let on some about these other things you've learned today. I think his cooperation is key."

"Okay, I can work on him. How about the others?"

"Do what you do best. Find out all you can about Zacaari and Amed. Especially Amed's operation which is right here in town." Jesse looked at his watch. "I'm going to Orlando now to see if I can confront Zacaari." He opened the car door. "Are you okay with this?"

Reid, still making notes, looked up. "You bet. I've gone about as far as I can with the senator for the moment. Need new leads. Sounds good." He held his hand out and Jesse took it and squeezed hard. "Let's stay in touch."

Jesse got in the car and inserted the ignition key. He looked at Reid through the open window. "Curious, Reid. Just how did you find about Provident?"

Reid smiled. "Can't reveal my source, Jesse." He placed the pen in his pocket. "Reporters have ethics too, you know."

CHAPTER 60

Jesse took the ticket from the lady in the booth and entered Florida's turnpike headed for Orlando. He set the cruise control and settled into the seat for the tiring trip. He was unsure exactly what he hoped to gain from a conference with Abdullah, assuming he could even get one. He went over Abdullah's return in his mind. The front page showed nothing unusual; salary, interest, dividends. The copy of the W-2 showed him that Abdullah was in fact employed by the university in Orlando. What was his connection to all this? He was not on the board of Allied or any of the other entities. The only connection seemed to be the receipt of funds from Hemisphere, which indicated some sort of relationship with Rabia. What were the funds used for? That was the big question and the one Jesse hoped he could use for leverage.

The account name, Operation Inner City flashed across his mind, and he gasped as he remembered his children. If there was going to be a holocaust, when was it to be? He picked up the phone and dialed his lawyer's number.

The secretary answered, "Lewis, Wilkins and Mahoney. Can I help you?"

"Good morning. This is Jesse Hawkins. Can I speak with Mr. Lewis?"

"Good morning, Mr. Hawkins. May I tell him the purpose of your call?"

"I'd like to talk with him about my children. He handled my divorce two years ago."

Gerald Lewis spoke into the phone. "Yes, Mr. Hawkins, how can I help you?"

"Gerry, this is Jesse, the IRS agent – the pilot. You park your plane right next to mine."

"Oh hell, Jesse. Been doing any flying? Every time I go up to the airport, your plane is there. When are we going back to the Keys?"

"Been busy as a bee here lately. I did take a trip to Nassau couple of weeks ago, but not much since then. I've got to get back in the air, though. How about you?"

"I try to get up there at least once a week. Are you calling about your divorce? Problems?"

"Yeah. Thelma, er, my ex-wife has moved to New York. She took the children without even discussing it with me. If I understand the decree right, she's not supposed to do that. What can I do about it? Didn't she have to get my permission to take them out of the county?"

"That's usually the case, but let me pull your file to be sure. I can call you back after lunch. Is that okay?"

"Sure. I'm on my way to Orlando but I have the phone with me. Thanks, Gerry. See you in the air."

He dialed Thelma's number. No answer. He stewed for a minute then forced himself to let up. Get on through today's business then take care of other matters. He'd go to New York if necessary.

Jesse tapped the brake with the idea of turning off at the rest stop, decided against it and was just beginning to reaccelerate when a car entering the turnpike cut in front of him. He slammed on the brakes and just barely avoided a broadside collision. The driver looked at Jesse and sped away, unable to hear Jesse's tirade. "You son of a . . . ."

Jesse was still trembling from the sudden reaction to disaster when he realized what he'd just seen. The car, Jesse's dream, a light-blue BMW, the driver, a man with dark skin and a square face. God Almighty, he'd know that face anywhere. That was the man who tried to kill him twice. What was he up to? Trying to do it again?

Jesse stepped on the gas pedal and accelerated to ninety in an attempt to catch the BMW, but it was nowhere in sight. Flashing lights in the southbound lane caused him to ease off on the gas. The officer appeared to be writing a ticket.

It was nearing three o'clock when Jesse turned onto the university grounds; he was making his way towards the buildings when he spotted the BMW parked behind another vehicle on the other side of the plaza. His throat constricted and he gasped for air. What could the murderer be doing on the campus grounds? He slowed to a crawl as he searched the students scattered around the area in various modes of repose – some sprawled on the neat, trimmed grass, others sitting on benches, still others strolling here and there.

As Jesse neared the BMW, he saw an elderly man dressed in a suit, walking towards a man sitting on a bench under a large oak tree. As Jesse drew nearer his throat constricted again. The man on the bench was the square-faced killer. Who was the well-dressed man? Could he be Abdullah Zacaari? Was he the one who ordered the killings? Jesse had to get as close as he could. He parked behind another car where he could plainly see the men without standing out.

CHAPTER 61

Hamza was gazing across the plaza at the soccer field as Abdullah approached the bench from the opposite direction. Abdullah looked at his watch. He had an unscheduled meeting in forty-five minutes, but he had to make time to be sure Hamza understood the plan and the use of the weapon completely. The young man, for all his beastliness, had a good brain, was more than capable of absorbing information quickly, and was a solid Muslim, too.

Hamza turned and stood as Abdullah said, "Hamza, you are right on time, as always." Hamza seemed unfazed by the sudden intrusion on his thoughts. Abdullah touched Hamza's arm. "Come, let us sit. You are well?"

"Yes, sir. I *am* ready. I have the assurance of Allah and I'm awaiting instructions. Is all in order? I'm eager to begin my mission."

Abdullah patted Hamza's knee. "That is good. We will transfer the device to your car in a minute, but first let me explain what you are to do and what will happen." He studied the calm face and knew that he had chosen the right person for the job.

"The suitcase you will take contains a nuclear bomb. You will set it off on a busy intersection in Times Square. You will do this at exactly four o'clock in the afternoon on Friday." Hamza started to speak but Abdullah continued. "One hour before that, you will call the telephone numbers I give you and simply say '9999'. Others receiving that call will set off bombs in other areas of New York to draw attention away from you. You should be able to casually stroll out to the intersection and follow the prescribed directions."

Hamza eased to the edge of the seat, his eagerness getting the better of his usual calm and self-control. "How many will be killed? Is the bomb easy to use?"

"There are two switches on the outside of the suitcase both of which you will activate. The one on the left causes certain liquids to mix and the one on the right will allow the bomb to explode. It will take twenty minutes to go off after the turn of the left switch. You must position yourself in the Square so as to not attract attention while you wait for the action." Hamza now stood, eager and ready to go.

Abdullah continued, "You must control your emotions and think. You must find a parking space where you will not be questioned by the police. The usual detectors expected in parking garages should not penetrate the material covering the suitcase. But you may wish to choose other parking arrangements. I will leave that decision to your good judgment." Hamza beamed.

Abdullah looked at his watch. "Do you have any questions? Need me to go over any parts of the plan?"

"No, sir." Hamza went on to repeat the instructions word for word. "I'm eager to get started." He hesitated. "One question. Why do I have to wait until Friday? I will be in New York way before that."

"The time has been set. I want you to take your time going up there. We cannot afford for you to get stopped by the police. Time has been allotted for you to enjoy your last days and you may wish to visit a mosque on the way. You should not reach New York before Friday. There are many things to see along the way." Abdullah stood. "Enjoy yourself, Hamza." He smiled and touched Hamza's arm. "Come, let us transfer the suitcase. I have parked my car behind yours."

As the BMW pulled away, Jesse got out of his car and followed the well-dressed man, staying far enough behind and mingling in with others. His first reaction when seeing the transfer of the suitcase was to follow the BMW. He suspected the suitcase represented a bomb of some sort, but he had to find out if this man was Abdullah Zacaari and then try again to find someone to act. He now believed it was Abdullah who controlled the man in the BMW and was therefore responsible for the killings and the attempts on his own life. If it was in fact a bomb, where would it be set off? Hamza was from South Florida. Was the target Miami?

Inside the building, Jesse yelled at the man to hold the elevator, and squeezed past the closing door. "Thank you, sir." Jesse looked into the dark eyes of a sixty-year-old man of obvious Arab descent. "Hope I didn't put you out." He noted the selected floor was three, and pressed it again.

Abdullah seemed impatient. "That's quite all right, young man. Are you a student here?"

Jesse's insides began to tingle. He had to be careful. "No, sir. Just visiting for the day."

They both exited on the third floor and Jesse went in the opposite direction from Abdullah. A bit down the hall, he turned and watched Abdullah enter an office. Jesse turned around and, as he strolled by the door, read the title, Professor Abdullah Zacaari.

CHAPTER **62**

Jesse couldn't think straight. He felt certain there was going to be some sort of attack, but the known facts kept jumping in front of one another, and he couldn't come up with a decisive conclusion. He was sure the professor was in control of all the others. The meeting today with the square-faced Arab, the killer, was the prelude to the plan. Where was the attack going to happen, and when? He expected it to be in a large city, and had originally suspected New York. The World Trade Center came to mind, but he knew it was going to be a much greater disaster. But the square-faced man was from down south. Why was he chosen? *Good God. Why can't I think straight?* He pounded the steering wheel as he made the turn onto the turnpike and headed south.

If the attack was going to be in New York, how could he convince Thelma of the danger they were in, when he didn't know for sure himself? He slapped the steering wheel again. He wasn't even sure there was going to be a disaster.

His phone chimed and he noted the name of his lawyer. "Yes, Gerry. Good news?"

"Your ex-wife is definitely acting contrary to the agreement and therefore I feel that any judge will order her to return to the county with your children. The problem is—"

"Yeah, I know. How to enforce it. Would I be breaking the law if I went up there and stole them?"

"It's probably not the smart thing to do without the court's prior permission, but . . . I think you might not be breaking the law. To be certain I'd have to do a little research. Are you thinking of doing that?"

"I've been thinking about it, but hold off on the research for now. I'll get back to you. Thanks a lot, Gerry." He pushed the end button and entered Thelma's numbers.

After five rings and a long silence there was a connection. He blurted, "Thelma, I need to—"

Thelma's voice came as a shout. "What is it now, Jesse? I told you before; I'm not coming back to Florida. Now leave me alone."

"Hold on, Thelma. I talked to my lawyer and he said you're breaking the law. I can get a court order you know. Let me talk to my children." The phone went dead. He pushed the numbers in again and listened woefully to the rings. He pounded the steering wheel. *Damn. Damn.* What was he going to do? What could he do? *I've got to save my children.*

With his mind blazing with confusing ideas and thoughts, Jesse figured there had to be someone in government willing to sort through the facts and see the possible result. He entered the reporter's number and the response came after the first ring.

"Hey, Jesse. How did your trip go? Did you meet with the Professor?"

Now how in the world did Reid know that Zacaari was a professor so soon? "No, I didn't meet with him, but I saw him having a meeting with the person who tried to kill me before. I—"

"Tried to kill you? When? You never told me about that. Are you—?"

"Hold on, Reid. That was several weeks ago. He hasn't tried again lately. Don't know why, but I suspect he's Zacaari's hit man, and that they're planning something else."

"What makes you think that?"

"A suitcase wrapped in plastic was transferred from Zacaari's car to his. Again, I don't know why, and that's one of the reasons I called you today. We need someone in government with more experience to listen, or we need to get better intelligence ourselves. Have you made any contact with Rabia and Amed?"

"As of today, I haven't been able to make contact with either of them, but I'm watching Rabia's office as we speak. I haven't seen him at all today."

"I think he's the most important. Don't know if he's in on the plot, but he could be the help we need if he is. Do you know anybody in government who might be able to help?"

"I have contacts all over, but it'll take time to reach them. Let me think on it. Maybe I can come up with a plan."

"Okay. Thanks, Reid. Keep in touch." Jesse's children jumped into his mind. "We may not have much time." *How about the senator? Will he listen?*

CHAPTER 63

Abdullah hurried across campus to the convention center where he was to make a presentation in the absence of the scheduled professor. These fill-ins happened on rare occasions, but it always peeved him when notification didn't arrive until the last hour. This one was especially trying with all the other activity in his mind.

Hamza had seemed unable to contain his enthusiasm for the task ahead and really became aroused when told that millions would be killed. Abdullah hoped that Hamza would take his time to enjoy himself along the way and not do something foolish that could jeopardize the mission. Abdullah could clearly see Hamza standing in Times Square with the suitcase in hand, hundreds of people milling about in their normal fashion, then, the blast that vaporized Hamza and the people nearby, and razed all the buildings within sight. He stopped short, his daughter replacing all other visions. She was riding on his knee, laughing gleefully. How was he to save her? He entered her telephone number and listened to the rings, and then, at the tone, left a message for her to call him.

Abdullah gazed out across the campus, his mind trying to accept the facts and stay calm. His daughter being vaporized along with the others filled his mind; a fear like he'd never known took hold and he trembled visibly. How could he save her? He couldn't reverse his command to Hamza and his commitment to the *Mujahadeen* – and especially to Allah. It was a holy order to rid the world of The Great Satan. But he had to save his daughter somehow. He knew that even when he reached her he wouldn't be able to change her mind. She had her duties there and was steadfast.

He began to walk again when the thought hit him. Syed had always voiced a deep abhorrence for all aspects of the operation and especially for the idea of killing millions. Maybe he should give him all the facts. He entered Syed's telephone number.

Syed paced back and forth behind the desk in his den at home. He had told Mary that something drastic was about to happen, but had delayed telling her of the possibility of a nuclear blast and its related consequences, unable to bring himself to that. She had advised telling the authorities before it was too late. That was his dilemma now. How was he to turn his back on Abdullah – on his religion – on his promise? What was to happen to his business that he'd worked so diligently to foster? He thought of the revenue agent and his promise to work with the authorities to mitigate the possible criminal penalties. The phone rang and jerked him back to the present.

He noted the name and pressed the talk button. "Yes, Abdullah. Are you near?"

"Syed, it is nice to hear your voice. I have been thinking that I should be completely open with you. You should prepare yourself. The holocaust will occur at four o'clock this Friday."

The voice paused and Syed drew in a deep breath. *Why is he telling me this now?*

Abdullah continued, "Hamza is on his way to New York with the nuclear bomb and will arrive there Friday morning."

Syed gulped audibly. *I should've known.* Abdullah had met with Hamza in Miami. That had been his main reason for going. "Abdullah, are you sure you wish to continue with this plan?"

"It is my duty, and it is the order from above. I have no choice."

"Isn't your daughter in New York? What about her? Will this affect her? What about her children?"

"I have no choice. Goodbye, Syed. Allah be praised."

CHAPTER 64

Jesse stopped at the booth, paid his toll, and headed for home. He ought to call Amy, but a glance at the sun near the westerly horizon, his weariness, bodily and spiritually, all negated that idea. The question about the senator wouldn't let go. The need to find someone with influence was paramount if he was to save his children. Should he fly to Washington D.C. and try for an audience with him?

He thought of his offer to help Syed Rabia if he would cooperate and share any useful information. The senator's tax return was already at CID, but Jesse felt sure he could convince Singleton to treat the monies received from Allied as going into his campaign fund rather than to him. While the purchase of the house was definitely a bribe, the actual transaction could be treated simply as the sale of his personal residence. If the senator could see through all the negatives and visualize the plot, Jesse felt sure access to the highest level of government officials would be at his disposal.

Jesse put in a call to Feldman and when there was no answer, realized the office was closed for the day. He called Amy.

"Hello, Jesse. You've been gone all day. Where are you now?"

"I just turned off the turnpike. Been to Orlando to visit with a professor there. Wait till you here what I found out." He paused, wondering if he should plan to have a snack with her before turning in. "Heard anything from the FBI?"

"No, there's no news. Gary called over there again, but it looks like they're dead on the issue." Amy paused. "I'm sorry, Jesse. What're you going to do?"

"Look, you want to grab a bite somewhere?"

"Yes, I'd like that. Like to hear what you learned in Orlando, too."

"Okay, meet me at the plane. I want to get it gassed up before tomorrow."

"Dulles Tower. 8425 Delta request permission to land." Jesse spoke into the mouthpiece attached to his head. He needed to get out and stretch. The trip from West Palm Beach had taken seven hours, and although the trip had been pleasant with open ocean and beautiful scenery, he was beat. The beautiful rising sun peaking from behind a serene ocean had been replaced by a harsh one, now tipping to the west.

"8425 Delta cleared to land, Runway One Eight Zero."

"Roger, Dulles, two-five Delta, copy that, One Eight Zero." Jesse maintained his northwesterly heading, turned downwind after passing the northerly end of runway 180, and finally lined up on the assigned runway. He executed a perfect landing and continued smiling as he turned onto the taxiway and made his way to the parking area.

At the airport he made expeditious use of the facilities, had a quick bite at the diner there, and hailed a taxi. He was in awe at the enormity of the Capitol Building and stood there gawking for five minutes. A glance at his watch and his mission quickly gained his attention – one-thirty. No time to waste.

In short order, after passing inspection and getting directions from the guards at the entrance, he walked down the hall towards the senator's office. His stomach churned. He had never been in the presence of a United States Senator, especially under today's circumstances. Was the senator in? Would he be able to see him? *Will I have the guts to face him?*

Will he believe as I do?

Jesse stopped at the door with the senator's name emboldened in large black letters and was about to reach for the knob when the door opened suddenly and a nice-looking lady stepped into the hallway, almost bumping into him.

She seemed distraught, controlled herself and said, "Ooh, I'm sorry, sir. May I help you? I'm Senator Walker's secretary."

"Forgive me, ma'am." Jesse backed out of the way. "I was hoping to see the senator today."

"I'm sorry, but I don't recall any appointments for this afternoon." She closed the door. "Did you talk directly to the senator? Your name, please."

"I'm Jesse Hawkins. No, I didn't speak directly with the senator, but . . . ." Jesse's mind raced. This woman seemed in a hurry to leave, and if she left without giving him permission to enter, the trip would be a complete waste. He reached into his coat pocket and removed his ID card. He presented the card and said, "I'm with the Internal Revenue Service and I've come all the way from Florida to speak with the senator. I don't—"

"I heard he was being audited. He's not in any trouble is he?" The woman was shaking. She moved away from the door and took a few steps down the hall. "Mr. Hawkins, maybe you can help me." She motioned for Jesse to follow. "I'm afraid." She paused as if trying to force herself to talk with a stranger. "But someone has to do something or I'm afraid he will . . . ."

"You're afraid he'll do *what*, Miss . . . ." Jesse was now beginning to get alarmed himself. What had he stepped into? The woman's face looked like it was going to erupt.

"You're a government man. I'll trust that you'll do the right thing." She paused again to gather her strength. "I don't usually leave the office until after five. Today the senator ordered me to leave now. He was visibly upset. I don't know what to do, and I don't want to bring the police in on something I'm not sure of." She paused and stared into Jesse's eyes. "I'm afraid he might try to harm himself."

"What do you mean, harm himself? You mean—"

"During the past few weeks he's been very distraught." She wiped her teary eyes with a handkerchief and seemed ready to break down completely. "He has a gun in his desk." Her free hand covered her mouth.

Jesse moved to the door and opened it a bit. "Where is he?"

"He's probably in his office, just to the left of my desk. Please be careful, Mr. Hawkins." She began to quietly sob.

"You go on home now, Miss. Let me see what I can do."

CHAPTER 65

Jesse entered the outer office. The door to the left was closed. He moved to it and placed his hand on the knob. The knot in his gut seemed to enlarge. He was treading on unfamiliar ground – about to enter the office of a United States Senator unannounced. *Have I lost my mind?* The words "he has a gun in his desk" resounded in his ears. But the secretary's concern for the senator trumped his fear. *I must go in.* Jesse turned the knob slowly and moved the door open a slight amount – it squeaked.

The senator, with a gun to his head, spun around to face Jesse. "What the hell? Who the hell are you?" He pointed the gun at Jesse.

Jesse recoiled. "Whoa. Hold on there, sir. Put that gun away." Jesse raised his arms to show that he had no weapons. "I'm not here to hurt you. I just flew up from Florida to discuss a dire issue with you."

Senator Walker continued to point the gun at Jesse's head – the hand on the gun unwavering.

"Please, sir, point the gun away from me."

"What do you want? Who are you?"

Jesse's throat felt dry. He tried to speak but no words would come.

"Speak up, man. Identify yourself."

"I'm Jesse Hawkins with the Internal Revenue Service. I have information you need to hear. You're the only person I know that can save this country from the disaster it faces. You must—"

"What do you mean the disaster the country faces?" The gun lowered for a moment then returned to pointing directly at Jesse's face. "By God. You're the agent that's causing me all my troubles." Walker cocked the gun. "Boy, you better get the hell out of here while the getting's good. You've caused me enough trouble."

Jesse's throat constricted from extreme panic. None of his close calls in the air or with the terrorists equaled what he now felt. It looked like he was a goner for sure. "Hold on, Senator. I'm going." He started to back out the door when a push from the other side stopped him. He turned to see a young man enter the room.

Tom Benson cried out, "Senator Walker, what's going on? What are you doing with that gun?" Benson glanced at Jesse questioningly, then back at the senator.

"What are you doing here, Tom? You were supposed to be gone for the week." The gun lowered slightly. Jesse stared at the two men talking business while his insides crawled.

"I forgot to take care of a critical detail. Wanted to ask you a question before I left for the weekend." Benson moved toward the senator. The gun rose.

"Stop right there, Tom. I want both of you out of here . . . now."

Benson stopped short. "What is it, Senator? Our problems aren't enough to send you to this . . . are they?"

"Enough talk. Get out of here. Now." The gun hand trembled. Jesse moved, and Walker diverted his eyes toward him. Benson lunged forward and knocked the gun out of Walker's hand. It clattered to the floor and fired, the bullet harmlessly hitting the wall behind the desk. Jesse jerked involuntarily and Benson clasped both arms around the senator. They stood that way for a long moment.

Jesse, finally able to calm himself but still unable to comprehend what was going on, watched as the two men stood there; the senator with arms hanging limp by his side, tears flowing from his eyes, Benson with both arms still holding tightly to the senator. Neither man spoke and Jesse, fighting the urge to intercede, remained silent and waited for the drama to play out.

Benson removed his arms and led the senator to a guest chair where he slumped and hung his head. Benson looked at Jesse, then picked the gun off the floor and removed the bullets, looking at the gun for a long time as if wondering what would have happened had he not come in when he did. He walked around the desk and placed the gun in the drawer. The senator remained slumped over.

Benson looked at Jesse and asked, "Where's Mrs. Morrison. Did she let you in? Do you have an appointment?"

Jesse, feeling much better, remained standing by the door, several feet from the desk and the slumped back of the senator. "No, I didn't have an appointment. I flew up here today to see Senator Walker and met the secretary at the door. She said the senator may have problems and asked if I would help. When I came into the room, the senator had the gun to his head, then aimed it at me and ordered me out. That's when you came in." Walker raised his head but remained silent. Jesse said, "And I want to thank you, sir, for coming in when you did. You may've saved my life. I—"

Senator Walker, speaking to no one in particular, said, "He's the revenue agent from Florida."

"Revenue Agent?" Benson faced Jesse. "Is that why you're here? I thought that was being taken care of by the accountant in Florida."

"I came up here primarily to get Senator Walker to help me make contact with government officials to hear what I have to report. I believe an attack against the country is imminent. I figured I could help—"

"An attack against the country?" Senator Walker roared, jerked around in the chair and stared directly at Jesse. "What the hell are you talking about? An attack? What sort of attack?" He stood and his eyes demanded an immediate answer.

Jesse, startled by the outburst, hesitated for a moment and before he could speak, Benson put his hand on Walker's shoulder to calm him and said to Jesse, "Wait a minute, let me get this right. You're not here about his tax return but about some plot to attack the United States?" Walker started to speak again and Benson patted his shoulder. "This seems a bit ridiculous, but let's stay calm and hear him out. It's not likely he would've come all this way on some lark. Go ahead Mr. uhh . . . ."

"Jesse Hawkins." He extracted his ID card, walked across the room and held it out for Senator Walker. Benson took the card, read the information and passed it to the senator, who glanced at it and handed it back to Jesse. "As you know, I've audited the senator and Allied Paint Corporation, and both of those cases are now in the hands of the Criminal Investigation Division." Benson started to interrupt but Jesse continued, "In addition, because of ties to those examinations, I've audited two mosques and two other entities all controlled by persons of Arab descent." The faces of both men reflected confusion and disinterest – a familiar reaction of all the others he had tried to explain the facts to. "The results of the examinations lead to my conclusions that we are about to be attacked – worse than 9/11."

Walker and Benson looked at each other. Walker said, "You'll have to be much more explicit than that, Mr. Hawkins. I haven't heard anything yet that would lead me to your conclusion." He moved around the desk, glanced down at the drawer holding the gun and took his normal chair. "Besides, why are you bringing it to me? Why not go directly to Homeland Security or other responsible agencies?"

"I've contacted the FBI in Florida and they say they can't take action because of some court order. I figured someone with your stature could get through to them . . . if I could convince you." Jesse moved to the chair and started to sit. "May I?"

Walker nodded and Benson took the other chair.

Jesse continued, "Let me recap the story for you." He went on to relate the facts from the killing of Mendez and the revenue agent, the attacks on his life, the connections between all the entities, his recent sighting of Abdullah and Hamza, the transfer of the suitcase and his various attempts to get others interested.

Both men paid close attention, and Walker asked, "Assuming you're correct in everything you say, and accepting your conclusion for a moment, what's in the suitcase and where's it going?"

A small frown creased Jesse's brow and he said, "Unfortunately that's where my expertise peaks and the need for others comes into play." He noted frowns on both men's faces. "But, I do know that the person who took the suitcase is the same man that tried to kill me on two separate occasions, and I figure he lives somewhere in South Florida. I also believe an attack is likely to happen in a large city – maybe Miami." Jesse read the lack of enthusiasm on their faces. *Here we go again.* "But, I have a strong sense, though, that it's going to occur in New York City."

The two men looked at each other. Benson said, "What do you think, sir?"

Walker looked directly at Jesse. "I appreciate what you're trying to do, young man. I wish we had more like you, but I wonder if there's enough evidence to obtain action. We don't know where, when, or even if an attack will come. Do you have anything else?"

Jesse's phone chimed. He placed his hand on it and looked to the senator for approval to answer. Walker nodded and Jesse took the call. "Yes, Reid. What've you got?" Maybe this was the information he needed.

"Jesse, where are you?"

"I'm in D.C . . . with Senator Walker."

"With Senator Walker? Good gosh. What're you doing there?"

"Trying to get him to intervene with government agencies." Jesse looked intently at the senator. "But he says I don't have enough information to get action. Were you able to contact Mr. Rabia?"

"The reason for my call. I'm with him now and he has something to say to you. Hold on."

"You're starting to break up, Reid. Can you hear me?"

"Jesse, you . . . ." The phone went dead.

Jesse panicked and said out loud, "Damn it. Damn it." He dialed Reid's cell number. Reid, breaking up, tried to speak but Jesse overrode him. "Reid, call the senator's number." Jesse looked to the senator, got the number and relayed it to Reid. The phone went dead. Jesse said to the senator. "Lost the damn phone connection. That was Arthur Reid, the reporter with the *Washington Post*. He's—"

"Reporter? He the one writing the articles about me?" Walker glanced at Benson, at the bottom drawer of the desk, then back to Jesse. "What's he calling you for? Have you been giving him information about me?"

"No, sir. That's confidential and I'd never do that, but . . . since I've been unable to get anyone else to listen to me . . . I tried to get him interested in my attack theory without revealing personal information. When he called he was with one of the main Arab participants I've been trying to put pressure on, hoping he would give me something more tangible. Reid sounded positive. Maybe he can reach me on your phone."

The door opened and the secretary peeked around. "Uh . . . Senator . . . ."

Walker, apparently agitated at the interruption, said, "What are you doing here, Sylvia? I thought you had gone home. You—"

"I got half way to my car, but just had to come back. I was worried about you. Are you all right?"

"Yes. I'm fine. You ought to go on home now." He looked at Jesse, then at the phone, then directly at Sylvia. "Stick around for a bit, Sylvia. May need you. We'll be just a few more minutes."

Walker's phone rang. He looked at Jesse, reached for it and pressed a button. Sylvia exited the room.

Reid's voice came over the intercom. "Jesse, are you there?"

Jesse's heart leapt into his throat. *Maybe, just maybe.* "Yes, Reid, I'm here with the senator and his associate. You're on the speaker. Go ahead."

"Okay. I'm here with Mr. Rabia and his wife. He has something to say to you. I think you'll like it. Here he is."

Syed said, "Mr. Hawkins. I have received word from Abdullah Zacaari and, after discussing it with my wife and Mr. Reid, I thought it best to share it with you without further delay." Syed hesitated and Jesse fretted and looked hopefully at the senator.

Syed continued, "A blue BMW, carrying a suitcase containing a nuclear weapon is headed for New York City." The faces of all the men in the room reflected unfettered amazement. Syed continued, "The device left Orlando Wednesday afternoon and is destined to be exploded in Times Square Friday at four o'clock in the afternoon." Syed choked up and mumbled something unintelligible. "There likely will be other explosions around the city as a prelude to the major blast."

Jesse struggled to catch his breath and looked at the two men. Senator Walker, sitting straight up in his chair, seemed eager to take the phone and place the necessary call. Jesse said, "Mr. Rabia, is there anything else?"

"No, that is all the information I have, and it has taken all my courage to part with it."

"I understand, sir." Jesse could hardly control himself. The looks of acceptance on the two faces were almost beyond belief. He had done it. "I cannot thank you enough, Mr. Rabia." He looked directly at Senator Walker. "I guarantee you that I will provide you with all the protection I can muster. Thanks again, sir." Senator Walker nodded slightly and Jesse smiled.

The reporter came on the phone. "Senator Walker, I'm sorry for the trouble I've caused you, but I beg you now, to put Jesse in touch with the right people and prevent this horrible act."

"Do not berate yourself, young man. You and Mr. Hawkins have done your jobs well. Now I'll do mine." Walker slammed shut the drawer holding the gun and grabbed the telephone.

"The BMW seems to be slowing." The helicopter hovered high and far to the right of I-95, just south of Trenton, New Jersey. "Looks like it's getting ready to pull into the rest stop. Yes, it has turned in. Move in but keep out of sight."

The line of police cars maintained their distance, but an unmarked car containing several FBI agents, also turned off, passed the BMW, and parked farther to the south.

The helicopter reported, "The driver is walking toward the restaurant building. Coordinate with the others. I'll maintain cover from here."

The agents followed Hamza into the building as the police cars circled the BMW.

-EPILOGUE-

"Cast your line over there, Amy. See the ripple. Fish under there." The sun hovered near the eastern horizon. The refreshing cool breeze zipping into the inlet from the Atlantic Ocean warded off what few mosquitoes there were.

Amy reeled in her line and recast it as directed. She moved to the stern to be with Jesse and they both sipped their coffee. She said, "That was some article in Friday's paper, but they didn't even mention your name. Just said that because Senator Martin Walker alerted Homeland Security based on a tip from the Internal Revenue Service, New York City was saved from a nuclear holocaust." She sipped her coffee. "You did all the work and got no recognition. How come?"

"Didn't want any. I told Arthur and the senator to keep my name anonymous at all costs." Jesse grinned. "Just doing my job, Amy." Jesse's line jerked. He tightened his grip; then the line went limp. "Thought I had one."

"What about the senator's return? Allied Paint?' Amy grinned. "Are we going to work those?"

"Allied, definitely. They've conspired to keep their profits overseas – a criminal offence without question. We'll eat those buggers alive. Can't wait to get started. But—"

"And the senator? You're not succumbing to pressures from above are you?" Her brow squinched; then she grinned. "Just kidding." She looked seriously at Jesse. "But what's to happen . . . ?"

"I know what you mean. But if it hadn't been for him, the terrorists would've had their way. I have to admit I've changed my attitude toward him. We had a long conversation after he called the authorities and I began to think that I might've been a tad harsh on him in my thinking."

Amy poured them more coffee. "I always thought your case against him was a bit weak, but it was so complicated I figured it was worth digging into. What particulars changed your mind?"

Jesse reeled his line in a little. "He and his aide proved to me that the $150,000 went into the campaign fund the same as all other such receipts in past years. He told me that Allied contributed substantial funds over the years to different campaign committees, and that fact strengthens our case against Allied, especially if they treated the outgo as expense, which I bet they did. Since the senator never used any of that money personally, and they pretty well convinced me of that, I think we'll likely lose there, too." Jesse took a sip of coffee and tossed the rest over the side. "I don't know what the cost of his house is and whether the sale will produce a profit. He was still married at the time of the sale and if the profit's not more than $500,000, it's not reportable." He stood and stretched. "The senator's career is definitely over. Even though he didn't take anything personally, other than his house proceeds, he knew what was going on, and that's why he planned to kill himself. What do you think?"

"I tend to agree, but we still have a good case against Allied. What about the mosques? Any chances there? I guess they might lose their tax exemption, huh?" She threw the balance of her coffee over the side, too.

"The Faroque mosque definitely will. That was a sham from the beginning."

"What's to happen to Syed Rabia? You always expressed a deep respect for him even though he seemed to be as wrapped up in the scheme as all the rest. How about the other two?"

311

"I'm not sure about Amed Imraaz. He seemed to be pretty much a dupe in the actual plan to set off the bomb, but he played a big part in the collection of money and the purchase of businesses around the country. That will take others to unravel just what that was all about. I hope they don't do like they did before, and let the likes of him go free. There's no question that Abdullah Zacaari will be prosecuted to the full extent of the law. He was the mastermind in the country. His life, for all extents and purposes, is over. He will likely spend the rest of his life in prison."

"And Rabia? Didn't he indicate that there were cells all over the country ready to act against the country?"

"Yes, and the senator said enforcement agencies would take the necessary action to root them out, which means . . . probably working closely with Zacaari." He grimaced and looked out to sea, then back to Amy.

Her eyes widened. "You mean they may let him off?"

"I doubt that, but that part is beyond me."

"Will Rabia go to prison?"

"I certainly hope not and the senator assured me that he would do everything within his power to negate any such action. As a matter of fact, he plans to meet personally with Syed to thank him for his disclosures and to get to know him better." Jesse smiled with satisfaction that his promise to Syed may yet work out and his good name and devotion to this country might be preserved. "Although Syed agreed to wash money for the purchase of businesses, I'm convinced he was not really a part of the plot to destroy the United States until the very end. I think it was his devotion to his religion and his home country and family that did him in." Jesse reeled in his line, replaced the bait and tossed it far away from the boat. "But I have a lot of confidence the senator will work it all out. Let's hope so."

"Whew. That was some job you took on. Ready for another?"

"You bet, and this time you're going to be with me all the way and . . . ." He winked at her and she stood as he moved toward her. He took her in his arms. "I mean all the way."

She nestled her face on his chest and murmured, "Thank God, your children are all right."

Jesse grimaced. "Yeah. That's my next job."

Amy's line sank beneath the calm water. Jesse shouted, "You got one. Pull it in."

ERNEST HAMILTON

Made in the USA
Charleston, SC
08 November 2016